Manuscript Mysteries at the Robin Hood Club

The Robin Hood Club – Book 1

Jennifer Ash

Copyright © Jennifer Ash 2024

All rights reserved. No part of this book may be copied, or transmitted in any form or by any means, electronic, electrostatic, magnetic tape, mechanical, photocopying, recording or otherwise, without the written permission of Jennifer Ash www.jenniferash.co.uk

The stories contained within this book are works of fiction. Names and characters are the product of the authors' imaginations and any resemblance to actual persons, living or dead, is entirely coincidental.

Dedication

In memory of Richard 'Kip' Carpenter.
Thank you for the continuing joy your creations bring.
Nothing's forgotten.

Acknowledgements

I doff my hat (Lincoln green, naturally) to the attendees of every conference that I've ever been to – Robin Hood related or otherwise. You all inspired the writing of this book.

A special mention must go to Barnaby Eaton-Jones for introducing me to his amazing Hooded Man events, which allowed me to indulge my passion for all things Robin Hood. This book would never have been written without the experiences I've had since Barnaby walked into my world and allowed me to not only meet the cast and crew of the best Robin Hood adaptation ever – *Robin of Sherwood* – but to write audio dramas and novels for them as well. (Dream job!!!)

Thank you to Alison Knight for her editing eye, encouragement, and coffee fuelled catch ups. Also to Lucy Felthouse for her expert formatting and proofing skills.

Finally, a huge thank you to Suzanne Hodgson-Cox, for her invaluable advice when it came to the world of self-publishing. I'd have been lost without you.

Prologue

April 28th

```
Found: Previously undiscovered Robin
Hood Ballad...
```
    Dr Harriet Danby, known to her friends as Hari, hovered her hand over the computer mouse. Telling herself that the notification on the Medieval Scholars Facebook page was bound to be spam, Hari clicked on the post anyway. Mentally crossing her fingers, hoping she hadn't just unleashed a social media virus upon her laptop, Hari's jaw dropped as she read the press release that filled her screen.

    Two minutes later she picked up the telephone. The call had barely connected before, not bothering with a hello, she blurted out, 'Neil, have you seen…'

    'Harriet! I was about to call you.'

    Detecting an edge of excitement in her former university professor's voice, Hari said, 'You've seen the report then?'

    'I have.'

    'A new Robin Hood ballad!'

    Neil cleared his throat, just managing to keep his enthusiasm in check. 'It would be nice if it was genuine, but if it does turn out to be a hoax, it'll still give us something new to talk about at the Robin Hood Club convention. You are coming, *aren't* you?'

The emailed invitation sat open on Hari's laptop.

    The Robin Hood Club: 28th – 30th May.

    Dear Dr Harriet Danby,

    You are invited (along with a guest of your choice), to this three-day event at the beautiful Harmen Hotel, Buxton, within the stunning Peak District, Derbyshire.

As the writer and creator of the hit television series – Return to Sherwood – we'd be delighted if you could join us for this fans' convention to celebrate your amazing show. We would love it if you would agree to be interviewed by myself, Jeremiah Barnes, about your work and passion for all things Robin Hood.

I can confirm that your leading lady – Scarlett Hann – and your leading man – Lee Stoneman – have already agreed to attend.

You'll find a rough outline of the convention timetable attached to this message. A more detailed running order of events will be available nearer the time.

Please email your response at your earliest convenience.

Yours,
Jeremiah Barnes

Hari opened the attachment and took a ragged breath as she found herself face to face with an invitation to a medieval banquet on the Saturday evening and (worse) a disco on the Sunday evening and (worse still) an interview before all the guests as the "Headline Event" on the Monday.

Why do they want me as the featured speaker when the stars of the show will be there?

Averting her gaze from the laptop screen, she picked up a framed photograph of herself, Scarlett Hann and Lee Stoneman – known to millions as Mathilda of Sherwood and Will Scathlock. It had been taken during the filming of the first episode of *Return to Sherwood*.

'I suppose if you two are attending, it would be odd if I wasn't there.' She focused her gaze on her leading man's grey eyes. 'And who knows, Lee, you might even acknowledge my existence as a human being this time.'

Returning to the laptop, Hari typed out her acceptance, doing her best to ignore the nerves that were already stirring in her stomach.

'At least Neil will be there and, as he said, if a new Robin Hood ballad has been found, it'll be the talk of the weekend, taking the focus off me.'

As she pressed send, Hari addressed the posters of various Robin Hoods that plastered her study walls. 'I blame you lot for this, you know. Every single one of you!'

Chapter One

May 21st

Hari had wanted to call her television series *Mathilda's Sherwood*. It *had* been *Mathilda's Sherwood* right up until the money men (and they were men in this instance), declared that *Return to Sherwood* would be a more viable title.

She had come to hate the word viable. Television executives used it in so many differing and conflicting ways that Hari suspected they did not know what it actually meant.

Crossing her living room, she ran a finger along her bookshelf.

If I'd known how much you'd change my life, would I still have invented you?

Writing the first Mathilda story had been a hobby – an outlet for her inner Robin Hood love. It had been something to do to take the edge off the stresses of the day job as a history tutor at the university where she'd once been a student. But, as the words had stacked up, her best friend, Dot, had persuaded her to contact a few publishers.

A year later, she'd signed a contract for her first novel and two sequels. Hari had entertained no visions of success beyond perhaps accruing a small Robin Hood fan-based readership. She'd been warned more than once by her editor that success was down to luck as much as talent.

But luck had come quickly. Before Hari had realised what was happening, she'd been picked up by an agent and was suddenly on a rollercoaster ride that appeared to have no brakes. There were already six Mathilda novels, with two more slated to be written.

Novelists waited their whole lives for book deals, let alone television deals, and she'd come along and simply got both. Hari winced as she considered how much her fellow authors must hate her. Dot was convinced she was paranoid. Hari knew she wasn't.

'Well, we'll find out, won't we?' She spoke to an exquisite stylised pencil drawing of Robin and Marion that Dot had bought for her on a visit to Nottingham. 'According to the timetable attached, I'm not the only writer going to the Robin Hood Club convention.'

Deciding she'd feel less anxious about the prospect of the forthcoming weekend if she did something productive, Hari moved into the bedroom to pack. Unhooking two shirts from the wardrobe, she asked the posters on the walls, 'What do you think, boys and girls? Shall we take bets on how many seconds it will be after entering the hotel, before someone asks me why I set *Return to Sherwood* in the fourteenth century rather than during the reign of King Richard and Prince John?'

Richard Todd and Joan Rice, from Disney's version of the legend, conferred within the confines of a large framed photograph. *Maybe sixty. Ninety seconds at a push.*

'I reckon thirty. Mind you, there is one question I'll be asked before that. A question that will be repeated on and off all weekend if any of the other public appearances I've made are anything to go by.' Hari paused. 'No, I'm wrong. There'll be one question asked and one statement spoken. It is anyone's guess which way around they'll be delivered.'

Go on. The knitted Robin Hood toy that took centre stage on her bed looked at her expectantly. *Tell me.*

'The statement will be, "I really enjoyed your series, but it's a shame it's not as good as *Robin of*

Sherwood*", which, I grant you is fair, because nothing will ever beat that. And the question will be, "Why is there no Robin Hood in *Return to Sherwood*?"'

Having fought – and won – the battle not to transplant all of Mathilda's adventures from the fourteenth century to the twelfth, she'd been surprised that the lack of a Robin Hood within the stories hadn't been a problem to the producers. They'd liked the originality of it. And the female lead. They said things like, "A fresh take on a timeless tale," and "Outlaws in the time of equality." Hari had quite liked the original label. She'd been less keen on the equality quip, but, as her best friend, Dot, had pointed out, she'd have been foolish to bite the hand that fed her.

Hari's heart hammered in her chest as she folded a spare pair of jeans and placed them in a mini suitcase. 'The people who come won't be fans of me, but of the show. I've no need to be nervous. What the attendees think of me personally doesn't matter.'

She added her cosiest jumper to her packing in case the early blast of summer sunshine they'd been experiencing reverted to the arctic chill that had lasted through most of the spring.

'Who am I kidding? Of course it matters.' Hari thumped her backside onto the edge of the bed. 'I'm not sure I can do this. All the previous gigs I've done have been book related. It's been just authors and readers – not TV show fans. What if everyone hates me?'

You can do this, and you'll have a ball. A whole conference full of Robin Hood fans, who want to see you.

Hari smiled at the final framed photo on the bookshelf. It was her favourite. The male contingent of the cast of *Robin of Sherwood*, with – in this case – Jason Connery in the lead role. She could have sworn she heard Ray Winstone's Will Scarlet whisper, 'Have a good time – and if you ain't well treated, give 'em hell, girl.'

An hour later, having done as much packing as was possible for her trip, Hari was busy plotting the murder of a tanner which was to feature in her next novel, when the announcement of a WhatsApp video call popped up on her phone's screen.

'Neil.' Hari saved her work before accepting the call. 'You've rescued me from the agony of working out the method of death for my latest victim.'

Rather than responding to her comment, Neil asked, 'Have you seen it yet?'

'Seen what?'

'The ballad that's been found. What else?!'

'Of course I haven't seen it.' Hari knocked a long, stray black hair from her face as she propped her phone up against the laptop's screen. 'I'm a *former* historian. The powers that be are hardly going to invite someone who writes fiction to see a lost manuscript.'

'*Robin Hood and the Carter*. Sounds like fiction to me.' Professor Neil Frampton waved the latest newspaper to run a feature on the new discovery at the phone screen. 'Would you like to see it?'

'Ask a silly question! But I'm unlikely to get the chance. Not until it's put on display somewhere.'

'Harriet, you might be a fiction writer now, but you have a proven academic record, with a dozen learned papers on ballad history to your name. Why wouldn't they let you see it? Want your opinion even.'

Suddenly suspicious, she tilted her head to one side. 'Professor Frampton, you haven't told anyone I have an opinion worth giving, have you?'

Neil ran a hand over his poorly shaved chin. 'You

only call me by my official title when you're cross with me.'

'I'm not sure if I'm cross with you, yet. Have you said I'll examine it?'

'They asked for both of us.'

'*They*?' Hari felt the ever-present butterflies in her stomach flutter into action. 'Who is this *they*?'

'You're coming up to Buxton on Saturday, aren't you?'

'You know I am, although I'm nervous as hell.'

'There's absolutely no need to be. Jez is a lovely bloke, and the fans are a friendly bunch. On the whole. You always get one or two purists who want nothing more than the original texts to be portrayed again and again with no wavering from the *Holy Canon*– and even then, they can be sniffy about anything post-sixteenth century.' Neil raised his eyes to the heavens, his arms following in mock despair. 'Talk about being stuck in the past!'

Hari chuckled. 'If being a writer has taught me anything, it's that pleasing everyone is impossible.'

'It's the same for most walks of life.'

'Probably.' Hari's grin faltered. 'How do these Robin Hood Club weekends work then?'

'It's very simple. The fans come to listen to a series of talks about Robin Hood or medieval England in general, along with interviews with stars from the featured show – in this case, your *Return to Sherwood*. There are scheduled timeslots where they can get autographs from said stars, and sessions where they can have their photograph taken with them.'

'And while all that is happening, what do we do?'

'You, I imagine, will sell and sign books while chatting to fans in the trading area. Speakers like me, invited for our knowledge and not our fame, are largely ignored until our moment. We get the choice to either attend for the whole weekend, or hide in the Green Room, or slope off into the wonders of Buxton until we're needed.'

'You can always join Dot and me by the books. She's coming to help me do the sales thing.'

'I might well do that, in between hiding in my room and marking exam scripts, that is. Be great to see Dot again. I trust she'll bring a cookie supply from her biscuit-selling empire.'

'I'm banking on it!' Hari's smile dipped. 'You can help Dot shield me from the other author going. Frank Lister.'

Neil grunted a sharp laugh. 'Ah yes, Frank. I met him last year at the RHC event in Oxford. He'll be okay. Bit of a chip on his shoulder about how much success you've had with your books compared to him, but that's his problem, not yours.'

'I suppose...'

Not wanting to give Hari the chance to start overthinking where her fellow author was concerned, Neil jumped in. 'How about you come to see this ballad with me then? They've had some experts in already, but the more opinions the better.'

Hari sucked her bottom lip. 'The newspapers have suggested it's sixteenth century. Is that what they think at the Buxton Archive?'

'That's the impression I got. About 1530 is the current estimate, going by the material and the language.'

'And the ink used would support that?'
'Appears so. They're planning tests.'
Hari frowned. 'Gut instinct – genuine or hoax?'
'I want it to be genuine, but until we see it...'
'Quite.' Hari picked up a pen and pulled a sheet of

scrap paper towards her. 'The various reports describe a story not dissimilar to *Robin Hood and the Potter*, which dates to approximately 1503. If the Carter story is real, it could be an "inspired by" ballad.'

'That would be my guess. The Potter story was popular at the time, so it makes sense that a new story was created along the same lines but featuring a different craft. Writers have always liked to cash in on the success of others' words.'

'Ouch!'

'Oh, you know what I mean.' Neil winked.

Hari chuckled as she pondered. 'Or, perhaps *Robin Hood and the Carter* came first, but just happened to be written down later than *Robin Hood and the Potter*. Maybe there were earlier versions of this ballad that simply haven't survived. It could have a thirteenth or fourteenth century origin and only have been written down in the sixteenth.'

'Unlikely we'll ever know.'

'It'll come down to the language used.' Hari scribbled *1503-1530?* in her ever-present notebook. 'I assume people from the National Archive and British Museum have seen it?'

'They have. They wanted to take it away for safekeeping, but Buxton were insistent on keeping it until they have it in writing that the manuscript will be returned to them after the science bods have done their bit.'

'Can't say I blame them. Be good for their future funding bids, having a previously undiscovered work of literature on the premises.' Hari paused. 'I'm assuming they are housing it in suitable conditions?'

'I'm assured they are. Where it was found doesn't seem to have done it much harm. Some parts are faded, apparently, but it's in no worse a state than you'd expect for any other manuscript of the age.'

'How was it found?' Hari doodled a tree as she listened to her friend.

'The chief archivist, Christine Spencer, was tackling some old stock mending. Found it inside a copy of Volume Four of *Henry Knighton's Chronicon* that had been sent down to await a new spine some months earlier.'

'Odd.'

'How odd?'

'Wouldn't the archive want Knighton's complete work available to its users? It's a stock reference book for medievalists, after all. I'd have thought, if it was damaged, it would be mended at once and put back on display.'

'They have another full copy from the 1652 print run.'

'Really? Impressive.'

'The broken one was a reprint from the 1850s.'

'I see.' Hari made some more notes. 'Funny it was found in Volume Four. Quite a coincidence.'

'How do you mean?'

'That's the one containing first-hand insights into the fourteenth century. A time when many of the Robin stories are believed to have been created.'

'So it does. As you say, a coincidence, surely.'

'Unless it's a fake.'

Neil pulled a face. 'If you faked something like that, wouldn't you leave it in a less historically connected volume to avoid suspicion?'

'I don't know…'

'You've got your, "I've thought of something" expression on, Harriet. What is it?'

'I just wondered — if it is a fake — does the forger want us to know it's a fake?'

'And they left it in Knighton as a clue?'

'Maybe.'

'That's a bit of a leap. I mean, why bother creating a fake and then say it's a fake?'

'No idea. But if I went to the trouble of forging something like that, I'd only do it if I had a buyer already lined up. It would all stay private until money had exchanged hands and it was too late to start questioning its provenance.'

'Good point. And I suppose the library aren't likely to have gone public with its discovery if they didn't think it was real.' Neil relaxed back in his seat. 'So, I'll see you there then?'

The excitement at the prospect of being one of the few people allowed to study this new ballad conflicted with Hari's inner demons. 'Are you absolutely *sure* they asked for me? It wasn't more a case of you saying you'd only visit if I came too?'

'On Robin Hood's life.'

'Then how can I refuse?'

'Excellent.' Neil grinned. 'Christine Spencer has asked us to attend on Saturday afternoon, at 6 o'clock.'

'That's an odd time for a meeting in a library. Won't it be closing about then?'

'I get the impression that it's after hours because Miss Spencer wants to keep our visit quiet, so she doesn't have every historian in the country asking to take a look. She did ask me not to let anyone else know we were coming. If we're lucky, we can drag things out and miss the evening banquet!'

'Perfect!'

Chapter Two

Saturday 28th May

'Wow!' Dot let out a low whistle as she led Hari into the Harmen Hotel's reception area.

'Woah...' Hari stood stock still; nerves somersaulted within her stomach.

Just inside the hotel foyer's sliding glass doors, two huge freestanding banners, both emblazoned with the title of Hari's television show, *Return to Sherwood,* dominated the scene. Then, against a suitably medieval forest backdrop, two further banners hung from the ceiling. The nearest showed Mathilda in the foreground — the actress Scarlett Hann at her most ethereal — clutching a longbow and staring into the distance. The second banner had Will Scathlock centre stage. Actor Lee Stoneman glowered roguishly, looking past his fellow outlaw actors with a confidence that Hari could only envy.

In every direction, Hari saw tables covered in photographs of her cast leaders waiting to be signed. There were posters everywhere; most of which advertised her show or her novels, with only the occasional flyer showcasing Frank Lister's work.

Hari was trying not to worry about how the other author might feel about being second fiddle to a show that didn't feature a Robin Hood, when she became aware of the number of people in the hotel; many of whom were heading her way.

'Harriet's here!'

'It's Dr Danby...'

'Harriet Danby! Come on, let's say hello...'

The words acted like ripples in a pond, and suddenly Hari was surrounded by eager faces, looking at her expectantly.

'Oh... hello everyone.' Searching frantically for Dot, who'd been cut off from her as quickly as an island in a rising tide, Hari rallied and plastered on a smile. 'Pleased to meet you all.'

Finding her nervous smile becoming genuine in the presence of so many happy faces, Hari realised they were all waiting for her to say something else.

'Ummm... thank you for giving up your time to come and see me — well, the event I mean.'

'We love it. Come every year.' A girl with shockingly bright green hair spoke up as her companions beamed behind her. 'Wouldn't miss it. We arrived yesterday so we didn't have to get up at the crack of dawn to travel here. Just had breakfast.'

'You're all Robin Hood fans?'

'Big time.' The green-haired girl oozed enthusiasm. 'Especially your series. You are going to write another one for the telly, aren't you?'

'Well...'

'Sharman.'

'Sharman, that's kind of you, but I can't say as yet. If the TV company want me to, then I will adapt some more of the books. It isn't down to me.'

'It's a great series, I'm sure they will.' Sharman pushed a stray curl of tangled hair from her forehead. 'What do you think of this new ballad then? Real or fake?'

'Obviously, I'd love it to be...'

'Oh! It's Lee!'

Hari found her words fading into oblivion as Sharman's attention abruptly switched to the automatic doors as they swished open. She watched the combined gaze of the group of fans before her become focused, glaringly so in some cases, on her leading man as he walked into the hotel, towing a wheeled suitcase behind him.

In less than three seconds, everyone had gone.

'He's more handsome in real life than I expected,' Dot whispered.

'Yup, he's a looker all right.'

Dot linked arms with her friend. 'I think we should escape and find our host while we can. It won't be long before you're mobbed again.'

'Good idea.' Hari kept her eyes on her leading man. If Lee was annoyed that he hadn't had the chance to check in at the hotel desk before being badgered for selfies, he wasn't showing it. Unable to decide if he was simply being professional, or if he was lapping up the attention like a jilted teenager, she followed Dot across the foyer.

Jeremiah Barnes was not what Hari had been expecting. Although, she wasn't sure what she had been expecting, but the giant of a man with big hands, a grizzled grey beard and a large Indiana Jones-style fedora wasn't it. She would have cast him as Little John in any appropriate production, not as the host to a Robin Hood fan gathering.

'How wonderful of you to come along. I'm Jeremiah, or Jez – happy with either name. And you are Harriet and…'

'Dot.' Resting back on the table which they'd been allocated to trade from, Dot added, 'I'm Hari's right-hand saleswoman and cookie creator extraordinaire.'

'Cookie creator?'

Hari smiled. 'Dot is the head honcho of Cookie Creations.'

'No way! I love those. I'm rather partial to your ginger cup cookies.' Jez patted his robust waistline. 'As you can possibly tell.'

Dot chuckled. 'Always nice to meet a fan.'

'I think you'll find many of us have a weakness for your wares.' He chuckled warmly, before turning to Hari and nodding towards the rectangular table behind them. 'I hope this will be enough space.'

'Plenty, thank you. You've been very generous.' Hari noted that her table was twice big as the already stocked one on the opposite side of the room. 'Are you sure the other trader won't mind me having more space than them?'

'You're the star of the show this time, and you have more to sell than them, so don't you worry about that.'

Not commenting on the fact Jez hadn't actually reassured her that the other seller wouldn't mind, Hari said, 'Dot and I will go and get our boxes of stock from the car, then…'

'Absolutely, but first, I'll just run through a few things with you, Hari, if that's okay?'

'No problem.'

Dot took her car keys from her bag. 'I'll go and fetch some stock while you chat.'

Jez smiled appreciatively at Dot as she headed off, humming happily to herself. 'So, Hari, doors officially open at ten, that's in just over an hour, but as you can see, many fans are already here. Many of those who've travelled long distances booked into the hotel last night.'

'It's good of them not to come through into here.'

'This area, and the conference room beyond,' Jez waved an arm towards a set of double doors on the far side of the room, 'are out of bounds until kick off. If you need to escape from fans, stay in here until ten. After that, you and Dot are free to use the Green Room if you need some peace and quiet. It's on the first floor, third door on the left after the lift. The door is labelled; you can't miss it.'

'Green Room? Surely that's for the actors?'

'It's for all our guests. That includes you.'

'Oh.'

Jez smiled. 'You didn't think we'd take care of you?'

'I'm just a writer.'

Privately wishing that all his writing guests felt the same way, the host said, 'You're the writer of a successful TV show and several books. Trust me, not everyone came here because of the stars — lots of folk are here to meet you. They'll want to know where you get your ideas from and share their own ideas for episodes with you, to see if the creative magic you have will rub off on them.'

'Really?' Hari felt her muscles clench with nerves.

As if understanding her anxiety, Jez added, 'No need to worry, everyone will love you. All you have to do is help Dot sell your stuff, chat to anyone who wants to chat to you, and do your interview on Monday.'

'As simple as that?'

'Yes, and if it doesn't stay simple, come and talk to me.'

'Right. Sounds good.'

'You're bound to be asked about this alleged new ballad.'

'Fear not, I've done my research.'

'I knew you wouldn't let me down.' Jez grinned as he asked, 'So, what do you think, real or…?' His phone burst into life before Hari could reply.

A second later he'd disappeared beyond the swinging double doors.

The time between fetching in their final box of stock

and opening time at ten o'clock disappeared like sand through Hari and Dot's fingers.

'There's a massive queue building just outside the doors!'

On hearing Hari's nervous squeak, Dot glanced up from where she was organising the cash float. She could see a few eager faces peering through a small glass window in the doors. 'Awesome. I expect they'll traipse through to the welcoming ceremony in the conference room. Meaning they will get a good look at what we have to sell on the way.'

'Thank goodness you're here.'

Dot paused in the middle of counting ten pence pieces into a tray. 'Come on, Hari, you'd have been just fine without me. You saw how happy those fans were to see you. They weren't scary, they were just nice.'

'Until Lee came in.'

'You don't mind that they dashed off to see him, do you?'

'Not in the least. But it does show how people see things. Lee and Scarlett *are* the show. No question.'

'But without you, it wouldn't happen.'

Hari gave a rueful grin. 'Come off it, you know as well as I do, that is not how it works. It doesn't matter how kind Jez is, or how clearly a few fans see things, I'm the backroom girl. Mostly, that suits me fine.' Making sure they weren't being overheard, she mumbled, 'I'm not madly comfortable with sticking my head over the parapet like this.'

'I know.' Dot reached out and squeezed her friend's arm. 'You've got used to working alone.'

'I have. Plus, the modern world is all image and celebrity and social media. Sometimes it feels as if intelligence is out of fashion. It gets me down.'

Dot laughed as she gave her friend a hug. 'Maybe it

is, but not for everyone. Lots of folk are here for the scholarly side of things.'

'Ignore me, I'm being gloomy.' She shrugged. 'You know me, if I'm prepared for the worst-case scenario – like being totally ignored or ridiculed for my work – then it might not happen.'

Shaking her head at her friend's cynical self-view, Dot stepped in front of the stall to critically examine the display. 'This is good.'

'And yet you're still fiddling with it.' Hari smiled as Dot moved two copies of *Mathilda's Outlaw* forward half an inch. 'You've worked wonders. Thank you.'

Picking up a mug with *Mathilda's Sherwood* written on one side, and a cover of the associated book on the other, Dot chewed her lip. 'I think you should charge a tenner for these, rather than eight quid.'

'I want them to sell.'

'Oh, they'll sell. For a start, the other stall has no mugs on it. In fact, it has no merch at all. Just books.' Dot tutted. 'Missed opportunities everywhere.'

Thanking her lucky stars that her friend was so marketing savvy, and that she had listened to her advice concerning the merchandise side of things, Hari asked, 'Have you got your cookie flyers out?'

'Not yet. Are you sure you're okay with me advertising my business too? This is your moment, not mine.'

'I'm positive.'

'Thanks hun.' Dot was about to fish a pile of leaflets advertising Cookie Creations, and offering a discount on any goods ordered that weekend, from her bag when the doors that separated the trading room from the hotel's bar area flew open and, resplendent in his hat, Jeremiah Barnes led a procession of eager people into the conference room.

Shrinking back behind her stall, glad of the barrier it provided, Hari found herself smiling at everyone. Many attendees shared a cheery hello as they passed. Soon, the queue slowed, as people went to take their seats, and a bottleneck of attendees loitered happily before her stand.

Dot immediately engaged people in discussions about what was on offer. Hari was amazed to see two books sold before the opening ceremony had even taken place. Finding herself promising to sign them once the inaugural address was over, the crowd moved on, but not before she overheard a fan say to his partner:

'It's good and everything, *Return to Sherwood*, but nothing like as good as *Robin of Sherwood*.'

'Might have been better if she'd set it in the correct historical period.'

'In King Richard's time, you mean? Yeah, that Harriet missed a trick there. Maybe we should tell her later.'

'And perhaps, if there'd been a Robin Hood in it...'

Chapter Three

'All I'm saying, Jez, is that I ought to have as much table space as Harriet Danby, and it seems rather unfair that she is slated to give a fifty-minute interview on Monday, when I'm down for just twenty-five minutes today.'

Jez adopted his most understanding tone as he listened patiently to the Robin Hood Club's longest serving guest moan. 'I totally sympathise, Frank, but as you can see, Harriet has written more books than you, and she has a range of merchandise that the fans will expect to see and be able to buy.'

'I've been in this business far longer than her. It's not—'

'Not long before your interview in front of the fans? Absolutely right. Just two hours in fact,' Jez cut in before Frank Lister threw the final toy from his pram. 'And we are expecting quite a crowd. Your Robin Hood adventures are popular.'

'But not popular enough to be given equal billing to—'

Jez's free hand clenched and unclenched as he forced himself to relax. 'Frank, you must understand that this particular Robin Hood Club convention is centred around *Return to Sherwood*. It's Hari's turn to have the top of the bill talk on our last day. We focused on your work three years ago.'

'And ever since then we've talked about doing another one featuring my work, but it hasn't happened.'

'Because there are a great many Robin Hood related things out there. That means everyone has to take a back seat as well as having their moment in the limelight.'

'Well, I don't think—'

'Luckily for you, I do think, Frank. And right now, I think you should take advantage of the lull in here and think about your interview. I'm sure everyone will want to know about your next book.'

Before Frank had the chance to say anything else, Jez moved away, crossing the room as quickly as he could.

I bet there is no new book – again. Every year he promises one, and every year it remains in the planning stages.

He hadn't taken many steps across the deeply carpeted floor when his phone rang. 'Hello, Jeremiah Barnes.'

'Hey, Jez, it's Maisie.'

The organiser's heart sank at the sound of his least favourite agent's grating voice coming down the line. 'Hello, Maisie, how can I help?'

'Roger's just told me about the convention's schedule. I'm pretty sure you know what I'm going to say.'

Jez sighed. 'Ummm... no, actually.'

'Darling, although he, like me, is *thrilled* you have Harriet Danby on site, he is not happy about being interviewed separately to Lee and Scarlett. You're treating Roger like he's just an occasional character from *Return to Sherwood*.'

'But *he is* an occasional actor on the show.'

'Roger Striver is a *star,* darling. He was almost Frank Lister's Robin Hood, you know.'

Yes, I do know, because you, Frank and Roger tell me every time I see you.

'I can't deny that, Maisie, but the fact remains, he *didn't* play Robin, because the series was never made.' Jez hurried on before Maisie could chip in. 'I have no doubt Roger would have been wonderful in the role, but

I can't schedule his contribution on the panels according to work he *didn't* do. Please tell Roger we're all looking forward to seeing him tomorrow, and that his role as Cedric, the cunning potter, in episodes three and four of *Return to Sherwood* are among the fans' favourites. Now, if you'll excuse me, I have lots to do.'

Having hung up, Jez made another attempt to get to the bar for a much-needed coffee when his phone rang again.

For heaven's sake! What now!

He frowned as an unknown number appeared on the screen. 'Hello, Jeremiah Barnes.'

'Mr Barnes, sorry to disturb you. My name is Christine Spencer. I'm calling from the Buxton Library Archive. I believe you left a message for me?'

Jez stopped moving. 'Yes, indeed. Many thanks for calling back. It was about the new Robin Hood manuscript.'

'Indeed. My colleague says you run the Robin Hood Club. I'm sorry, I'm not familiar with it.'

Unsure if the crisp tone to the archivist's voice was just her way, or if she was being deliberately offhand, Jez explained, 'There's no reason why you should. The word "club" was perhaps a mistake on my part. Makes it sound rather child-like. We are, in fact, a group of people all connected with a passion for the stories of Robin Hood, not to mention other medieval outlaw or society tales such as Adam Bell, Clim of Clough and so on; in short, all things medieval with strong literary links. That passion also includes the more modern retellings of the story, be they in book, television or film format – but at heart, we're all enthusiasts for the legend at its root level.'

Christine Spencer's tone thawed. 'I sense you've given that speech once or twice before.'

'Once or twice, yes.' Jez relaxed. 'I will confess to occasionally becoming tired of the assumptions people make about what we do.'

A gentle laugh came down the line. 'Preconceptions are dangerous things. Who'd have thought an archivist could sit in an office and work at a computer screen all day? Surely I should be sat in a dusty library – oak-panelled, naturally – making copious notes with a fountain pen on vellum.'

Jez felt the last traces of tension lift from his shoulders. 'You mean that's not what you do all day?!'

'If only.' She paused, before going back into professional mode. 'So, how can I help?'

'To be honest, you probably can't, but I'd be lax in my responsibilities if I didn't at least ask…'

'You want to come and see the *Robin Hood and the Carter* manuscript.'

'I'd love to, but I'm not that ambitious. I wondered if there were any photographs of it that I could share with my guests. This year's Robin Hood Club convention is under way right now — in Buxton, as luck would have it.'

'It is?'

'We meet in a different location each year, usually somewhere with a connection, however tenuous, with the legend in some way, or someone who may have influenced said legend.'

'You can't beat the Peak District for that.'

'I agree.'

Jez sensed a new warmth to Christine's voice as she said, 'I've made a complete photographic record of the ballad. I'm only allowing small portions of these photographs to circulate in the media, but I'd be willing to allow you to display a few at your event.'

'Well, that's extremely kind. I'm honoured.'

Christine sighed. 'I'm under pressure to send the manuscript to London for examination. We have people here who could work on the manuscript, but well…'

'I totally understand.'

'Things do tend to go political if we aren't careful.'

'Doesn't everything?'

'Ironic, really. I can't help thinking Robin Hood would be against red tape.'

Jez laughed down the phone line. 'Can't argue with you there. I hope you didn't mind me asking.'

'Not at all. I have a couple of experts coming to see the ballad today, in the early evening. If you're in the area, why not come too? I'm sure no one would mind.'

Jez surveyed the scene around him. 'I would love to, but I've so much to do here, and it's just me doing it.'

'That's a shame.'

'I appreciate the offer, though.'

'Not at all.' There was a rustle down the line, and Jez had the feeling the archivist had sat up straight and was flicking through some papers. 'How about I get back to you about sending over some photographs for your guests to peruse?'

'I'd be very grateful. The finding of the ballad is on the lips of nearly everyone here.'

'And I see no harm in you personally seeing the complete photographed record. I'll bring it all with me, but for your eyes only.'

Jez approached Hari as she said goodbye to her latest customer. 'Fabulous to see you so busy. Surviving the event so far?'

'Day one has gone in a flash! It's been so busy with sales and chatting to fans that I haven't made it to a single event. I hope Frank Lister didn't think I was being rude by not attending his talk. I just couldn't get away.'

'I'm sure he will be fine with that.' Jez hoped he sounded more sincere than he felt.

'Hopefully I'll get to hear some talks tomorrow. I'm sure most people have already bought what they want from me now.'

'It's often the way. Folk come with money to buy Robin Hood stuff burning a hole in their pockets. I know a few of the regulars have a special savings account they use just for these events, and when they get here, boy, do they spend that money fast!'

Hari laughed. 'I can't complain. Dot's just gone to the car to get fresh copies of the first two novels in the series. We're all out in here.'

'I'm so pleased it's working for you.' Jez's eyes twinkled. 'I expect lots of people have been asking you about the ballad, too.'

'Quite a few, yes — although I know no more than anyone else.'

Jez nodded. 'I was just talking to the archivist in Buxton. I'm hoping she'll have some photos to show us tomorrow.'

'That reminds me.' Hari felt herself blush. 'I meant to say, well, ask really, would you mind if I skipped the banquet? Between ourselves, I've been asked to view the ballad this evening and…'

'You're one of the experts!' Jez's eyebrows rose in delight. 'Miss Spencer asked me to come along too, but obviously I can't escape.' He raised his arms up to encompass his surroundings.

Hari lowered her voice. 'I wasn't supposed to tell anyone, but I didn't want to just disappear and let you down. Nor did I want to lie to you about my absence. I'm an appalling liar, I go bright red!'

Chapter Four

Having arrived early, so she could be sure to get into the library before it closed at six, Hari inhaled deeply. She savoured the bookish atmosphere as she pushed open the heavy wooden double doors that took her into the library. Admiring the building's mix of original features, ranging from Regency, Georgian, Edwardian to Victorian architecture, Hari instantly loved the historical hotch-potch the structure represented — as if it was trying to echo the ages of the vast range of period documents and books it housed. Letting the blessed silence of quiet industry, punctuated occasionally by the turn of page or the click of a computer keyboard wash over her, she smiled. It felt like coming home.

Resolving, as she always did whenever she was in such a place, to spend more time getting back to her grass roots and researching original medieval sources for her next book – a resolution that would always falter when it came to the actual writing.

I'm so out of practice. What if I say something about the ballad, and I'm proved wrong?

Reminding herself that she'd been invited to be there, and was both wanted and expected, she headed to the reception. She had only taken two steps when a familiar voice called out, 'Harriet!'

Neil's whippet-thin frame was striding towards her. 'Hi there,' she mouthed quietly. 'Good timing.'

'Ready to be amazed?'

Christine Spencer had said very little since greeting them and leading the way into an office-cum-workroom, and to her prize exhibit.

Three pieces of parchment, each approximately forty-by-twenty centimetres in size, lay on a crisp white table covering. Three sets of gloves waited in sanitised packets next to the table, where a state-of-the-art magnifier and a wide screen microscope were connected to a nearby computer.

For a moment, no one spoke. They just stared at the beige pages and faded brown ink script before them. The letters themselves, sloping to the right, were tightly packed together, while each stanza of verse was spaced to clearly define the end of each section or verse. Spotted, as if with age, there was a small piece torn off across the right top hand corner of the second page, suggesting it had been caught in a drawer or the equivalent at some time.

'It's perfect… almost.' Neil broke the silence as he stepped closer, picking up a packet of gloves and ripping it open. 'That tear appears to be recent. The area where the parchment is damaged isn't the same colour as the rest of the document.'

'I agree,' Hari whispered, feeling somewhat in awe of the item before her. 'I'd guess the blemish is less than a year old… although I can't be completely sure, of course. Ummm… Is it too perfect?'

'That crossed my mind,' Christine slipped her own gloves on, 'and yet, somehow, it feels real.'

'I agree.' Neil crouched closer. 'It has a sense of age about it.' He paused before turning to Hari. 'You know that feeling you get when you sit with a thirteenth century court roll – or a fourteenth century one, come to that…'

'I know the one. You get a sense that you are privileged just to be in the same room as it. I always find myself picturing the clerk whose whole life was spent doing nothing but writing it; hearing the sounds of medieval life going on around me as I read.' Hari stopped talking; not looking at her colleagues in case they decided she was insane and unfit to examine the document. She focused on the first page. 'This has an atmosphere to it, but is that because we want it to be real, or because someone very clever has manufactured accurate ink and has applied it to some original material?'

'You think that the parchment is period?' Christine sat down and pulled her chair as close as possible to the table. 'The others who've seen it wouldn't commit themselves.'

'I'm not surprised. They have reputations to uphold. I'm just a writer, so I've less face to lose. And I can't swear to it, but I'd be very surprised if this parchment wasn't sixteenth century.' Wary of touching the document unless she had to, even with gloves on, Hari asked, 'Who found it? The newspapers were very cagey on that front.'

Christine smiled. 'Actually, I did, but I'd appreciate it if you kept that quiet. I don't need the press on my front doorstep.'

'Wow! That must have felt amazing.' Hari asked, 'How on earth have you managed to keep that a secret?'

'With difficulty. I will publicly confess to being the finder if it's confirmed as genuine. If it isn't, then I might tell my friends, but otherwise I'll stay quiet. I'm not keen on being associated with a fraud.'

'Understandable.' Neil stared at the lettering. 'The opening line is clear enough... *"In spryng, when the buds appeare".*'

'Very like the Potter tale...' Hari slipped on her gloves. 'I can see why comparisons are being made.'

Neil agreed, 'That was, *"In schomer, when the leves spryng".*'

'They've just swapped the season. No one's mentioned that until now.' Christine sucked on her bottom lip. 'I've been led to understand by the three historians who viewed it before you, that many of the early ballads were similar; being retellings of each other.'

'It was the same then as it is now.' Hari focused her gaze on the title, placed slightly off centre on the first page. 'We're still doing it, taking the original stories and reworking them to suit our audiences. New characters are added, but they are often simply reflections of those from the first texts. Take Mathilda from my novels; everyone knows she is a reworking of Maid Marion.'

'I hadn't thought of it like that.' Christine observed her visitors as they peered at the documents.

Hari asked, 'What's the current thinking? Fake or real?'

'As I said, no one will commit themselves. Not until the paper is analysed.'

'Wise.' Neil kept his gaze on the document. 'But their gut feelings?'

'Two-to-one in favour.'

'Fair enough.' Hari held a magnifying glass up to her eye and focused on the capital R of Roben. 'At least if it is a fake, they've remembered to use an e instead of an i in Robin.'

'Could have been a y or an e really.' Neil scrubbed a hand over his beard.

'True.' Hari paused, her focus moving back to take in the whole manuscript. 'I don't think analysing the paper will help. It's the ink and graphology that will tell the full story – quite literally in this case.'

'So, what do you really think?'

Hari guessed Neil had been dying to ask her that question ever since they'd left the library, but he knew her well enough to wait until they were sat with a cup of coffee apiece before quizzing her.

'We've talked in general terms, but now we are away from Christine – yes, or no? Fake or real?'

'No comment.' Hari picked up her coffee cup and took a lifesaving sip. 'You?'

'I don't see how it was faked. It looks and feels so authentic. And yet…'

Hari nodded. 'My mind keeps coming back to how well it has survived considering how it was found. What was it Christine said? She was going through the books that needed mending — many of which had been waiting for attention for years — and found it.'

'How long was the mending archive undisturbed, though? And how come it ended up in a book and no one noticed?'

'It wouldn't have been visible, though. The *Knighton* volumes are large, at least fifty-by-thirty centimetres in size. That's big enough to conceal the document's three pages without folding them or having their edges poking out.'

Neil leant back while a waitress delivered two plates of jacket potatoes topped with tuna. He thanked her before saying, 'We could do with knowing when the *Knighton* volume was first consigned to the mending pile.'

'We could. I am also curious about the parchment itself. I'd stake what little reputation I have in historical circles that it is original, so where did it come from, if the ballad was faked?'

'You think forensic analysis will find older, faded writing under what is there now?'

'It might, or it might have been a blank page torn from another volume.'

'A flyleaf from an old book?'

Hari shuddered at the idea of such desecration. 'Three flyleaves – and that's assuming they didn't have a practise first.'

'*If* it's a fake.'

'Yes.'

'Is that yes to *if,* or yes to you are sure it's a fake?'

'No comment!' Hari laughed as she forked up some potato and tuna. 'Don't get me wrong, I'd love it to be real, but…'

'I know. The chances of finding an original document, in that condition, in such a book…'

'Are a million to one.'

'But if it is real?'

Despite her misgivings, Hari couldn't help but be excited by the prospect. 'It would be amazing. Especially for the historian and archive team who'd get to work on it.'

'You'd be hanging up your writing hat and applying for the job?'

Hari sat back in surprise. 'As if! I'm one of those awful writer types who has diluted the Robin Hood canon.'

Neil laughed. 'You're so paranoid! Why not dream anyway? You never know, if it is the real deal, you could retrieve the imagined damage to your reputation by doing some research into this new story.'

Hari suddenly looked up towards the window, making Neil turn sharply in that direction.

'What is it, what did you see?'

'I was just checking to see if there were any pigs flying past the window.'

'Oh, ha-ha.' Neil took a gulp of his fast-cooling coffee.

Hari's smile dipped as she scooped up some more dinner. 'Can I ask you about the Robin Hood Club event?'

'The one we are currently skiving from?'

'The very same.' Hari tried to ignore the stab of guilt she felt at abandoning Dot to the medieval banquet alone. 'It isn't held at the same location each year, is it?'

'Moves around the UK. Jez tries to make it so that if regular attendees have a long drive, train trip, or whatever one year, then it's not so bad for them the next.'

'Nice of him.'

'And a real pain in the arse, I imagine. Not many hotels have enough room for everyone, as well as sales and conference space. Not to mention parking, access to major roads and rail networks and the likes.'

'I hadn't considered any of that.'

'So, what is it you were thinking?' Neil put down his fork. 'You've got your "I'm on the trail of something" face on. I've not seen that since you were doing your PhD and found a crime recorded in a gaol delivery roll that was previously unconnected to outlaw activity in the Peak District.'

Hari rolled her cup between her palms. 'Between you and me, I was thinking what a lucky coincidence it is that we are here, a mass of Robin Hood fans and scholars, on the doorstep of the place where and when such a document was found.'

Chapter Five

The medieval banquet — which wasn't a medieval banquet at all, but a roast dinner eaten by people wearing fancy dress — was in full flow. If anyone noticed the absence of a roasting pig on a spit or endless flagons of ale, no one was saying so.

Dot grinned at the eager faces fixed on her, as they sat around one end of a long, thin table. 'I must say, it hadn't crossed my mind that anyone would want to talk to me! I'm only here as Hari's helper.'

'Of course we want to talk to you.' Sharman swept her straggly mass of hair back, catching a tress that had escaped her bottle-green headband; the clash with her lime hair was remarkable to say the least. 'Not only are you the best friend of the guest of honour, but you make the most delicious cookies on the planet.'

'You're very kind.' Dot shovelled up a forkful of roast potato. 'I must admit, when Hari invited me to bring some flyers along, I never dreamt they'd be so popular. Everyone seems to be ordering. It's rather wonderful.'

'We do like a biscuit or three here.' The woman sat next to Sharman smiled shyly. 'I love the ones you do with melted dark chocolate in the middle best.'

'Oh yes.' Her neighbour leant forward, accidentally dipping the wide sleeve of her Disney princess outfit into her gravy. 'The melty in the middle cookies are fabulous, although the orange and milk chocolate one is my personal favourite.'

'What got you into cookies, Dot?' Sharman poured some wine into her glass.

'The inability to afford nice biscuits when I was a student.' Wary of boring her companions, Dot asked, 'Wouldn't you rather talk about the new ballad or

Robin Hood or something? My business story isn't exactly riveting.'

'We can do that all day.' The woman in the princess outfit smiled. 'I'm Clara, by the way.'

'Dot. Pleased to meet you.'

'And I'm Penny.' The younger woman next to Sharman gave a small wave from the other side of the table.

'And you all catch up here every year?'

'Wherever the Robin Hood Club meets, yep.' Sharman pushed her headband higher up her forehead. 'Never miss one.'

'It's the only time we see each other.' Clara raised a glass to her friends. 'I'm from Dorset, Penny lives in Norfolk, and Sharman's all the way up in Oldham.'

'Geography not on your side, meeting up wise, then.' Dot smiled.

'Nope. But we all eat your biscuits, just like we all read Harriet's books and watch her TV show.'

'I'd never thought of it like that.' Dot paused as she felt a new marketing idea spin through her head. 'Uniting people through cookies…'

'And biscuits and books go so well together, don't you think?' Sharman added.

'I certainly do.'

'I often have a box delivered to the shop.'

Dot laid down her cutlery. 'You manage a shop?'

Clara smiled at her friend. 'Sharman runs a bookshop. It's awesome.'

Sharman chuckled. 'You've never been there, Clara.'

'I've seen photos on Facebook, and I've heard you talk about it. It sounds wonderful. *Parchment and Paper*. A real mix of new and second-hand books.'

'That's a great name for a bookshop.' Dot raised

her glass in approval.

'It's a bit of a treasure trove. A muddle of small rooms all jammed with books, but I love it.' Sharman dragged the headband off her head, pulling a face. 'But I hate this thing. God knows why I bothered to put it on. Every year I try it, and every year it's off before the dessert course.'

'You were telling us why you sell cookies, Dot.' Penny wiped absentmindedly at her gravy-spattered sleeve.

'Okay, but don't say I didn't warn you. It's not an exciting tale.'

Sharman laughed. 'Consider us warned.'

Taking a draft from her wine glass, Dot launched into her story. 'It's simple, really. It was almost time to leave uni; that's where I met Hari. She knew what she wanted to do with her life, to be a medieval historian, but I didn't. We were sat in a pub one day and I was mithering over what I'd do once I'd got my business degree. Hari asked what I loved most in life, and I said cake, books, and biscuits.' Dot patted her rounded waistline. 'As perhaps you can tell!'

'And so say all of us!' Penny winked. 'Go on.'

'Hari suggested I build a career around one of those. I'd always intended to run my own business, but I hadn't a clue doing what. I can't write and I couldn't think of an angle with cake that hadn't been done to death, so I considered cookies. The cheap ones are okay, but often lack flavour, and the nice ones can be stupidly expensive, or they are in packs of five or six that go soft very quickly if you don't eat them all in one go.'

'I'm guilty of eating a whole packet at once!' Sharman took a sip of wine.

'Me too!' Dot laughed. 'But even when I mainlined

them in one go, the last cookie always felt a bit limp, if that makes sense.'

Penny winked. 'Nothing worse than a limp biscuit.'

'Oh, I don't know!' Clara giggled. 'I can think of something worse.'

Digging her friend in the ribs, Sharman laughed. 'That's a different kind of limp crisis altogether.'

'Ignore them, Dot!' Penny rolled her eyes. 'So you decided to supply small packs of fresh cookies direct from the bakery to the customer via mail order?'

'That was the plan. Took me a long time to find a recipe that worked; a cookie with the right amount of snap, but which also kept some softness which would last once the packet was opened. The last thing I wanted was to produce a biscuit that was the same as something that could be picked up in a supermarket. Although, since the business took off, I have noticed a few of the supermarkets have upped their game, starting their own line in superior cookies, which are annoyingly like mine.' Dot sighed. 'Anyway, I had to make sure they would stay intact through the postal service too. When I started, I didn't have the likes of Uber or Deliveroo on hand, it was just the posties.'

'Cookie Creations is a far better biscuit supplier than anywhere else.' Sharman spoke so decisively that Dot was taken aback.

'Why, thank you. We work very hard. I can only take the credit for the running of the business and tasting the stock. It's my bakers, dotted all over the country, who are the magicians here.'

As the waiters and waitresses began to clear the tables around them, Sharman asked, 'Where's the nearest bakery to here then? The one who is producing your delicious biscuits this weekend?'

'*Pearce Bakes* in Bakewell – so not too far away.

They, like all the other bakeries I pay to create my biscuits, dedicate a small part of their enterprise to creating my cookie on an order-by-order basis – with a few of the most popular flavours constantly in stock.'

'No wonder they taste so fresh.' Penny looked at the dishes of apple pie and ice cream that the waiting staff were depositing in front of them. 'Not out of a wholesaler's freezer department like this lot!'

Clara sank a spoon into the over-sugared pie crust. 'Shame we aren't having your cookies and ice cream. That would taste amazing.'

Dot played her spoon through her fingers. 'Depends on the flavour of cookie. I had wondered about proposing a frozen dessert to some supermarkets, but I'm not sure the quality of the biscuit would hold.'

'Probably not, but it's a lovely thought.' Clara sighed. 'Got any new flavours on the go?'

'I've just signed off on some cappuccino ones and some chilli and ginger ones. Hari usually gives me the last word on whether the flavours work or not.'

'Now that's a job I wouldn't mind having!' Penny rubbed her hands together. 'A Cookie Creations taste tester! Better than being an admin clerk for sure!'

Dot chuckled. 'Be careful what you wish for! I'm always after opinions when I trial new flavours.'

'What flavours do you have in mind to add to the range next then?' Sharman scooped up some pie.

'I've been toying with a few ideas. I'd quite like to do a range with nuts in – peanuts, almonds and so on – but it's such a minefield for allergies.'

'Makes the food preparation more complex.' Sharman pulled a face. 'I can't have anything with nuts in.'

'Oh, I love almonds!' Penny wiped her mouth with her serviette. 'I'd buy almond cookies like a shot.'

'Me too. The folks in the staff room at the school where I'm a teaching assistant love a biscuit at breaktime. I bet they'd like almond ones.' Clara pushed her half-eaten pie away with a wrinkle of her nose. 'Mind you, anything would be better than that!'

'Not great, is it.' Dot finished her ice cream, leaving her pie largely untouched. 'There's a costing issue with nut-flavoured biscuits too. I can't claim a nut-free environment for the other cookies if some do have nuts in, so I'd need to pay for separate baking space.'

'Which costs money.' Sharman grimaced. 'Business is never straightforward. I'd love a small café in my bookshop, but the health and safety hoops you have to jump through are insane.'

Dot nodded. 'That's one of the reasons I don't have a café outlet, but I won't rule the idea out forever.'

'Ooohhh... a Cookie Creations café!' Penny's eyes shone. 'I'd be there like a shot.'

'Me too.' Sharman threw down her spoon in defeat. 'Shame Harriet missed this evening, apart from the pie, obviously. Will she be back soon?'

Dot gave a friendly shrug of her shoulders. 'I hope so, but I wouldn't be that surprised if we didn't see her again until tomorrow.'

'Where is she, anyway?' Sharman grabbed hold of her wine glass so the waitress clearing their table didn't take it away.

'Out with Professor Harman.'

Penny blushed. 'He's nice. I always go to the professor's talks. Handsome and clever. What more could a girl ask for?'

Dot smiled. 'He was Hari's tutor at uni. They go way back, but rarely get time to catch up.'

'How wonderful. I had no idea Professor Harman

was connected to Harriet.'

Penny's over-plucked eyebrows rose. 'It must be nice for her to escape all of us for a bit too.'

'I always feel a bit sorry for the guests here.' Sharman laughed. 'We can be a bit full on!'

Dot hurriedly defended her friend. 'It isn't that Hari wanted time out from you guys, I promise. She's quite shy, but has been having a great time.'

'She certainly appears to be happy.'

'Bit overwhelmed, perhaps. Hari was gobsmacked to be asked to come in the first place, and rather nervous. That's one reason I'm here; moral support.'

'Can't see why she was gobsmacked,' Penny said. 'Even if she wasn't here as an author, she'd be a great guest as a Robin Hood expert. Her academic record speaks for itself.'

Clara nodded. 'I've read all her papers on medieval literature.'

'Have you?' Dot was surprised.

'Loads of us here study history as a hobby. Inspired by our love of the Robin Hood story.' Sharman drained her glass. 'I've got my degree, but I'm longing to do a PhD. It's just a case of money.'

Penny's nose wrinkled. 'It does cost a fortune if you can't find funding.'

Dot gave a sympathetic nod. She knew from conversations with Hari how difficult it was to find postgraduate funding for humanities subjects. 'Would you like to give up the bookshop and study then, Sharman?'

'I'd do both. I love the bookshop, but if I could get a doctorate, then I'd be able to get papers published. Be a proper historian.'

Dot's forehead creased into a frown. 'You don't need to have qualifications to be a historian, do you?'

'To be respected and taken seriously you do. I mean, take Frank. He's very knowledgeable, but he has no qualifications, so he tends to get overlooked on academic matters.'

Having heard Hari say as much in the past about other authors with vast knowledge but only fiction as proof of their intelligence, Dot conceded the point.

Sharman pushed back her chair as she made ready to leave the table. 'Still, I may well have a breakthrough on the money front soon.'

'How exciting! I'll keep my fingers crossed for you.' Dot stood up. 'I hoped Hari would be back by now.'

Clara glanced hopefully towards the door. 'It would be great if she could join us. I've a few questions about this new ballad. Do you think she knows much about it?'

Mentally crossing her fingers behind her back, Dot said, 'No more than anyone else at this stage, but obviously she's taking an interest.'

'I'm sure.' Clara hooked up her long skirts as they wove through the fast-emptying tables and chairs. 'I hope it's real. It would be wonderful to have a new story to enjoy.'

Checking her watch, Hari experienced a fresh stab of guilt. She'd promised Dot she'd rescue her before the end of the evening. 'I ought to get back. I've a feeling the banquet will be over by now.'

'It's usually done and dusted by nine.'

'You've been to one before?'

'Just once.' Neil picked up his pint of beer. 'The food is generally the poor end of mass catering. Most people eat as fast as they can and escape in favour of the bar and chatter.'

'You aren't selling it to me.' Hari sucked in her bottom lip. 'Poor Dot.'

'She'll be in her element. Dot's a people person.'

'Unlike me.' Hari pulled a face. 'The whole thing's been nicer than I imagined so far, though. Everyone's so friendly.'

'Even Frank Lister?'

'I've not spoken to him yet. The chance hasn't arisen, thankfully.'

'You think he'll resent you for having a TV show when he never got his?'

'I'd put money on it.'

Neil got to his feet. 'Then, for goodness' sake, don't let him know you've seen the new ballad. He's an expert on this stuff too. Real or fake, his ego would not welcome the fact that you've seen it before him.'

Chapter Six

Sunday May 29th

Hari sat down for the first time since breakfast with a grateful sigh. 'I can't deny this is massive fun, but boy do I appreciate it when everyone disappears to listen to a talk or get themselves photographed with a star and we get five minutes to breathe!'

Dot laughed. 'Have you eaten?'

'Not since I had a couple of slices of toast at eight, but then, neither have you. If I haven't been signing books, you've been selling them. Thank goodness we brought so many.' Hari gestured to the doors. 'Fancy some chips or something from the bar?'

'Hell yes, I'm famished. I'll go. You ought to be here in case anyone wants a signed copy.'

'Okay.'

'No need to look so worried.'

Hari grimaced. 'But what if…'

'You're going to have to talk to Frank eventually.' Dot gave her friend a gentle smile.

'But you've seen the disapproving looks he's been throwing this way.'

'Envy. His problem, not yours.'

'I ought to have gone and said hello to him the minute we arrived, but what with sorting the books and everything, it's been a day and a half already and—'

'I know you're convinced he'll hate you, Hari, but there is no reason why he should.'

'Actually, there's a very good reason.' Hari's stomach interrupted her, giving a deep growl of hunger. 'But if I don't eat soon, I'll feel faint, and that won't help anyone.'

Dot winked. 'Then just be grateful you've got

halfway through the three-day event without talking to him and pull your big girl pants up.'

Dot hadn't been gone more than thirty seconds when the inevitable happened. Out of the corner of her eye, she saw Frank put down his mobile and cross the room, his purpose clear.

He had been watching the comings and goings at her table from the safety of the opposite side of the room since the doors opened four hours ago. Hari suspected he believed his frequent glimpses to be covert, but James Bond he was not.

'Mr Lister.' Hari reached out a hand. 'It's a pleasure to meet you. I'm sorry I haven't been over to introduce myself, but—'

'You've been busy. Yes. I saw.' Frank pushed his hands deep into the pockets of his leather jacket that was designed for a man far younger than he was. 'You'd think our esteemed host would have taken the trouble to introduce us on day one. It seems I'm not even worth that courtesy these days.'

Rather taken aback by Frank's open attack on Jez, Hari found herself floundering. 'He is rather busy. In fact, he apologised for not having time to introduce us formally.'

'Apologised to you, but not to me.' Frank grunted. 'Sounds about right.'

Realising her attempt at conciliation had had the opposite than planned effect, Hari felt pinpricks of nervous perspiration gather on the back of her neck. 'It's been rather overwhelming, all this. I didn't feel I could abandon people who'd paid to be here to come and say hello. I'm sorry if I offended you.'

'Oh.' Frank looked surprised, as if he'd expected confrontation rather than an apology.

Ploughing on, so Frank couldn't get another dig in, Hari said, 'I expect it was like that for you the first time you came to the Robin Hood Club. The fans are so keen. It's unbelievable.'

'Well, yes... I suppose it was.' He dragged a hand through his closely-cropped hair. 'That was a few years ago now. Before—'

'Before I came along and ruined it all?' Hari held up her hands as she jumped in, stalling his chance to accuse her of ruining his life by cutting to the chase. 'I'm *really* sorry. I had no idea my books would be successful. It's all been rather a whirlwind – a surprising whirlwind at that.' Wishing Dot would hurry up, Hari added quickly, 'I love your books, by the way. I've read them all.'

'Have you? Then why didn't you come to my talk?'

'Well, I was rather occupied here.'

'Of course you were,' Frank snapped. 'When?'

'Pardon?'

'When did you read my books? Before or *after* you wrote yours?'

It took Hari a few seconds to understand what Frank Lister was implying. 'Oh my God! You don't think I'd...'

Frank's voice dropped to a quiet hiss, the menace in his words unmistakeable. 'If I discover that you have ripped off my stories and made them your own, just by swapping a Robin for your blessed Mathilda, I'll...'

Hari's mouth was opening and closing so fast, she wasn't sure which words of denial to utter first. The whole idea was insane. *As if I'd plagiarise!* She'd always gone on at her former students to be original, however old the source of their work, and...

The abrupt sound of fast-approaching, heavy-soled boots pulled Hari's stupefied gaze away from her companion.

'Harriet! Harriet. Can I quickly grab your autograph before I go and have my photos signed by Lee?'

The attendee with the shocking green hair that she remembered from the first day was descending on them fast, waving a copy of *Mathilda's Sherwood* in her hands. 'Hi, Frank, how's it going?'

'Good, thank you, Sharman. I see you've had another trip to the hairdresser since last year's meet up.'

'Nah. Do it meself.'

'You don't say.'

Horrified at Frank's offhand manner towards their visitor, Hari felt two high spots of pink hit her cheeks; taking the embarrassment he should feel as her own.

As Frank stomped off, Sharman laughed. 'Don't you mind him, Harriet. He's a right old stick in the mud. Positively medieval in attitude.'

'He was so rude to you.'

'He's rude to everyone.' She patted her hair. 'But to his credit, Frank comes back every year and he always remembers the attendees who've been before by name. Roger Striver does too. I know Roger can also be annoying in his own special way, but he makes sure he knows who's who at events like this.' Sharman smirked. 'Roger's a bit of a lapdog when it comes to Frank, but that is one positive trait he's picked up from him at least.'

'That's quite something.' Nerves danced in Hari's stomach as Sharman talked about one of her series' recurring actors that she knew was due to join them the following day. 'There are hundreds of you. I'm struggling with names. I hope people don't think I'm being rude, especially as I wasn't at the dinner last night.'

'Not at all. Dot explained you were catching up with the professor. Everyone needs time out from this for a while. Even attendees like me try and escape for a few hours over the three days.' Sharman lifted her book up hopefully. 'Would you mind? I'm happy to pay for the signature.'

'Pay for it?' Hari paused in the act of grabbing her pen.

'Yeah. We pay for all the autographs we get here.'

Hari took hold of the novel. 'But you paid for the book, and you paid to be here. How can anyone justify asking for more money for a two second signature?'

Sharman shrugged. 'It's just what happens.'

'Well, I'm not charging for signatures.'

'Thanks. That's great.'

'I did wonder why so many people were querying the price when they paid me yesterday.'

'Probably expecting you to add a tenner for the signing. Didn't Jez tell you that's how it works?'

'A tenner! Jez didn't say anything.'

'He probably assumed you knew.' Sharman laughed. 'Frank charges a fiver. Makes it sound like a bargain.'

Hari groaned. 'Another reason for him not to like me.'

Sharman brushed a strand of green hair from her eyes and tucked it behind her ear. 'Like I said, don't worry about it. Frank has fans, and most of them are here. But we tend to like his work, not him as a person.'

Hari passed the newly-signed book back to its owner. 'That's sad, really.'

'His doing.' Sharman checked her phone for the time. 'I must dash, if I don't want to miss my chance to get a photo with Lee. Thanks, Harriet!'

***

Dot plonked two takeaway-style boxes of chips onto the edge of the table and sank onto her seat with relief. 'It's insane out there!'

'Lots of hungry people.'

'You aren't wrong.' Dot opened the nearest box and gobbled down two hot chips. 'Umm... worth the wait, though. These are lovely.'

Hari opened her box, but her appetite had deserted her. 'They smell great.'

'Tuck in before I eat yours too.'

'You go first. One of us should have clean hands in case a customer comes along.'

'Good thinking.' Dot stuffed another chip into her mouth. 'But you should eat too. I'll have a few, clean my hands, then you have a few.'

'Actually, I'm not sure I could eat.' Hari pulled a face. 'Thanks for getting them, though.'

'Why?' Dot paused mid-chew. 'What's happened?'

'Frank Lister. He implied that I stole his ideas for my book. As I've read them, I must therefore have been influenced by them.'

'You're not serious?'

'Deadly.' Hari swallowed. 'I knew he might be difficult, but he was properly hostile. I tried to be nice. Supportive, even. Told him I'd enjoyed his books.'

'And he jumped on that as an excuse to add credence to his paranoia.' Dot stared across the room. 'Creep.'

'What if he tries to prove it, though? What if he goes all legal on me?'

'He'd be an utter fool to try.' Dot closed the lid of her chip box. 'And, forgive me if I'm wrong, but your books and Frank's have nothing in common, bar a few overlapping names; Will, John and so. And those names are in the public domain anyway.'

'I suppose so.'

'Suppose nothing.' Dot glared across the room. 'I've read your books and his books. They're nothing like each other. Ignore him, Hari.'

'Easier said.'

'There's a lull now while everyone grabs food. Why not head up to the Green Room? Grab some quiet time. You were nonstop yesterday, and it's been busy this morning. Take half an hour.'

'Would you mind?'

'Not at all. And take your chips with you.'

Plastering on a smile, waving back as fans waved to her as she passed through the hotel towards the stairs to the upper floor, Hari tried to calm down.

Dot is right. There is no way Frank could officially accuse me of theft of his work. I wish he wasn't quite so hostile, though.

Pushing through the swing door to the stairwell, Hari inhaled the beautiful silence as the bustling noise of the guests was shut away behind her. Avoiding the temptation to sit on the stairs and eat her chips there, Hari moved on, driven by the desire for a cup of coffee to accompany her lunch.

Glad to find the corridor that led to the Green Room empty, Hari nervously peered around the appropriately-labelled door. She was immediately confronted with rows of sandwiches and cakes, alongside two huge catering flasks of tea and coffee. Feeling like an interloper, Hari slipped inside and started to pour a coffee.

'Who the bloody hell are you?'

Hari's cheeks infused with a red heat as she spun around, slopping her half-full coffee cup over her legs.

Lee Stoneman was sat in the furthest corner of the

room, his arms and legs crossed. He looked angry and bored. 'This room is for stars only. Bugger off.'

Dropping her cup onto the table with a clatter, embarrassed that the star of her own show didn't recognise her, Hari felt her shoulders start to shake as Scarlett Hann strolled into the room.

'Hi, Harriet. Good to see you.'

'Hi. Yes.' Giving her Mathilda a half smile, Hari stuttered, 'I was… I was just going.' Then she ran from the room.

Chapter Seven

The nearest exit led Hari down some stark back stairs and into a large, pub-style garden which backed onto the rear of the hotel. Full of attendees to the event, all chatting happily as they tucked into their sandwiches and pints of beer, Hari tried to smile as they waved at her, hoping they wouldn't notice the distress she was trying to hide.

How could my own leading man not know who I am?

Moving forward, blindly heading onwards, her trainers padded across the soft grass. She clutched the box of chips, crushing its edge in her grip as she stumbled towards a solitary bench, half hidden by an overgrown hedge at the very back of the hotel's garden.

Frank Lister hates me, and now my Will Scathlock has dismissed me. I was right. I'm not cut out for this sort of thing. I should have stayed at home.

Closing her eyes, Hari took some long, deep breaths and mumbled, 'I am here because my work is popular. I am not an imposter. I am *not* an imposter.'

Not entirely believing what she was telling herself, Hari opened her eyes and glanced back at the people sat chatting around the pub garden tables. *They all seem happy. Dot would say that I'd helped make them happy.*

Hari was halfway through exhaling another heavy sigh, when a figure at the far edge of the pub garden, seemingly trying not to be seen, caught her eye. 'Roger?'

Jez doffed his hat as he approached Dot. 'How's everything going? Need anything? Help required?'

'All great, thanks.' Dot smiled up at the host's impressive frame. 'I was just indulging in a sneaky sit down while everyone's elsewhere.'

'Wise.'

'It's been a while since I helped Hari sell her books. I'd forgotten how tiring being behind a stall was.'

'And where is the lovely Dr Danby?' Jez looked about him. 'I thought, now I have two minutes, I'd get the introduction to Frank over with before someone else needs me for something.'

Dot wrinkled her nose. 'He beat you to it. Not the friendliest encounter, from what Hari tells me. She's gone to the Green Room for some recovery time.'

Pulling off his fedora, Jez played the rim through his hands, muttering under his breath. 'Damn that man. Honestly, he simply can't take that other people write Robin Hood books. You'd think he'd written the originals, the way he goes on.'

'It's ironic, as Hari rather likes his work.' Dot paused, uncertain if she should go on, but going on anyway. 'Frank gave Hari the impression that he thinks she stole the idea for Mathilda from him, and that her success should have been his.'

Jez gave a resigned groan. 'I'd better go and find her, then I'll talk to him.'

Dot sat up straight. 'I am not sure Hari would want you to. She very much favours the no ripples on the pond method of living.'

'Me too...' Jez lowered his voice as he added, 'So why I put myself through this every year, I don't know. The price of it is crippling me, the guests can be prickly, and... oh well...'

Dot gave him a gentle smile as she saw the concern in his tired eyes. 'You do it because it makes a lot of people happy, and you're clearly a good person.'

'Oh, ummm, thank you.' Taken aback, Jez looked

intently at Dot for a moment, before averting his gaze to the book stock on the dark-green tableclothed display that divided them. 'Apart from Frank being bitter, how's it going?'

'Sales wise, very well.' Dot stared past Jez to the table on the opposite side of the room. She could hear Frank in full historian mode, explaining to an eager fan why his Robin Hood was very probably *the* Robin Hood. 'How about you do me a favour?'

Jez pushed his hat back into place. 'If I can.'

'It comes with the added bonus of being able to sit down for five minutes.'

'Now you're talking.'

'Hari said she'd be thirty minutes, but she's been gone almost an hour. That's ages for her. Normally her crushing sense of duty allows no more than a fifteen-minute lunchbreak. I'd like to see if she's alright.'

'You want me to watch the stall?'

'Please. I'll be quick.' Dot pointed to the cash box. 'You won't have to worry about the card machine. If anyone wants a book, say it's cash only until I get back. If that's okay?'

'Sure.' Jez checked his watch. 'But sadly, it can only be five minutes. I need to meet Professor Frampton in Reception before his talk.'

'Understood. There are some cookies under the counter. Help yourself; you could say I have access to a bottomless supply.'

Hari kept her eyes fixed on the view of the countryside that ran beyond the back of the pub garden as Dot plonked herself onto the bench next to her. 'I'm sorry. I lost track of time.'

'Uh huh.' Dot followed Hari's eyeline onto the Peaks. 'I assumed you'd be in the Green Room, so I went there first. I found Scarlett. She told me what happened.'

'Oh.'

'Sorry, Hari. That must have hurt.'

'It did a bit, but I've been thinking about it, and it was my fault.'

'How is Lee being rude to you, your fault?'

'The rudeness, not so much, but the fact he didn't know who I was – that's what got to me. That's why I came out here for some space. That and Frank.' Hari gripped the box of chips in her lap. 'Lee didn't recognise me because I hide all the time. I know my books are all over social media, but I'm not – as a person, I mean. He's unlikely to follow me anyway. Whenever he's passed through the trading area to get to the hall, he's been deep in conversation with Jez or Scarlett. Before this weekend, I've only met him once before, and that was in a rehearsal room full of new cast members. I was there as a courtesy to the writer thing. I wasn't really wanted. You know how it is, once the thing is adapted for TV, the original writer is superfluous.'

'But *you* did the adaptation.'

'Even so. As soon as the script is sorted and the cast is picked, writers are simply people who get in the way. I soon discovered that I was better off sitting at home and waiting for the outcome like everyone else.'

Unsure what to say for a moment, Dot quickly rallied. 'That's worse, then. If Lee thought you were a fan, he definitely shouldn't have spoken to you like that.'

'True.' Hari waved a hand towards the glimpse of rolling countryside in the distance. 'I was contemplating disappearing onto the Peaks. The Coterel brothers would have walked around here. Maybe across this very stretch of land. They were real outlaws.'

'Murderers, thieves and thugs.' Dot nudged her friend playfully as she went on, 'Three brothers who ruled the Bakewell area with fear. Not very Robin Hood.'

'You listen when I talk!' Hari teased, before conceding, 'That's true. But they were, I'm sure, the inspiration for many outlaw stories nonetheless.'

'Including yours.'

'And maybe the Robin Hood ballads themselves.'

'*Maybe*?' Dot cocked her head to one side. 'Not like you to sound unsure about that. You've always said that criminal activities of the lower noble criminal families, like the Coterels, influenced the latter stories; once they began to be written down, that is.'

'Probably rather than maybe, then.' Hari raised a smile as she heard Dot quote her own words back at her from many lectures on the subject. 'But we'll never prove it, which is just as well. Part of the magic of Robin Hood is *not* knowing. Once the quest to find him is over, the magic will die. Although, if you listen to Frank Lister, you'd think the mystery was long solved.'

'By him, presumably.'

'Who else?' Hari shrugged.

'He was having such a discussion with a fan earlier.'

'And he could be right. The Robin Frank focuses on did exist on a human being level. There's no way to prove he wasn't *the* Robin Hood, and I wouldn't want to. Just because Frank clearly has an axe to grind with me, doesn't mean I would take his belief away. I just wish he wouldn't belittle everyone else's.'

'I doubt he has any idea he's doing that. He's very—'

'Single-minded?'

'I was going to say arrogant, but that too.'

Hari kept her gaze on the horizon. 'Time I pulled myself together, stopped hallucinating actors, and went back inside.'

'Hallucinating actors?'

'Which actor would I absolutely not want to see before I have to?'

'Roger Striver, obviously. Your cruel potter. His presence is bound to send Frank into one of his, "You'd have made a good Robin Hood" speeches.'

'I could have sworn I saw Roger earlier.'

'I didn't think he was due until tomorrow.'

Hari shrugged. 'I was in a bit of a state, so my imagination probably invented him.'

'Are you okay now?'

'Yeah.' Hari looked embarrassed. 'Imposter syndrome attack. Sorry, Dot.'

'No worries. As long as you're alright. Neil is talking soon, and you ought to be there to support him.'

She checked her watch. 'Blimey, I didn't realise I'd been here that long!' Immediately feeling guilty, Hari gave her friend a hug. 'I'm sorry I've dumped so much on you, especially after abandoning you at the banquet.'

'Don't be daft. I'm having a great time — and you would not believe how many cookies I've sold! I think the girls I met last night would be up for testing duties.'

'Seriously? Thank goodness you brought so many boxes to sell with you.'

'Not enough, though! I've asked the guys at *Pearce Bakes* to do a few extra flavours today to try out here. They'll be delivered later.'

'That's fantastic! I'm so glad you came. I'll keep my eyes open for delivery folk weaving through the crowds.' Hari tucked her knees up onto the bench and hugged them to her chest. 'I know I ought to come back in, but I don't want to, even though I do want to be there for Neil.'

'Look hun,' Dot paused, 'don't let the likes of Frank and Lee get to you. This is your moment! This whole event is based around your work. What *you* have achieved. Your contribution to the Robin story. Don't let them rob that from you.'

'Thanks, Dot.' Hari whispered, 'I love my fans and stuff, but...'

'I know. It's a bit different from sitting in your study all day surrounded by photographs of various Robin Hoods.'

Hari grimaced. 'I think I was cut out for fiction, rather than reality.'

'These days I wonder if there is much difference.' Dot chuckled. 'Come on, we ought to get back to your stall.'

'Oh my goodness, I was so wrapped up in myself that I forgot about the stall!'

'Don't worry. Jez held the fort for a while, then when I couldn't find you in the Green Room, we handed it over to Sharman while I hunted for you. Bit of a star, that girl. When I sat with her at dinner last night, she told me that she runs a bookshop in Oldham.'

'That's so kind.' Hari felt a new flush of shame wash over her. 'Whatever must she think of me, running off like this?'

'She hasn't a clue. I told her you had a call with your agent you couldn't avoid. No one knows the truth apart from Jez and Neil, who arrived in the middle of all this, plus that prat Lee, and Scarlett. She's worried about you, by the way. Nice woman.'

'She is.'

Dot tapped the box of chips. 'Have you eaten anything?'

'Not much.'

'Eat them. Even if they're cold, you're going to need the fuel.'

Hari reluctantly opened the box, surprised to find a faint trace of warmth left as she took a bite from a long chip. 'Oh, actually, these are lovely.'

Dot gently wiggled the takeout coffee cup she'd come armed with. 'Get some caffeine down you, too.'

'What would I do without you?'

Dot gave her friend a gentle nudge. 'Eat fewer cookies?'

Chapter Eight

'Thank you so much.' Hari focused her attention on Sharman, rather than letting her eyes stray to Frank Lister or his stall. 'Not just for helping out now, but for keeping Dot company while I was busy last night.'

'My pleasure.' Sharman rose from the seat behind the books. 'It's been fun being on the other side of things for a while. Oh, and Dot, you've had a delivery.'

'Already!' Dot beamed. 'The don't waste time at Pearce's!'

Sharman picked up a stout paper bag she'd hidden behind the stall. 'Are these the trial flavours we were discussing last night?'

'Should be.' Dot peered into the bag to see three red and white striped boxes of cookies, each emblazoned with the familiar Cookie Creations logo. 'Yep – one set of lemon and white chocolate, one batch of maple syrup—'

'That's the flavour you thought might go soggy too fast, right?'

'That's the one.' Dot smiled at Sharman as she checked the last box. 'And then there's almond and pistachio.'

Crossing herself, Sharman took a step backwards. 'Be gone, foul fiend!'

Hari frowned. 'Not a fan of pistachio, Sharman?'

'Nuts hate me.'

'Sorry yes, you did say.'

'I'm sure I'd be okay with the lemon ones.'

'Sorry hun, no can do. They shouldn't have been in contact with each other at the bakery, but I'm not prepared to risk anything now they've been in the same bag as the nutty ones. I'll order you some other cookies instead.'

'There's no need.' Sharman sunk her hands into the huge pockets that hung off her purple dungarees. 'I'm used to going without in case of nut issues.'

'Nonsense, you've been so kind and helpful. What's your favourite flavour? Orange and milk chocolate, wasn't it?'

'They are delicious, but that's Clara's fav. Mine are the caramel and choc melty middle ones!'

'Dark or milk chocolate?'

'Either. Love both.'

'Then, if you give me your room number, I'll get some delivered to you directly.'

Having promised to autograph a dozen books for Sharman to take back to her bookshop to sell on as signed copies, as an additional thank you for saving the day, Hari reinstated herself back behind the stall with Dot.

Immediately pounced upon by three fans who'd bought novels in her absence and wanted them dedicating, Hari had no chance to talk to Neil before his talk as she saw him and Jez pass through the trading area towards the conference room.

Suddenly, a stream of fans surged by in a concentrated rush for seats.

'Neil's talk looks like it's going to be popular.' Dot tidied a pile of *Mathilda and the Earl of Huntingdon* back into order as a sea of happy faces passed by. 'You should go in. It'll be quiet while he's talking and I'm sure Neil would appreciate your support.' Dot gave the table display a critical stare. 'It'll give me a chance to redo this. It's a bit haphazard after so many sales.'

'Always the businesswoman.' Hari hugged her friend again. 'I'll wait until everyone is in and settled, then I'll slip in and sit at the back.'

'Neil is bound to be asked about the new ballad. He might need you to help him.'

Hari blanched. 'But no one is supposed to know we've seen it.'

'I haven't had the chance to ask, how did sleuthing at the archive go?'

'Interesting. Hence me not getting back to the banquet last night. Neil and I had a lot to talk about and then I wanted to do some thinking about it.'

'Genuine?'

'Well, that would—'

A palm suddenly slammed against their table, making both women spin round. 'Are you telling me you've seen the missing ballad?'

Dot pulled herself up to her full five feet and levelled her gaze on Frank Lister. 'No. My friend was telling *me*. If Hari had wanted to speak to you, she'd have come to see you.' Turning to Hari, she said, 'You should go, or you'll miss Neil.'

'Are you sure?' Hari gave Frank an uneasy look.

'Perfectly.'

Frank glared at Dot, before saying, 'I ought to go and listen, too. Make sure Frampton doesn't rubbish my Robin.'

'Why on earth would he do that?' Dot crossed her arms. 'Whatever you might think, Frank, both he and Hari like your work. They respect it. They respect your thinking concerning your Robin, too.'

'Well, they have a funny way of showing it!'

Stalking away, Frank Lister pushed his way through the double doors into the conference room, letting them swing violently behind him.

Hari couldn't relax. So much for no one knowing she'd seen the ballad. *Although, I can't see why it's that important whether I've seen it or not.*

She realised with a start that she was only half listening to Neil as he spoke about the history of Robin Hood's original ballad record. Frank had plonked himself onto the chair immediately in front of her, on the penultimate row of seats at the rear of the large conference room. Even though he'd not spoken a word since his arrival, she knew when Frank disagreed with something Neil said because his whole body twitched.

As soon as Neil wrapped up his talk, Jez opened the floor up to questions from the audience. Hari felt her stomach curl into tighter knots; convinced Frank would launch in for an attack.

The first question, however, came from someone sat near the front. Not surprisingly, it concerned the new ballad.

'Professor Frampton, what is your thinking concerning *Robin Hood and the Carter*?'

Neil was about to answer when Jez gently cut in. 'If you will forgive me, Professor, and you, Penny, before you receive an answer to that, I feel this is the perfect moment to announce that I have an extra treat for you this weekend. We are extraordinarily fortunate to be located so closely to where this ballad was discovered. I have arranged for photographs of the ballad to come to this event, here, to be displayed for all to see in the trading room tomorrow.'

A wave of excitement ran through the room. Hari saw Frank sit up a little straighter.

'While the original manuscript is due to head to London for forensic examination this very day, I am honoured that the chief archivist of Buxton library, Christine Spencer, along with Professor Frampton here, and our very own Dr Harriet Danby, will be talking about the implication of this find in here today. The time is still to be announced, so keep your ears open.'

Hari felt her mouth drop open. This was the first she'd heard of it. *Me? But...*

Jez was deferring back to Neil. 'My apologies for the interruption. It seemed a good moment to mention this extra treat.'

'Not at all.' Neil smiled as he turned from Jez to the fan who'd asked the question. 'At the risk of sitting on the fence about the ballad, I think it is either potentially sensational or potentially disappointing. Until we have scientific confirmation of the date of both ink and parchment, we can't afford to get too excited. But, as Jez says, more on that later today.'

Three more hands shot up, and Jez moved towards the nearest person ready to take their question, but Hari didn't hear it. All she could focus on was Frank's stiff body on the chair before her. She could hear his breathing. It was laboured and rough, as if he was having trouble controlling it – or maybe his anger.

Wondering what she was supposed to say to the eager fans sat around her, about a ballad she'd seen briefly only once, beyond, "It might be real, but it probably isn't," Hari suddenly felt her brain engage.

Lee's rudeness and Frank's paranoid anger slipped into insignificance as the thought that nagged at the back of her head took centre stage.

This ballad is going to cause trouble.

Dot wasn't surprised by the news of the ballad being featured at the event, nor that Hari was part of the discussion. She was, however, surprised that Hari appeared to be calm about it.

'Are you sure you're okay about the extra stage time? You said you were dreading doing your interview about Mathilda, and this is an extra public appearance.'

'I wish I'd been told about this one before it was announced, but I can hardly say I won't do it.'

'And Frank and Lee? You okay with them?'

'I'll avoid Lee as best I can, but I have a feeling Frank will be making his presence felt a little more. Once this is over, I'll never have to see Frank again at least. As to the crowds, I'm just out of practice. They are all so friendly and they seem to want me here.'

'Of course they do.' Dot gave her friend a searching look, noting a lack of nervousness. 'Who are you, and what have you done with Harriet Danby?'

'I've given her a good talking to. There's a time for being weak and feeble, and that time isn't now.'

Dot's forehead furrowed as she examined her friend's expression. 'You've got your historian on the scent of an undiscovered source face on.'

'Ummm. Neil said something similar when we saw the ballad.' Hari spoke more quietly in case anyone should pass them by. 'You know I said I've been thinking since I was with Neil last night, well this ballad, if it isn't real, then why go to so much trouble?'

Dot passed Hari a cookie from their private stash under the table. 'Why make it such a good fake, when it's bound to be subject to forensic tests, you mean? And why hide it where it might not have been found for a very long time?'

Hari nodded. 'Or where you were sure it *would* be found – and found now…'

'Now, as in, just before this weekend?'

'Neil thought it was just a coincidence, albeit a very lucky one.'

'You aren't convinced?'

Sucking in her bottom lip, Hari said, 'You've read Frank's books on Robin Hood, haven't you?'

'You know I have.'

'The new ballad is called *Robin Hood and the Carter*.'

'And?'

'Unless my memory is failing me, Frank has a carter in his series. A character that runs through the entire first book and features in the others. While his carter is not the main rival of the outlaws, he is a recurring thorn in their side.'

'So he is.' Dot drew in a sharp breath. 'You don't think Frank faked the ballad, do you?'

'He's a clever man, and very knowledgeable in his own field, but I was more wondering why he hasn't been shouting about the connection between his work and this find.'

'He hasn't seen it. He made his displeasure on that fact clear.'

'But the title, *Robin Hood and the Carter*, has been in all the papers.' Hari wished she had more time alone to think. 'Does it seem typical behaviour for Frank not to be shouting about the fact that a rare manuscript has been found, and not only is it a Robin Hood story, but it is one which features a character that is a major player in his stories?'

'Now you mention it, he was suspiciously quiet about the whole thing until he heard you'd seen it.' Dot mused, 'Even if it's a forgery, he could make it work for him. If it's fake, he can claim the forger was influenced by the power of his words, and if it's real, he can claim he has a close affinity to the medieval balladeers.'

'Precisely.' Hari considered Frank's body language while they'd been in the hall. 'And when it was announced that Christine was bringing photos of the ballad here, he went, well, rigid is the only way to describe it. I guessed he was angry. Hurt that he hasn't been asked for his professional opinion. But what if it isn't that?'

'So you *do* think that it was him who—'

'The manuscript has been sent to London. They will check for all sorts of things. But if I was the forger, there are two things that I'd be worried about them checking more than anything.'

'The language style and the ink?'

'No. I'd be worried about them testing the document for fingerprints and DNA.'

Chapter Nine

Jez gave Hari and Neil an award-winning smile as they gathered near the bar. 'Hari, I owe you an apology. I wanted to speak to you before I announced the extra talk, but you were busy with fans and Neil said you'd be okay with it.'

Hari punched her former tutor gently on the arm. 'Remind me to thank you for that later!'

Jez's jovial expression wavered. 'You don't really mind, do you?'

'Not at all.' Hari knew she could never let Jez down, even if she wanted to. 'Is Christine due soon?'

'Within the hour. I'm letting it be known that the talk will be at five. I thought we'd have a lightning-quick meeting over a cuppa to get our ducks in a row before she arrives. Is Dot okay on book sale duty?'

'She is.'

'Excellent, so,' Jez checked over his shoulder to make sure they weren't being overheard, 'Christine has said it's okay to admit you've both seen it, but we can't mention where the ballad has been taken, beyond it's in London. It's pretty obvious it's the British Library, but we can't state it for security reasons.'

Neil looked surprised. 'You don't think someone here would be mad enough to steal it, do you?'

'If not one of these good folks, then who?'

Hari raised her eyebrows. 'I'd rather assume no one here would stoop that low, if that's okay. Anyway, you couldn't sell it without drawing attention to yourself.'

'But what about those weird collectors?' Jez wrinkled his nose. 'You know, the sort of people that get off on owning things no one else has. They'd get it out, stroke it once in a while, just for the thrill of being the only ones who can see it, then hide it away again.'

'Some people are truly odd.' Hari shook her head. 'What would you like us to say when we talk about the ballad, Jez?'

'You can give your opinion as to its provenance, talk about the ballad itself, its condition, and the words themselves. Then answer questions you are asked within the boundaries dictated. As I said in the hall, Christine is bringing the photographs, which I'm going to display tomorrow.'

Hari bit her bottom lip. 'Do you think, out of courtesy, we should let Frank see the photos before everyone else?'

'That's very decent of you, and normally I'd play the nice guy, but he has been rather unpleasant towards you, and you're our special guest. This time, he'll have to muck in with the rest.'

Hoping her surprise at this decision didn't show, Hari was about to ask which of them was going to kick off the discussion once they were all seated on the stage, when a flurry of activity by the hotel's main door made them look towards the reception.

'Ah... here comes Roger.' Jez pushed his hat firmly in place. 'If you'll excuse me...'

Striding into the hotel's foyer, Roger Striver held his arms wide open, while steering a small, wheeled suitcase in each hand.

'I'm so sorry, everyone. I would have loved to be here yesterday, but I had an audition for *Anything Goes*. In London, don't you know! I can't wait to begin rehearsals.'

Hari couldn't prevent a grin crossing her face when she saw Jez do a covert eye roll. Her amusement abruptly ended when Roger spotted her from her place in the sidelines.

'Harriet! How wonderful.' Roger dashed past a gathering of hopeful fans, who'd been approaching one of *Return to Sherwood's* favourite guest actors in the hope of an early autograph, and engulfed an unsuspecting Hari in a hug.

'Hi, Roger.' Muffled against his arm, Hari had no option but to inhale a heavy dose of crisp cotton and a deodorant which was on the dangerous side of being too liberally applied.

Eventually stepping back, holding Hari's shoulders, so he had her at arm's length, Roger tilted his head to one side. 'And how's my favourite author, then?'

'Me?' Temporarily forgetting that the fans could hear her for a moment, Hari said, 'Don't let Frank hear you say that.'

'Frank's an old pussy cat, he'll be fine!'

Neil suppressed a chuckle as he came to his friend's side. 'I'll take this opportunity to grab us some coffees, Hari. I'll see you in the bar a minute.'

Grateful for Neil setting up an excuse for her to leave soon, Hari extracted herself as politely as she could from Roger's grasp and nodded to the group gathering around them. 'Your people await. I should let you get on.'

No sooner had she stepped back, then Roger, a Cheshire Cat expression on his face, twirled around to face the nearby group. 'My lovely fans, how wonderful of you to come all this way to see me. Let's regale to the bar, and we can do the chatty thing there.'

Jez and Hari watched the group go with differing levels of relief.

'Regale to the bar!' Jez gave a quiet tut. 'The boy thinks he's Laurence Olivier!'

Hari laughed. 'The fans like him.'

'Especially the women.' Jez shook his head. 'That

lad has had more girlfriends than I've had hot dinners.'

'Takes all sorts,' Hari muttered, her gaze on Roger's retreating figure as her mind had triggered into overdrive. She was aware of an undiscernible idea nagging at the back of her head as she mumbled, 'He did play the part of my potter well, but it wasn't exactly a big role.'

'And yet he makes it sound as if he was the lead.' Jez shrugged. 'His agent is still referring to him as "Frank's Robin Hood."'

Hari groaned. 'It's bad enough knowing that Frank isn't ever going to forgive me for stealing his big moment. The last thing I need is Roger's agent hating me too. Thank goodness they're not coming.'

'Ahh.'

'Ahh?'

'Maisie Flowers, said agent, does have a habit of popping up wherever Roger is. She hasn't officially been invited, and may not come along, but…'

'You're telling me that the chances are high that she will.' Hari gave an internal groan.

'Between us, I think she sees Roger as her last chance for mainstream success as an agent, and well,' Jez pulled a face, 'he does need keeping an eye on sometimes.'

'I see.' Hari was thoughtful. 'And he's in *Anything Goes*?'

'No, he said he had an audition for it – not the same thing.'

'He made it sound like a forgone conclusion.'

Jez took off his hat as they watched the activity at the bar on the far side of the reception. It was filling fast. 'He spends too much time with Frank. He is an expert at inflating Roger's ego – as if it needed help.'

'They stayed in touch, despite the series never

being made?'

'There's a lot of resentment there.'

'I noticed.' Hari sighed. 'I could have sworn I saw Roger here this afternoon – when I was having a break in the garden, but if he was in an audition in London this morning, then he couldn't have got here any earlier than now. I'm going mad.'

Jez waved his hat towards where he could see Neil at the bar. 'Come on. If you've been hallucinating Roger, then you need a drink a bit stronger than a coffee before our extra lecture. Maybe a double!'

'This is so kind of you, Sharman.' Dot passed the cash box to her temporary helper.

'Not at all. Least I can do after those cookies arrived for me this afternoon. It was a lovely surprise to find them on my doorstep when I nipped back to my room to drop off my signed photos just now. I'm planning a pig-out while I get ready for the dance this evening.'

'Glad they arrived so fast. The benefits of being located so close to the bakery that covers the region.' Dot picked up her mobile and hotel room key. 'I'm very grateful for your help. Neither Hari nor I imagined the sales side of things here would be so full on. I know there's only an hour left before we close for the day, but I must get some of my own work done, and Hari needs to chat with Neil before their extra talk.'

'If I'm honest, you're doing me a favour, too.' Sharman smiled. 'I could do with a sit down before the dance tonight. And if I'm here, I can't be tempted to buy more photos and autographs from Lee, Scarlett, and Roger!'

Neil placed two large coffees between himself and

Hari, with a Bailey's on the side for each of them.

'Thanks. I think I need both of those!' Hari lowered her voice. 'I've got something to tell you before Jez gets back. Actually, it's more an idea that won't stop niggling me.'

'And you want to share it while no one is listening?'

'Exactly.'

Moving his seating position, so he could see if anyone approached the table, Neil lifted his cup to his lips. 'I imagine we have about two minutes before we are no longer alone judging by the busy queue at the bar, so fire away.'

Hari felt a sip of Bailey's soothe her throat. 'You'll probably think I'm crazy, but Frank... do you think he might have forged the ballad?'

Neil regarded his companion carefully. 'You realise what you're saying?'

'I do. And I'm aware I sound paranoid, but now I've had the idea, it won't budge.'

Hunching his shoulders forward, attempting to keep their conversation as private as possible, Neil muttered, 'Let's see. He's an unqualified ballad historian, but widely acknowledged as being well informed. An expert, even.'

Hari agreed. 'He knows his stuff.'

'But that is a long way from him having the ability to forge something.'

'I know.' Hari gulped as she saw Frank at the bar, deep in conversation with Roger. 'The thing is, the more I think about it, the more he seems to be the only person with a motive.'

'And that motive is?'

'*Robin Hood and the Carter.* He has a whole book dedicated to a carter. Okay, so the novel in question is called *Robin Hood's Curse*, but there's no getting away from the fact, that the curse in question came from a carter.'

'True.' Neil took a sip from his drink. 'Coincidence?'

'What, like the coincidence of finding it here and now in Buxton, when we are all so conveniently placed?'

'When you put it like that, I…' Neil put his cup on the table. 'Don't look now, but Frank's coming this way.'

'Oh, it's okay.' Neil let out a slow release of breath as he saw Frank pull his mobile from the inside of his jacket pocket, read something on the screen, spin abruptly on the balls of his shoes, and head for the main doors. 'Looks like he's going outside to make a call.'

'I wonder who to?'

'Hari?'

'Something's not right here. Frank ought to be with his stall until five – unless he's got someone else watching it. Maybe Sharman is keeping an eye on his table as well as mine.' Hari picked her own phone up off the table. 'I need to text Dot.'

'What for?' Neil kept his eyes on Frank as he disappeared through the hotel's glass front doors.

'She was planning to work for a while. Her room is on the ground floor, near the fire exit, so she can get outside fast. I'd like her to take a quick walk in the hope of accidentally passing Frank as he chats, while keeping her ears open.'

'You're serious about him being involved in this ballad business, aren't you?'

'Deadly.'

Chapter Ten

Dot wasn't sure why she had agreed to spy on Frank. It felt both exciting and childish at the same time.

Having dashed outside on receiving Hari's text, Dot waited in the shadow of the clump of trees near to where her quarry was walking as he made his call. Keeping her own phone to her ear, ready to pretend she was deep in conversation if Frank saw her, Dot moved her lips silently, faking a work call.

As Frank got closer to where she hid, too consumed in his conversation to notice anyone or anything, Dot heard him say, 'Come on, darling, I could do with some support here. Join me for the dance tonight.'

Debating whether she should step out from her hiding place and walk casually forwards, or if she should continue to lurk in the shadows, the decision was made redundant as Frank said an abrupt 'Goodbye.' Then he closed his phone, put it back in his pocket, and marched back inside. The expression on his face convinced Dot that whoever he was appealing to for support was not forthcoming.

Letting out a rush of air, Dot contemplated following him into the bar – but if she did that, she'd end up having a drink with the attendees, and the time Sharman had given her to catch up on her emails would be wasted. Instead, Dot headed back inside, through the back door from which she'd emerged, texting as she went.

Didn't catch much. Was a call to someone he called darling – was asking her (I'm presuming a female) to come to the dance tonight. Expression on his face suggests that they said no. D x

'He must have a partner. I can't imagine him calling

anyone darling otherwise. It doesn't feel like the sort of word Frank would use as a casual greeting.'

Neil shrugged as Hari showed him Dot's message across the table. 'They say there's someone for everyone.'

Hari laughed. 'Not for me, there isn't. And before you say anything, I'm not looking.'

'Message received, loud and clear — although I live in hope that you'll live happily ever after one day.'

'With the person of my dreams?'

'Well, no, I grant that is unlikely.' Neil winked. 'Not unless Lincoln Green comes back into fashion.'

Sticking her tongue out at her friend, Hari sighed. 'I'm not sure what I expected Dot to hear, anyway. I'm probably being fanciful. This ballad business could be a coincidence after all, have nothing to do with Frank and everything to do with good luck.'

'You don't believe that for a minute.'

'The luck bit – no, I don't. As to Frank being involved; your guess is as good as mine.' Hari checked the time on her phone. 'Come on, let's go and see if Christine has arrived. I want to see the photos of the ballad before we talk to everyone.'

'Ready to go over the top?' Jez doffed his hat to Neil and Hari as he escorted Christine into the conference room ahead of the fans that were lining up on the other side of the double doors.

Hari felt her insides tie into knots as she saw the queue of people through the glass window in the door. 'As I'll ever be. I didn't think so many people would come, especially as they could spend the time in the bar talking to Scarlett, Lee and Roger instead.'

'I think you'll find that Scarlett, Lee and Roger intend to come and listen as well.' Jez ran a hand through his hat-flattened hair. 'You could argue that they have an investment in the ballad. They all play parts in a Robin Hood-inspired story. Whether the ballad is real or not, it will rub off on them. Celebrity magazines and chat shows are more likely to ask them about the story than get in an expert.'

Neil tutted. 'Sad, but true.'

Hari waved a hand towards the folder in Christine's hands. 'The photos?'

'Yes. I've one of each page and a couple of extras of the first page.' She held the folder out to Jeremiah. 'Do you want to display them somewhere?'

'I will tomorrow. If I put them out now, everyone will try to see them now instead of paying attention to what you guys have to say.'

'Makes sense.' Neil smiled as Jez led them towards a semi-circle of chairs on the stage.

'Could I take a quick peep at the photos now, Christine?' Hari tried not to see the rows of chairs laid out before the stage.

'Of course.'

Hari flicked through the photos until she reached the third page.

Making himself comfortable as a sound man applied a microphone to his lapel, Neil asked, 'Are you searching for anything in particular?'

'I'm not sure.' Hari scanned each line. 'There was something earlier, something I saw that's nagging at the back of my head.'

'Really? What sort of something?' Christine sat back as her microphone was fitted to the collar of her crisp white shirt.

'There was something about one of the lines... I can't put my finger on it.' The arrival of the sound man to fix her microphone in place curtailed Hari's investigation as Jez checked the time.

'Show time, folks.' He nodded to the photos. 'I'll take those from you in the bar afterwards, if that's okay, Christine?'

'I'll swap them for a large pinot!' The archivist glanced towards the doors as they opened. 'I reckon I'm going to need it.'

'So, it's written on parchment and not vellum?'

Hari faced her questioner; a lady on the third row of the audience, the tattoos on her arm boldly declaring that she was a fan of the show – or a fan of Lee Stoneman at least.

'As sure as I can be, although I should say that these days, the term *parchment* is often used in non-technical contexts to refer to any medium that involved the use of animal skin in its manufacture. I'm sure you all already know that said animal would have been a goat, sheep or cow. Such a skin, once it had been scraped or dried under tension, was then a very effective – and long lasting – resource for documentation.

'And, again, as I'm sure you know, vellum is the term used for finer quality material made from calfskin.' Hari turned to Neil. 'Am I right in thinking Shakespeare raised the subject of parchment in *Hamlet*?'

'He did.' Neil paused as he brought the verse to mind. 'Hamlet says to Horatio, "Is not parchment made of sheepskins?" and Horatio replies, "Ay, my lord, and of calves' skins too."'

Bolstered by the approving looks they were getting from Jez, Hari went on, 'Only scientific analysis can tell us which animal the parchment came from originally. The best we can say from an observation alone is that parchment in general is rather cruder than vellum, being thicker and less highly polished. As a result, historians and archivists tend to refer to all manuscript material as parchment, until the fact of it being vellum is officially confirmed.'

'In this instance,' Christine added, 'it is highly likely to be a simple parchment, as we suspect that the ballad paper is too thick to be vellum.'

A sea of hands shot up from the audience as the closest person to the front asked, 'But Professor Frampton, is it real? I mean, is it genuine?'

Neil responded, 'That's the question. We will soon find out. Not only have the relevant authorities agreed to do ink and parchment analysis, fingerprint and DNA tests are to be carried out.' He referred to Christine. 'You've already had a swab taken for elimination purposes, I believe?'

'I have.' The archivist beamed at the sea of eager faces. 'I have to confess to being extremely eager to discover the outcome. If it's a fake, then the criminal involved could be traced that way – but if it's real, this is a chance to learn a little about a scribe from the past.'

A voice from the back of the room cut through the growing bubble of excitement. 'Forgive me interrupting.' Lee's deep voice made every single person in the room turn to look at him. 'I may be wrong – too many detective programmes on the telly, perhaps – but won't DNA and fingerprints simply show up everyone who has touched it?'

Christine nodded. 'I wondered that about the fingerprints myself. Apparently, they will only be tested if it's assumed fake. Since it was found, everyone who has touched it has worn gloves. Although, obviously my prints will be on it, as I had no idea what I was holding the first time I picked it up. I soon dropped it when I did! The DNA they'll hunt for will be within the ink. Apparently, a certain amount of spittle is likely – human beings do leak dreadfully if you think about it.'

'Oh, we do.' The crowd chuckled as Lee added, 'Expensive, testing for DNA, I imagine.'

'I'm sure.' Christine gave a small shrug. 'When it comes to it, I imagine they'll make a judgement call on whether they spend out on such a test once the inks and parchment have been professionally examined. It may be that they decide it would be wasteful if the inks are found to be made of modern components.'

As Christine spoke, Hari found her eyes drawn to Frank. Rather than watching the stage, he was typing something into his mobile phone. She didn't have time to dwell on what Frank was looking up or who he was contacting, for Scarlett's voice was ringing out across the room.

'So, what do you all think then? Gut instinct – forgery, or the real deal?'

Flexing out his long legs as he rested back on the bucket chair, Neil held his hands out in front of him in a gesture Hari recognised from his lectures, which meant he was about to say something ambiguous. 'You will appreciate that we can't be certain – but my gut reaction says that if it isn't real, I will be taking my hat off to the forger. They've done an amazing job. As Harriet can tell you, it isn't easy to manufacture such things.'

A lady in the front row raised her hand as she asked, 'You've tried, Dr Danby?'

'In the course of my research, yes.' Hari settled back on her seat, focusing on the smiling woman, trying not to let her eyes stray to Frank's solemn expression as he sat in the seat behind. 'My aim at the time was to help my students to see how complex a process it was to create inks for a manuscript in the fourteenth century; not to mention using said inks to write on parchment neatly enough for the words to be legible.'

'Sounds fun, Hari.'

'It was. Although the mixing of the inks was really fiddly, but most satisfying, I would say that—'

'That you could forge a ballad?' A voice from the far side of the room made Hari peer to her left. Roger was stood against the wall, his hands tucked into his trouser pockets, the vision of a relaxed man. His expression suggested he was joking, and yet there was something about the glint in his eyes that made Hari's stomach do a backflip.

The audience laughed, but Hari struggled to keep hold of her smile as she caught Jez's uneasy expression as he watched the performance from the back of the room.

Eventually, she found her voice. 'I could certainly manufacture the inks, but thereafter I'd struggle.'

'Surely not.' Frank's voice cut across the room as he crossed his arms defensively across his chest. 'Everyone here would agree that you have more than enough talent to write a ballad – and get the style spot on, too.'

Before a flustered Hari could muster an answer, Christine came to her rescue. 'I don't think any of us would question that, Mr Lister. If it comes to it, I'm sure we'd also agree that you have sufficient wordsmithing skills and Robin Hood knowledge to invent such a story, too. Your books are most enjoyable, and clearly steeped in a love for the legend. I believe a carter features largely in your first novel, does it not?'

Hari could only imagine the expression on Frank's face as concurring murmurings swept the floor, as the archivist continued, her words firm but friendly. 'Yet, I think we'd also all agree that both you and Dr Danby care *far* too much about your discipline, the legend, and the historical record to do anything so underhand as forgery.' Christine smiled at the audience. 'Don't you agree, ladies and gentlemen?'

A round of applause swept the room. This time Hari risked a glimpse at Frank. He looked like he'd swallowed a particularly bitter lemon – or possibly an entire pineapple.

Chapter Eleven

The thud of the disco in the adjoining room vibrated through Hari's booted feet.

She sat at a table in the corner of the bar, a little cut off from the main hub of activity by some conveniently-placed pillars. Hari rubbed at her throat. It felt dry, despite the amount of water she'd drunk since she'd come off the stage.

'Here.' Dot rummaged in her handbag before shoving a packet of honey and lemon lozenges into Hari's hands. 'For your throat. I brought these in case you started to lose your voice. Talking isn't something you do a lot of, and today has been relentless.'

'You're amazing. You really have thought of everything.'

'Just think of me as your fairy godmother.' Dot shuffled her chair closer to Hari. 'Have you seen the woman Frank's with?'

'No, I haven't. He was on his own during the ballad talk. I haven't seen him since.' Hari covertly scanned the bar area until her eyes found Frank. He was on the opposite side of the room at a busy table, surrounded by fans. There was a tall, slim woman at his side. Clad in a shockingly pink jacket, a tumble of chestnut hair hung around her shoulders. She was doing a good impression of a fish out of water. 'She's stunning.'

Dot agreed, 'Whoever she is, if I was an unkind person, I'd say Frank was punching well above his weight.'

'Lucky you're nice then.'

'Also, lucky I'm still in spy mode.'

'Really?' Hari tore her eyes away from her fellow writer and focused on Dot.

'It might be unrelated. Frank and his companion

could have been talking about anything when they passed by me on their way to find a table.'

'But?'

'But I overheard Frank say, "I need it to be seen to be real."'

Hari's eyes narrowed. 'That has to be about the ballad.'

'It would be a huge coincidence if it wasn't. He put emphasis on the word *need*.' Dot pulled a face. 'I was queuing for a drink at the time and wasn't expecting them to be there, or I'd have been paying more attention and eavesdropped their whole conversation.'

'Ummm…' Hari whispered, 'Frank sent a text while he was listening to the ballad talk. Maybe he was summoning her.'

'It's possible.' Dot frowned. 'And I wonder if she is the same person he called darling earlier.'

'If she is, then why decline to come then, but appear by magic now?'

Dot cupped her hands around her empty coffee cup. 'After your talk on the ballad, you mean?'

'We could be reading way too much into this.'

'Or we might not be.' Dot focused her gaze on Frank and his companion. The writer was deep in conversation with a group of fans, Penny and Clara amongst them. The woman in pink sat silently by his side. 'I'd love to know what they're talking about.'

'Probably the ballad or Frank's books.'

'I'll ask Sharman tomorrow; her friends are with Frank now.' Dot turned back to her friend. 'She's promised to help with the stall again. Honestly, the woman is a star! I hope she enjoyed the cookies I ordered for her.'

'I haven't seen Sharman this evening.'

'She'll be dancing. She had plans to grab a dance

with Lee.'

Hari's eyebrows rose. 'Lee deigns to dance with the fans! Blimey.'

'So Sharman tells me.'

Seeing Christine and Neil heading in their direction, a tray of drinks in Neil's hands, Hari spoke quickly. 'Don't say anything about our theory concerning Frank in front of Christine. We have no proof he's connected to the ballad's sudden appearance.'

Dot's eyebrows rose. 'Why wouldn't you want Christine to know that we suspect Frank of being involved?'

Hari shielded her mouth with her hand as she said, 'What do we know about Christine? What if *she* is involved? What if she didn't just find it and—?'

'Great table!' Neil's arrival saw Hari abandon her queries as he slid the loaded tray onto the large, round surface. 'You were lucky to get it. Must be the only vaguely private spot in here.'

'I grabbed it the second I saw it was vacant.' Dot patted a pile of paperwork in front of her. 'Been sitting here doing some work while you guys did your academic bit and the fans got changed for the dance. Hari's been bringing me up to date on events.'

Staring out across the busy bar, and beyond, towards the hotel's reception, Hari waved at a tired-looking Jez. He was making his towards the adjoining room, where the disco was in full swing. 'Amazing how people have settled into friendship groups so easily here.'

Neil unloaded the tray. 'Some of the attendees have been coming to Jez's events for years. It's often the only time they meet in person. There have been some firm friendships forged during Robin Hood Club get-togethers — not to mention the odd romance.'

'Nice.' Dot heaped a spoonful of sugar into her hot chocolate. 'Sharman, Penny, and Clara were saying the same during dinner last night. There are some tight connections here.'

Christine picked up her large glass of white wine. 'I must admit that the talk we did had a nice family feel coming from the audience. Or it did, until Mr Striver made his ill-considered joke.'

'I doubt very much if it was a joke. It was just delivered as a joke.' Hari picked up a black coffee from the table, resting the base of the cup in her palm, feeling its warmth infuse her. 'Roger will do anything for attention.'

Neil's head tilted to one side. 'You think Frank put him up to it?'

'I wouldn't be surprised, but I can hardly ask him.' Hari nodded towards a folder that sat on the table in front of Christine. 'I don't suppose I could take another peep at the photos of the ballad?'

'Sure.' Christine put down her drink and opened the folder. 'We need to be careful we don't spill anything on them. Jez will be over to collect them soon, so if any of you want a personal viewing, this is your last chance.'

'Then let's see them!' Dot took a laminated photograph of the first page while Hari and Neil took the following two pages.

'I've read them and read them.' Christine held the third page up to the light, as if hoping the photograph would suddenly reveal some of the ballad's mystery. 'Yet nothing about them strikes me as anything other than authentic – and yet—'

Interrupting, her eyes focused on the page she was scanning, Hari said, 'Christine, can I ask you something?'

'Sure.'

'Did you know that The Robin Hood Club was coming to Buxton, before we all arrived?'

'I didn't. I love the Robin Hood story, but I'm not what you'd call a mega fan. I hadn't even heard of the club, to be honest.'

Hari swapped pages with Neil, her eyes scanning the stanzas as she asked, 'What made you go to the archive store that day? The day you found the ballad?'

'It's part of my job…' Christine faltered. 'You aren't thinking that I…'

'Oh no!' Hari's cheeks bloomed bright red, cursing her inability to lie effectively as Christine read her suspicious mind. 'Not at all. Forgive me if I gave that impression. I just wondered if something made you pick up that copy of *Knighton* that day, or if all this really was a coincidence. You finding the ballad, just as we all arrive on your doorstep.'

Christine drank deeply from her wine glass before answering. 'I've thought about that myself, but I can't recall anything specific that made me tackle that task on that day, other than it was unusually quiet and I had time to get on with those jobs that often get pushed to the back of the queue.'

Neil put down his lemonade. 'So, there were no convenient phone calls telling you to get all fourteenth century-related reference books out of circulation back in stock then?'

'Afraid not.' She tapped a red-painted fingernail on the photo before her. 'The only thing I remember being different from before I left was that the piles of books to mend had been tidied up. Usually they are all in a big box, rather randomly placed — or thrown in some cases — ready for mending or discarding. But the mending had been tidied into a neat pile.'

'With the copy of *Knighton* right on the top?' Dot spooned some cream from her hot chocolate into her mouth.

'Not on the top, but it wasn't too far down.' Christine paused. 'Now I come to think about it, the ones on top were all obvious throwaways. Beyond mending.'

Hari sucked on her bottom lip. 'So the *Knighton* was the first volume to command proper attention?'

'Yes, I suppose it was.' Christine's forehead creased as she examined the photo before her. 'You're saying I was set up to find it?'

'You, or someone else who works at the library.' Hari exchanged a look with Dot. 'Did you ask your colleagues about the tidy pile?'

'I didn't think to. It's only me who's qualified to mend spines and jacket tears at the moment.' She took out her phone. 'I'll email myself a message, so I remember to ask my colleagues if any of them have sorted through the mending tomorrow.'

Ignoring Hari's request not to point the finger, Dot blew across the top of her hot chocolate as she asked, 'I don't suppose Frank has been into the archive lately?'

Christine's eyebrows rose. 'You think it was—'

'We don't know... but he does have a motive.' Hari leant forward, her eyes darting anxiously around the room to make sure no one overheard them.

Dot added, 'Even if it wasn't him, I bet he enjoyed Roger laying suspicion on Hari. Frank might have asked him to say what he said.'

'We don't know that, Dot. It might simply have been Roger being Roger.'

'Possibly, but possibly not.' Dot shifted slightly to the left and looked out across the heaving bar. 'No sign of Roger out there, that I can see, anyway. He could be dancing, I suppose.'

Hari shivered. 'I know Frank doesn't like me, but would he go to so much trouble to discredit me? I can't see it.'

'Either way, I've not noticed him in the archive.' Christine swallowed another mouthful of pinot. 'But then, I had a week off prior to the day I found the ballad. Anyone could have come in while I was away. Although how they'd have managed to get into the store without anyone noticing, I couldn't say.'

'I don't suppose there are security cameras in the library?' Neil asked.

'No. Apparently we will be getting them one day. But then again, we've been told that almost monthly for three years now, so I'm not holding my breath.' Christine gave a nervous chuckle. 'This is all getting a bit *Scooby Doo*. Do you think I should tell the police about the tidying?'

'Only if it is a fake, and only if it wasn't a well-meaning colleague with five minutes to do odd jobs who tidied things up.' Neil drummed his slim fingers on the table. 'If it does come to police involvement, I'm not sure how seriously all this would be taken. It's not like anyone's been hurt, is it.'

'And it may be the real thing.' Christine returned her attention to the photos on the table.

Hari ran a single finger across the copy of the ballad's third page. 'I wish I could find what it was that's been nagging me about this. I'm sure that...' Her search stopped as she mouthed the words before her to herself.

'Hari?' Dot regarded her friend with concern. 'Are you alright?'

'It's here. This is what... Ouch!' Hari winced in

pain as a sharp kick met her leg.

'He's coming over.' Dot hurriedly apologised as Frank and his female companion approached the table. 'Quick, get the pages back in the folder, Hari. Something tells me it wouldn't be a good idea to let him see these yet.'

Chapter Twelve

'Elizabeth Jeffries, I'd like to introduce you to Christine Spencer, Harriet Danby, Professor Frampton—'

'Neil, please.' Neil rose, holding his hand out for their visitors to shake.

'Neil, then.' Ignoring the offered palm, Frank grunted, before switching his attention to Dot. 'I'm sorry, I've forgotten your name.'

No, you haven't forgotten — you never bothered asking what it is.

'Pleased to meet you, Elizabeth. I'm Dot. I help Hari out with the books and things.'

'Oh. How nice.' The older woman's tone dismissed Dot as unimportant as she focused on Christine. 'The ballad was found in your archive. That must have been exciting.'

'It was.' The archivist held Elizabeth's gaze. 'I just hope it's real.'

'As do we all.' A smile crossed the newcomer's face, instantly changing the rather uptight impression she'd been giving out to something much softer. 'Frank was telling me about the tests they're intending to do in London. Do you know when the results will come through?'

Before Christine could answer, Frank broke in, 'Oh, I imagine it will be ages. I know these things cost a lot, and I'm sure—'

'Tomorrow,' said Christine.

'Tomorrow!' Frank's eyebrows shot upwards.

'Some of them, at least.' Christine's voice was so cool and calm that Hari wanted to applaud. 'They're rushing things through – some fast-track funding has been found, apparently.'

'Really?' Elizabeth's perfectly plucked eyebrows

slanted. 'Convenient.'

'I assume they – and I'm guessing it'll be either the British Library or Museum – are paying above the odds, so they have a claim on keeping it in the collection if it's real.'

'A cynical opinion, Miss Spencer,' Frank blustered.

'A realistic one.' Christine drained her wine glass and picked up her folder. 'Now, if you'll excuse me, I need to get these pictures of the document in question to Mr Barnes before I head home.'

Elizabeth tucked a strand of glossy chestnut hair behind her ear. 'I was rather hoping for a peep. I don't suppose there's any chance?'

'Sorry. I promised Jez I'd keep them a surprise until he shows them tomorrow.'

'That's a shame. I love a good story.'

'Is that how you met Frank, through a mutual love of stories?' Hari asked.

'Frank's just a friend.'

Hari's eyes widened at the woman's blunt tone. 'I didn't mean to suggest otherwise.'

'I was just making it clear.'

Hari was sure she'd seen a hint of disquiet – possibly anger – flash through Frank's eyes before he guffawed, and Elizabeth regained control over her momentarily ruffled composure, the wrinkles that had appeared on her forehead disappearing as fast as they'd appeared. 'We've been friends for years.'

'Right.' Christine stood up, the folder firmly under her arm. 'Well, it was nice to meet you all. I'm sorry, Elizabeth, but if you want to see them, you'll have to come in tomorrow when they're out on display, assuming you have a ticket to the event.'

'Well, I—'

'Don't worry. You can come in with me. I'm sure

Jez won't mind.' Frank placed a palm on Elizabeth's shoulder.

'Thank you, Frank.' Elizabeth gave him a catlike grin. 'I'd like to be here when the results come in… if they do. All seems a bit rushed to me.'

Breaking the suddenly uncomfortable tension, Neil got to his feet. 'I'll walk with you to Jez, Christine. I want to thank him for a nice day before I head to my room.'

'Not staying for a dance at the disco?' Frank asked sarcastically.

'I think I've had enough excitement for one day.' Neil turned to Hari and Dot. 'I'll see you both tomorrow. I'm looking forward to your interview, Hari.'

'Hell!' Hari felt the colour drain from her face. 'What with all this talk of the ballad, I'd forgotten about that.'

Frank laughed. 'Don't tell me the great Dr Danby is nervous about giving an interview.'

'Of course I'm nervous.' Hari felt defensive. 'It's not unusual to be anxious about public speaking.'

'But, unless Frank was spinning me a line,' Elizabeth gave her companion a sideways stare, 'you're a former university tutor, so surely—'

Neil chipped in, 'Hari was an excellent tutor, but teaching about your subject is very different from talking to fans at a convention.' He gave his friend a reassuring smile as he and Christine worked their way out from the side of the table. 'I'll bid you all goodnight.'

'Well, if we aren't going to get a sneak peep of the ballad, I might as well go.' Elizabeth brushed her pink jacket down. 'I only came in the hope of having a glimpse.'

'You don't fancy a dance before you go?' Frank's tone was embarrassingly hopeful.

'I don't think so.' Twisting round on her heels without a backward glance, Elizabeth stalked her way through the crowds.

Feeling awkward, Hari found herself inviting Frank to join them as he stood staring at the space where Elizabeth had been.

'Umm... no. No, thank you. I ought to get back to my room. I'm part of the panel discussing who's the best onscreen Robin tomorrow morning. I'd better go and do my homework.'

Silence hung over the table as they watched Frank bustle into the crowd. It didn't last long, however, for seeing space at Hari's table, a group of *Return to Sherwood* viewers asked if they could join them. Within moments, the evening morphed into a happy succession of questions about Hari's show and books, most of which were so detailed that Hari herself had never considered them before.

Monday 30th May

Hari ran a fork through the substance on her plate that claimed to be scrambled egg – she was yet to be convinced. Even if the breakfast had been edible, her appetite eluded her as the words *the carter pushed her down, his ruddy face scowled in anger* played through her mind on a continuous loop.

'Where have I seen those words before?'

The previous evening, Hari's relief at having pinpointed the line in the ballad that had been bothering her, had been forgotten when Frank and Elizabeth had arrived in the bar. At three in the morning however, she'd woken with a start; the words on her lips and a headache pounding across her temples.

After two hours of tossing and turning against the mattress, and an hour of sitting in bed cuddling a mug of nasty hotel room coffee and dredging her memory for where she'd come across the words before, Hari had decided to get practical. Hooking the notebook that was waiting to be filled with ideas for the next Mathilda novel from her holdall, she'd found herself writing *Fake or Real?* in big letters on the first page.

Ten minutes later, she'd written a list of questions she wanted answers to concerning the ballad.

Now, as she buttered some toast, Hari silently read from the open notebook.

Who has the most to gain if it's a fake?
Coincidence that it has been found here, now?
Is there a connection to the RHC?
If there is a connection to RHC – what/who is it?
Who could have hidden it in the library store? Christine herself?

Hari paused as she read through her notes, picked up her pen with sticky fingers, and put a line through *Christine herself*, muttering, 'Her reputation is good, and the archive is well-funded in the grand scheme of things. She has nothing to gain.'

Frank? With/without Roger's help?
If it is fake, and it's not connected to anyone at the RHC, then was it deliberately planted in Buxton so that the club would be implicated?

Hari's egg-filled fork hovered in the air as she read her final point again, muttering, 'If that's the case, then who is the target? Is it Jez? Or the club as a whole?'

Deciding against the remaining egg, she took a bite of toast. 'Why would anyone want to incriminate the club?'

Realising she didn't know enough about the group

to answer that question, Hari closed the notebook. *I need to get a bit of background.* Refilling her cup of coffee, she looked up as Lee entered the restaurant. She was surprised to see her leading man making a beeline for her table.

'Harriet, I'm glad I found you alone. I owe you an apology.'

'Oh.'

Lee gave her the sort of smile that Hari knew his fans would kill for. 'Scarlett left me understanding, in no uncertain terms, just how rude I'd been.'

Feeling awkward as he towered over her, Hari brushed his apology away. 'I'm sure I just caught you at a bad time.'

'You did, but that's no excuse. I was going to apologise last night by asking you to dance, but I was rather cornered by fans to be honest.'

Taken aback, Hari felt a blush start in her cheeks. 'I bet your dance card was well marked. I know Sharman had designs on at least one dance with you.'

'Sharman?' Lee's forehead creased.

'Yes, the lass with the green hair. Heart of gold, that one.'

'I know Sharman. I didn't see her either.' He pulled out the chair opposite Hari and sat down. 'Do you mind me sitting with you?'

As he was already sat down, Hari didn't think she could say no. 'Be my guest. I should advise against the egg. It's a bit "school dinner", if you see what I mean.'

Lee's laugh rang out across the room. 'I'll consider myself warned.' He reached for the coffee jug and poured himself a cup. 'I think I'll stick to coffee. I've got to do a panel with Scarlett, Frank, and Roger at ten. Caffeine may be the only thing that gets me through.'

Hari was surprised. 'Don't you enjoy being on the

stage?'

'Not really. Not as myself, anyway.' Lee sipped at the strong coffee. 'It's different if you're pretending to be someone else.'

'I suppose it is.' Hari laid down her toast. 'I don't think I've ever had a chance to thank you.'

'Thank me?'

'For being such a good Will Scathlock. You bring him alive, straight from the page. Thank you.'

'Not at all.' Lee appeared to be genuinely taken aback. 'Thanks for such good words.'

Hari blushed. 'My pleasure. I still can't believe all this. I never saw a book contract coming, let alone a TV show.'

'I'm glad it happened for you.' Lee sighed as he saw Roger come in. 'Not just for you, but because it stopped *him* becoming Robin Hood.'

Not sure what to say, Hari refilled her own coffee cup. 'Oh?'

'The man is a leech. He…' Lee's voice petered out as Roger got closer. 'Here we go.'

'Morning, both!' Roger arrived at their side with an overloud greeting.

'Good morning.' Hari was suddenly glad that Lee had already sat down, as she had a feeling Roger would have happily installed himself with her.

'Looking as beautiful as ever, Harriet,' Roger gushed as he flicked his overlong fringe from his eyes.

'Hardly.' Hari took refuge in her coffee, hoping the caffeine might work some magic on the tired bags that hung under her eyes.

'I had hoped to dance at least half the night away with you last night, but you were nowhere to be seen.'

'Discos aren't my thing.'

'Nonsense! You'd have had fun. Our host was

doing a sterling job making sure everyone in there was joining in. You wouldn't think Jez had the energy, would you?'

Not responding to his insinuation, Hari waved at the food counter on the far side of the room. 'I'd grab some breakfast before it's all gone if I were you, Roger.'

'Trying to get rid of me?' His eyes flashed a teasing smile in her direction. 'Now then, you mustn't be cross with me for my little jest in the ballad talk yesterday. I was only joking.'

'A rather tasteless joke in the circumstance,' Lee answered for her. 'I'm assuming Frank put the idea in your head?'

Intrigued to find that Lee had had the same thought as her and Dot, Hari watched Roger closely.

'I am capable of my own jokes, you know.'

'You sound like a sulky child.' Lee shook his head. 'Now, if you don't mind, I was having a private chat with Harriet. Why don't you go and grab some eggs, I hear they're rather good today.'

Chapter Thirteen

'Lee did?' Dot knocked a pile of Cookie Creations flyers into order on the edge of Hari's book stall.

'Yep, he clearly has no time for Roger, and I'm not sure he cares for Frank much either.'

'Did he stay once Roger had gone?'

'He did. It crossed my mind that he might have known Roger was on his way and he only sat with me because it meant Roger couldn't join him for breakfast.' Hari undid the lid of a box of *Mathilda's Outlaw* novels and topped up the supply for sale. 'It was the first chance I've had to talk to Lee as himself. Before, we've only ever spoken when he was in character as Will, and then he was a bit frosty.'

'But he wasn't frosty today? He wanted to chat, Roger or no Roger?'

'To apologise for the Green Room incident. It appears that Lee's quite shy when he hasn't got a character to hide behind.'

'Is that so?' Dot gave her friend a knowing look. 'And you got on well?'

'Don't go all matchmaker on me, Dot. It was a chat between a writer and an actor. That's it.'

'Shame. He's a handsome boy.'

'What's that got to do with anything?'

'Nothing at all.' Dot winked. 'But it wouldn't hurt you to have some fun, you know.'

'He's my leading man. How inappropriate would that be? Anyway, I'm not—'

'In the market. Yeah.' Dot rolled her eyes.

'Can we change the subject?' Hari looked across the room as Frank arrived to set up his book stand for the day ahead. She lowered her voice. 'I've had a few ideas about the ballad.'

'Go on.'

'I couldn't sleep last night for thinking about everything.' Hari gestured to the bag slung on the back of her chair. 'There's a notebook in there.'

Stopping what she was doing, Dot retrieved the book and flicked to the first page. 'These are interesting questions.'

'I considered answers to some of them this morning. But each answer seems to lead to more questions. I didn't get as far as I'd have liked because Lee joined me.'

'Tempted as I am to break into song, *"There are more questions than answers…"*, I will refrain.' Dot regarded her friend. 'You're treating this like a story. I've seen your novel notebooks, they're full of hundreds of questions that need answering before you can make the plot work, and before—'

'Before I've worked out how the bad guy or girl did what they did.'

'And how Mathilda and Scathlock will capture them.'

'Exactly.' Hari hesitated. 'Not that I envisage doing any sort of capturing. I just want to know how this scam was pulled off and by whom. If it is a scam.'

'Come off it.' Dot double checked over her shoulder to make sure no one was in earshot. 'You wouldn't have made notes if you believed it was real. At least, not these types of notes.' Dot slid the notebook back into Hari's bag. 'I don't think any of us truly believe it's real. I'm more interested in why someone would do this. What's it all for?'

'Those are the big questions. Why? And what for?' Hari paused. 'Or are they the same question?'

'Possibly. We could add, "Why now?" to that list too.' Dot reached for the packet of cookies on her chair and passed it to Hari.

'Why now is easy.' Hari took an almond and pistachio biscuit and crunched through its centre. 'It *has* to be because of this – because the Robin Hood Club is here, now, this weekend.'

'But,' Dot moved nearer to her friend, 'how could it be guaranteed that the ballad would be found in time for this weekend?'

'That *is* a question that needs adding to the list. However it was done, the person behind this knew to make sure it was found somewhere where it would be seen for what it was – or what it might be – rather than being automatically discarded or ignored.'

'An archive.'

'Exactly.'

'But you don't think Christine is involved?'

'No – but I could be wrong. I was thinking,' Hari checked her watch as she spotted a queue of guests forming on the opposite side of the door to the trading area, 'how long ago did this begin? It's not a quick job putting a manuscript together, even if you aren't trying to hide what you are up to.'

'So, it could have been made ages ago and placed in the archive ages ago, too?'

Hari nodded. 'I checked on the Robin Hood Club website just now. The dates and venues for each gathering are advertised just under a year in advance of the actual meetings, so…'

'Someone who regularly attends would know that – and know how long they have to manufacture a ballad.'

'And that someone could have slipped it into the archive store in time for it to be found just prior to this weekend.'

Dot frowned. 'Sounds a bit convoluted.'

Hari sighed. 'The whole thing is convoluted.'

'Unless it's real.'

'Unless it's real.'

Changing the subject, Dot spoke through a mouthful of cookie. 'Are you going to watch the debate this morning?'

'I don't think so. Debates on who is, or was, the best onscreen Robin Hood always begin as a bit of fun but inevitably end in heated arguments.'

'I can imagine.'

Hari repositioned a stack of mugs as she went on, 'It always feels so personal when someone does down the Robin you like the best. It's like when anyone says that Tom Baker wasn't a good *Doctor Who* – it's like being slapped.'

Dot laughed. 'I hear you.' She checked her watch. 'Sharman offered to run the stall for us after the debate's finished. I'm planning a bit of hands-on cookie selling. A courier should be here within the hour with a new batch of boxes for me to knock out.'

'Awesome.' Hari brushed some crumbs from her chest. 'And I can prep for my talk.' She picked up another cookie with a smile. 'Brain fuel!'

Twenty minutes later, Hari, having done an about-turn on her decision to avoid the debate, found herself standing at the very back of the conference space. Hiding in the shadows, beyond the shining glow of the spotlights that were focused on the stage, so that no one asked her opinion as to who played the best Robin Hood, Hari watched Frank and Roger sat on the stage alongside Lee and Scarlett. Jez was with them, asking questions and sharing opinions from the floor.

If one of them is involved, then which one has the most to gain from the appearance of this ballad?

As Scarlett expertly fielded a question on which

Robin actor she fancied the most, Hari crossed her off the list of suspects. *Scarlett has a secure career in the acting world. She'd already had three leading roles in various series before she became my Mathilda, and there'll be more. There's no need for her to risk all she has for this.*

Hari's eyes roamed over Lee. *Could he benefit from Robin Hood having a resurgence of interest in the press?*

Again, she couldn't think of a reason why he'd want to go to all the bother of finding someone to fake a ballad. He was well established in his trade and had fans in his own right.

Whoever did this must be in it for the interest it would bring to the Robin Hood legend as a whole. There's too much going on in the real world to make a long-lost ballad newsworthy for long. It's in academia and the world of fandom where this matters the most.

As her gaze rested on Frank, his round face red under the heat of the lights, the line of ballad that had been bothering her came back to mind. *The carter pushed her down, his ruddy face scowled in anger.*

Having spent some time Googling every Robin Hood ballad, reading back through Child's and Ritson's acclaimed notes on the archives, as well as Dr Percy's *Reliques of Ancient Poetry*, Hari was sure it wasn't from a pre-established ballad, and yet its familiarity chimed so loudly.

Maybe... Hari froze. *Could it be as obvious as that? A line from Frank's books? Would he be arrogant enough to add a line from his own work to a ballad he's forged?*

Hari observed him more closely as he argued why his Robin Hood, had his series been made, would have been better than any that had been on TV before – an opinion that was making Roger visibly preen next to him.

Who am I kidding? Of course he'd be arrogant enough.

'Damn.'

'What is it?'

'I thought I'd worked it out, but it isn't here.'

'Worked what out? What isn't where?' Dot regarded her friend across the stall.

'I've been using the search function on my Kindle – searching for a line in one of Frank's novels.'

'That line from the ballad that keeps bugging you?'

'Yeah.' Hari sat down with a groan. 'I'm sure it isn't from an existing ballad, so I wondered if it might be from one of Frank's books.'

'Thank goodness he hasn't written many, or you'd still be searching.'

'True, but either way, it isn't there. Perhaps it *is* from a ballad after all, and I've just missed it.' Hari pulled a face. 'I've been out of the game a while now and there are far more retellings of Robin Hood than people realise. I could have missed one or two along the way. Some are really obscure. There's one called *The Pedigree, Education and Marriage of Robin Hood with Clorinda, Queen of Titbury-feast*.'

Dot's eyebrows rose. 'That tale certainly didn't make it into the mainstream!'

'Nor did *Robin Hood, Will Scarlet, and Little John's victory over the Prince of Arragon and the two Giants*.'

'Arragon? Seriously? That's a bit—'

'*Lord of the Rings*? Yep – *way* before Tolkien's time, though. The point is that I can't be sure I haven't missed something manuscript-wise.'

'Come off it, Hari. If it was from any existing Robin manuscript, you'd know — obscure or not.'

'Maybe.'

Dot patted the seat next to her, encouraging her friend to sit down. 'You don't think you might be getting a tiny bit obsessed with all this?'

'Well…'

'Why don't you just take a step back? Wait until we know for sure if it is forgery or not. It won't be long. Didn't Christine say the experts were on this?'

'We should have enough results by the end of the day to have an educated guess as to whether it's real or not.' Hari sank onto the offered chair. 'Of course, if it is fake, then more tests will be done, but…'

'Will they, though?' Dot became thoughtful. 'That sort of thing costs money. I know Christine said there was funding, but does anyone care enough to spend the money required to find out when there are undoubtedly real antiquities out there to spend research money on?'

'No idea.' Hari's forehead furrowed. 'It's not a world-shattering crime, but I'd like to think the police would care. That someone would try to get to the bottom of it.'

'That someone doesn't have to be you.' Dot smiled. 'Why not concentrate on the interview you are going to give later, rather than worry about what someone far less scrupulous than you may or may not have done.'

'I've been trying not to think about the talk!'

'You'll be fabulous. I'm looking forward to hearing it.'

'Are you sure you want to come? You've heard everything I've got to say about Mathilda and co.'

'Doesn't matter. Moral support. Sharman wants to see it too, so I'll close the stand up for a bit.'

'Thanks, Dot. It'll be good to see a friendly face in the audience.'

'They'll all be friendly.'

'Apart from Frank.'

'Okay, almost all friendly.' Dot surveyed the room. 'Have you seen Sharman? She said she'd help out this morning.'

'I haven't. Come to think of it, she wasn't watching the debate this morning.'

'Maybe you just didn't notice her?'

'Dot, the woman has bright green hair.'

'True. I wonder where she is?'

Chapter Fourteen

Hari spotted Dot sliding through the door into the conference room just as the lights went down and Jez picked up his microphone.

Forcing herself to face the crowded auditorium, she mouthed a few hellos to those she'd chatted to over the weekend so far. Hari was surprised to see a gap between Penny and Clara, who — if their constant glances to the closed conference room doors were anything to go by — were presumably waiting for Sharman to arrive.

Hari took a deep breath as Jez gave a thumbs up to the sound man at the back of the room to activate the microphones. It was time to be Dr Harriet Danby – author and medievalist, rather than Hari Danby – imposter syndrome-plagued writer and lapsed historian.

'Welcome, one and all.' Jez raised his arms in greeting. 'Somehow it is late morning on Monday already, and we only have this afternoon and early evening to go, before we bid each other farewell for another year – apart from those of you who are booked in for one more night in the hotel under your own steam, of course! I think you can agree that our Buxton Robin Hood Club get-together has been fabulous so far.'

A rousing cheer came from the audience, sending a shiver of apprehension through Hari.

'Our special guest speaker for the weekend, as you know, is the fabulous Dr Harriet Danby, known to her friends as Hari.' Jez turned to his guest. 'First of all, may I thank you on behalf of everyone for coming along to our small gathering.'

'It's my pleasure.' Hari felt her face glow and hoped her blushes would be hidden by the stark brightness of the room's lighting. 'You've all been so kind. It's been quite a revelation — and more than a little flattering — to see how much love there is for my stories.' Catching a disapproving glare from Frank, she hastily added, 'Although, I should say straight away that the most I can ever claim is to be the author of stories that *only* work because I was inspired by the Robin Hood tales written so many hundreds of years ago by others. Without those talented storytellers, I'd never have cobbled together Mathilda and Will's tales.'

Approving nods and whispers of appreciation rippled across the audience. Hari resolved to avoid looking in Frank's direction unless she had to, as Jez asked his first question.

'What was it about those early tales that drew you in?'

'Hope.'

Jez's smile broadened. 'That, I can see. There's no doubt that hope is the underlying theme of all the Robin Hood tales – at least, it's always seemed that way to me.'

'And to me.' Hari found herself relaxing as she spoke about her passion. 'It's no wonder that the Hood tales have lasted – and will continue to last. Every generation needs its own Robin, or equivalent thereof. Mathilda, in my case. We need them because there is always something bad happening that we need saving from. Look at the world around us; if ever we need a hero to believe in, it's now.'

'Do you think that's why every Robin through the ages, from the first ballads to the present day, is fractionally different from the one before?'

'Absolutely.' Hari motioned towards where Neil sat in the audience. 'As Professor Frampton was saying in his talk, the tale adapts to the world around it, because we, as readers, are influenced by the world we live in. We shape the tales to give us the Robin we need when we need him.'

'So,' Jez adjusted the rim of his fedora, 'in the 1980s, when the western world was obsessed with money and was undoubtedly fuelled by greed at a ruling level, it's perhaps no wonder that the Robin of the day was steeped as far away from that as possible, in magic and mysticism?'

'I think so. *Robin of Sherwood* – I assume that's what you're referring to – was very hope-focused. There was no hint of Robin or his men keeping anything back for themselves. All they had went to help others. If you go back to the original tales, Robin and his men took from those whom they considered cruel or greedy – not just from the rich – to teach them a lesson, just as most Robins do, including Richard Carpenter's *Robin of Sherwood*. But the early outlaw heroes kept some for themselves. It wasn't about taking from the rich to ensure the safety and health of the poor, it was about getting one up on the establishment.'

'You could argue that latter point for all the retellings, couldn't you, Hari?'

'You could. It is that which – alongside hope – holds the story together. The victory of the underdog over the oppressor, in whatever form that oppression might take.'

A hand shot up in the audience.

'Yes, Penny?' Jez moved the microphone nearer to his guest.

'Hi, Hari. I just wondered if it was due to the times we live in – when the rights of women to be treated as equals is an issue in the forefront of the public eye – that led you to have Mathilda – or Marion, if you like – as the lead in your tales, rather than a Robin?'

'In all honesty, no it wasn't. Although I can't deny that the timing has been fortuitous for me on that front. I simply felt that so many excellent novels had been written with the focus on Robin, or Robin and Marion as a unit, that it was time to have a go at something different. Take a story concept I love and change it a little – but not too much.'

'A fresh angle?' Jez chipped in.

'Precisely.' Hari focused on Penny. 'And Will was always my favourite character. It felt right to give him a leading role.'

'And a love interest?' Clara asked as she leant across her friend, towards Jez's outstretched microphone.

Hari laughed as Penny added, 'You must know we *all* want Mathilda and Will to get together. Any chance of that happening?'

'As if I'd say!' Hari had to suppress a giggle as she spotted Scarlett pull a face at the thought that Hari might write a scene which would mean her kissing Lee Stoneman.

Clara exchanged a hopeful look with Penny. 'That's not a "no" then.'

Moving back to the stage, Jez sat in an armchair next to Hari. 'You have experienced much success since your novels were commissioned to be made into a series. It is, after all, the appeal of *Return to Sherwood* that has brought you to us today. How did you feel when your agent first told you that your show had been optioned for television?'

Knowing it was inevitable that Jez would ask her this, Hari had prepared an answer already. She could feel Frank Lister's gaze start to bore into her, and a cold sweat crept up her spine.

Ignore him – it isn't your fault he didn't get his

show.

'It was one of those "this has to be a mistake" moments. I was sure I'd wake up the next day and find it was all a dream.'

'But it wasn't.'

'Incredibly, no, it wasn't. The email asking for a meeting with the production company arrived soon after the initial interest was flagged, and after that it all happened very quickly. Well, it took months – but that's quick in TV land.'

A hand shot up from the audience, and Jez moved forward to field it.

A gentleman Hari recognised as someone whom she'd signed a book for earlier in the weekend asked, 'Did you get a say in who was cast?'

'No,' Hari gestured towards Scarlett, 'but I wasn't disappointed. Casting directors know what they are doing, and I couldn't have wished for a better Mathilda or Will Scathlock.'

Hari found she'd braced herself for an acerbic comment from Roger, but the only one to speak was Jez.

'You'll find no argument from any of us, I'm sure.' A positive rumble of agreement ran through the audience. 'Lee and Scarlett are simply perfect, as are all of the supporting cast to date.'

When no heckle came from Roger to remind everyone, as usual, that he played the potter, Hari scanned the audience, and was relieved that Roger wasn't in the hall.

Not like him to miss the chance to promote himself.

'Would you say you had much input in the production of the television series?' Jez asked, bringing Hari back to the present.

'None whatsoever. I'm just the writer. I'm the one

who converts the novels into scripts, but after that, I'm not needed. I simply trust the cast to do me proud – which they always have – and then I start on the next novel.'

'Talking of which,' Jez patted a pile of Hari's novels that had been set out on the coffee table between their armchairs, 'what next for Mathilda and Will?'

'Obviously I can't tell you too much. I'd hate to give out spoilers, but I can say that a chap called John will crop up soon,' more smiles of approval floated across the audience as Hari went on, 'and as with all the other novels, I've used a crime I've found within the real documentary records of the day as the initial spark of the next story.'

'The Gaol Delivery Rolls from the fourteenth century?'

Ignoring the soft sound of the main door opening, assuming it was a latecomer to the talk tiptoeing in, Hari answered the question. 'Not this time, although they have been my source until now. On this occasion I've used some court records.'

A hand shot up from the audience, and a young woman smiled broadly as Jez came to her side with the microphone.

'Can I ask, why the fourteenth century? Traditionally the stories are set during the time of King Richard and Prince John.'

Not looking at Dot, knowing she would have been timing how long it took someone to ask her that question, Hari launched into a well-worn response. 'In one of the earliest printed ballads, the *Lytell Geste*, it is King Edward who is the featured king. Which one of the three Edwards has often been a matter for debate, but I've gone with Edward II and into Edward the III's reign because…'

Hari stopped talking as she noticed Jez's eyes flick from her to the door.

'Umm… forgive me, Hari. Everyone.'

As their host's attention moved away from the stage, the entire audience followed his gaze and turned to see the hotel's manager beckoning to Jez from the half-open doorway. Stood by the manager's side was a tall, slim man, wearing a suit that was fractionally too big for him; a small rucksack was slung over his shoulder.

As Jez went to see what was going on, a buzz of rumour and conversation erupted through the audience. Exchanging glances with Dot, a sense of unease crept over Hari as she went to her friend's side.

A second later, Jez, his countenance pale, returned to the stage. His steps were slower, his bounce gone.

'Ladies and gentlemen, if I could ask you to remain in your seats for the time being. I'm afraid there has been an… an incident, and it would be extremely helpful if you could co-operate.'

'Co-operate with what, Jez?' Frank broke his silence from the far edge of the room just as the man in the ill-fitting suit strode forward.

'With my enquiries, sir.'

'What enquiries?' Frank's eyes narrowed.

As the hotel manager retreated from the room, the suited man faced almost three hundred, strangely silent, Robin Hood fans. 'My name is Detective Inspector Shaw, and I'm here because a dead body has been found in the hotel.'

Chapter Fifteen

'Mr Barnes.' Detective Inspector Shaw ushered Jez out of the hall and into the trading area. It was deserted but for a uniformed constable guarding the dividing door. 'If I could have a brief word before we start taking general statements from everyone?'

'Yes… umm… yes. Right.' Jez gulped. 'Who…?' He found he couldn't go further with his question. 'Is the… are they… were they part of the convention, or a regular guest at the hotel?'

'The cleaner who made the discovery says they were part of the Robin Hood Club.'

'Oh.' Jez sank onto the nearest chair with a thud. 'I'd hoped…'

'I'm sorry, sir.' Inspector Shaw pulled out a chair and sat down. 'Would you say you know everyone here well? You're the organiser, I believe.'

'I am, but as to if I know everyone well; the regulars certainly. Others I've either just met or know on a "hope you're having a good time" level.'

Shaw nodded. 'We need a formal ID, and I wondered…'

'Oh, hell. Yes, I suppose. But as I said, I may not know them beyond saying they're part of the conference, although I have a spreadsheet with everyone's names, of course, so…'

'We will need a copy of that, please.'

'Of course.'

'Do you have an emergency contact number for everyone?'

'Not everyone. There's a box on the application form to add one, but some people don't have anyone, and others chose not to fill it in regardless of whether they do or not.'

'I understand, sir. I'd like the forms anyway. One of my colleagues will collect them from you shortly.'

'They're in my room.' Jez worked the brim of his hat around in his large palms. 'How do you think… I mean… A heart attack, maybe?'

'Sir, they don't—'

Finishing the detective's sentence for him, Jez plonked his hat onto his head with a sigh. 'Call the police in for a heart attack. No. I know that, Inspector. I was clutching at straws.'

Giving the organiser a kind smile, Shaw spoke softly. 'The cause of death has yet to be established. It could be that we are looking at accidental death. Until we're sure, then…'

'Yes, I see.'

'There's no blood, sir, if that's what's bothering you about the ID.'

'I wasn't too keen on seeing… but I suppose I should. Better me than one of my guests.' Jez made to stand, but the policeman waved him back down.

'It's okay, Mr Barnes—'

'Jez, please.'

'Very well, Jez. I have a picture of the deceased on my tablet. Can't have you wandering all over the scene, just in case it wasn't an accident.'

'No… no… it's not like on the telly, is it?'

'Very rarely.' The detective pulled a tablet from his rucksack. 'Are you ready?'

Hari unhooked the microphone from her shirt's lapel. Glancing around to make sure it was safe to speak, she whispered to Dot, 'Roger?'

Dot, her eyes wide, shrugged as she surveyed the audience. 'He certainly isn't here, but then neither is Lee.'

The hush that had descended over the room had been replaced by a vibration of hushed conversations that spread like a spider's web across the rows of chairs. As they listened to the growing speculation around them, Hari whispered, 'The detective said a dead body.'

Dot frowned. 'I know, I heard him.'

'I mean, he didn't say there had been an accident or that someone had passed away.'

'Oh.' Dot pulled a biscuit out of her bag and took a giant bite. 'I see what you mean. That's not good. Cookie?'

'How can you eat now?'

'Helps me to keep calm.'

'Fair enough.' Hari dived her hand into the box of cookies as she found herself watching Frank. He was sat at the end of a row a few rows in front of them, facing bolt forward, just as he had been through her talk, with no one sat next to him on his right side. 'I wonder how long we'll have to stay here?'

'Could be ages.' Scarlett suddenly dropped into the empty seat next to Hari.

Hari jumped, making a few of the audience members turn around in alarm. 'You startled me!'

'Sorry, Hari.'

'Not to worry. I guess we're all a bit edgy. One minute I'm talking about Mathilda, and the next... Thanks for coming to my talk. It's good of you to support me.'

'My pleasure. You wrote the best role I've ever had. I love being Mathilda.' Scarlett peered around, her voice dropping to a level that was barely audible. 'Umm... Lee said he was coming this morning. You don't think...'

Hari shook her head. 'He probably just wanted to

take a break.'

Please don't let it be Lee...

'Or maybe Lee assumed Roger would be here and wanted to avoid him?' Dot mused.

Scarlett's face paled further. 'Roger not being with Frank is a bit weird. They're normally joined at the hip.'

'We thought that,' Dot muttered, 'but then, not every guest is in here. I mean, where's…?'

'Oh, God.' Hari's gaze reached the empty seat between Penny and Clara at the same time as Dot's did.

Jez downed the glass of water Inspector Shaw had requested for him in one go. Its refreshing chill felt at odds with the situation.

'Thank you, Inspector. I didn't expect to feel so sick.' He ran a hand through his beard. 'How you chaps do it, I don't know. A violent death must be—'

'Utterly horrendous. Yes. But luckily we aren't in that territory today, although I don't imagine it was a peaceful death either.'

Contrite, Jez mumbled, 'No… no, I suppose not. So, what happens now?'

'Now, we take a statement from everyone here. We request that no one leaves the hotel for the remainder of the day. Those due to check out will have to stay on until we can verify their contact details.'

'Quite a few people attending the conference have booked to stay overnight anyway.'

'Even the guest speakers?' Inspector Shaw asked.

'I don't know.' Jez scratched his head. 'I think Professor Frampton – Neil Frampton – is due to leave today. I couldn't say for certain about Roger Striver.'

'The actor? The one who played the potter in *Return to Sherwood*?'

Jez regarded the detective with surprise. 'The very

same. Are you a fan of the show?'

Making sure his colleagues were out of earshot, Daniel Shaw admitted, 'I'm a huge fan. I had hoped to come along to the event. I'd love to meet Dr Danby, but I couldn't get the weekend off.'

'Well, now you'll be meeting her anyway. It was her interview you just interrupted.'

Dot's words fell out of her mouth with a hushed urgency. 'Sharman said she wanted to come to your talk.'

'It doesn't mean she's the…' Hari's thoughts tailed off as she observed the anxious looks Penny and Clara were giving each other. 'I don't think we should jump to conclusions. It could be anyone.'

'But Sharman especially said she'd come. That's why we closed the book stall, so she could be here too.'

The door to the conference room opened, and Inspector Shaw stepped inside. Every person in the room swivelled around as a fresh hush descended.

'Is there a Miss Dorothy-Ann Henderson here, please? I'd like to talk to her.'

Chapter Sixteen

The hush of the conference room felt tactile as Dot got to her feet. 'How can I help, Inspector?'

'If you could come this way? Nothing to worry about, madam.'

Concerned by Dot's suddenly grey complexion, Hari raised her hand. 'Inspector, may I accompany my friend?'

'And you are?'

'Hari Danby.'

'Dr Harriet Danby, the writer?' The inspector's grave countenance softened as she nodded. 'You may.'

The scrape of a seat being pushed backwards was followed by Frank clambering to his feet. 'In that case, Inspector, may I come too? I'm also a writer. Frank Lister.'

'I'm sorry, sir, but if you could remain here.' Inspector Shaw held up a hand. 'I'd just like to talk to—'

'But you're letting her leave! She's no better a writer than I am!'

Not knowing where to look, hating seeing Frank make a fool of himself, Hari dropped her gaze to the policeman's shiny black Dr Martens, which appeared incongruously out of place with his suit.

'Dr Danby is an excellent writer, sir, and I'm sure you are, too. But that is not the issue at this time. I wished to speak to Miss Henderson first and then Dr Danby, as I have already been informed they are friends and are attending this event together. It makes some sense to speak to them at the same time in this first instance.'

'Well, I… okay.' Frank, his face beetroot red, slumped back into his seat. 'I… the deceased… Could you…? I wondered…' He groaned, the sound echoing through the room as everyone waited to hear whom the subject of the inspector's interest was. 'I was expecting a friend to join me, and they aren't here. I'm a little anxious that maybe—'

'I understand, sir.' Inspector Shaw gave a reassuring smile before raising his head to address the whole room. 'As soon as the next of kin have been informed, I'll release the name. I know it's a big ask, ladies and gentlemen, but try not to worry. I'll be in a position to let you out of this room very soon. I am thankful to you all for your patience.'

Dot hugged Hari to her side as they followed Inspector Shaw from the conference room, through the trading area, and into the bar area of the hotel's reception. It was spookily quiet.

'Thanks for asking to come with me.'

'I wouldn't have let you go alone.' Hari mused, 'Why do they want to talk to us first; you then me?'

'I've no idea, but I think we are about to find out.' Dot gestured towards the semi secluded bar table where, only hours before, they'd enjoyed a drink with Neil and Christine. 'Jez is already here.'

Inspector Shaw beckoned them forwards. 'Please, come and sit down.'

As they sat, wary and uncertain, Hari asked a pale Jez, 'Are you okay?'

'Not really, lass.' He donned his hat in the direction of the detective. 'I suggested you two would be good people to talk to before everyone else. You can confirm the ID, and well, it seemed cruel to call on her friends.'

Hari grabbed hold of Dot's arm as they realised their suspicions had been correct. 'Sharman?'

Jez's sombre expression confirmed their fears as he

spoke to Dot. 'You sent her some cookies, didn't you?'

'I did. A thank you gift. She's been a star and...' Dot found her throat closing in on itself as she sat down. 'I've only known her a minute. She's a good person. Kind. Was kind.'

'She was.' Hari wrapped her arms around herself. 'Sharman really put herself out for us, when she could have been having a good time with her friends.'

'In what way?' Inspector Shaw took a notebook from his pocket.

'She took care of the stall sometimes. She runs — ran — a bookshop, you see; knew how to sell. I got the impression that books were as much her passion as Robin Hood was.'

'Hari's right.' Dot took a gulp from a glass of water in front of her. 'She was at home behind the counter. Hari gave her some signed copies of her books for free, so she could sell them in her shop as a thank you.'

'And did you give her anything, Miss Henderson?'

Dot gave Hari a sideways look. 'Like Jez said, I ordered her some cookies. She loved biscuits, but couldn't have any that had been prepared around nuts.'

'So you kindly ordered her a special batch?'

'Yes.' Dot felt her head begin to thud as she reached a hand out to Hari. 'That was okay, wasn't it?'

'It was a kind thing to do.' Inspector Shaw scribbled a note on his pad. 'Jez tells me that you are the owner – creator, even – of Cookie Creations. Is that right?'

'Yes.' Dot nodded. 'Jez was kind enough to let me promote my cookies here this weekend. They've been very popular.'

Hari leant forward. 'That's why Sharman offered to help with the stall at first. Dot was so busy with the influx of cookie orders that she needed a bit of time away from the stall to work at the same time as I was needed elsewhere. Sharman held the fort.'

A silence, broken only by the scratch of the policeman's pen against his notebook, cloaked the bar. Hari felt her gaze drawn towards one of the large posters displaying a scene from *Return to Sherwood*. Lee and Scarlett were shown as Will and Mathilda, side by side, swords drawn, ready to dive into whatever danger lurked offscreen.

Eventually, the inspector spoke again. 'Jez, this event, while not being expensive in general event terms, is still not cheap to attend. You told me earlier that Sharman was one of your regulars, and sadly, running an independent bookshop is unlikely to make her a rich woman – although she may have had private means that we have yet to uncover. What I'm asking is, would it have been in character for her to pay to come here, and then willingly miss out on features of the weekend to, effectively, do her day job?'

'Well, I...' Jez turned to Hari. 'That's a good question. Did Sharman say why she was willing to help?'

'Said it would save her some money. That it would stop her buying more signed photos when she had loads already. She seemed happy to help.'

'I'm sure she was.' Shaw switched to his tablet, tapping onto its screen.

'Inspector,' Hari's pulse thumped in her neck, 'why are you asking us this? I mean, yes, I know you must learn as much about Sharman as you can, but you'd only be asking us questions — those questions — if you believed them to be connected to her death.'

Daniel Shaw laid down his tablet. 'You're as intelligent as I imagined you would be, Dr Danby.'

'You imagined me?'

'Between the three of us, I'm something of a fan.' He peered over his shoulder. 'I'd be grateful if you kept that between us. My colleagues are liable to take the mick at any given opportunity.'

'I see.' Unsure what else to say, Hari was grateful when the inspector continued to speak.

'Your new friend was found in her room this morning by the lass on housekeeping duty. Sharman was curled up on the floor with a half-eaten cookie in her hand. There was packaging by the bed, showing that it was from your Cookie Creations empire, Miss Henderson.'

Dot's already pale face went puce. 'Like I said, it was a thank you and—'

'There was a note, thanking Sharman for helping with the stall in the box – typed.'

'Yes. I asked for that to be added. We do gift boxes. Anyone can have any message they want added.'

'So, you are confirming that the box of cookies came from you?'

As her friend nodded dumbly in confirmation, Hari asked, 'Are you telling us that Sharman died while eating one of Dot's cookies?'

'That appears to be the case. Can I ask, Miss Henderson — Dot — which flavour cookies did you order for Sharman?'

'Caramel with melted chocolate in the middle. Dark chocolate.'

'The cookie in her hand was certainly chocolatey, but judging by her reaction to eating it, we assume it contained nuts.' Shaw's expression became set. 'Until the pathologist has done their job, we can't be sure of anything, but their first reaction on viewing your friend was death via a severe allergic reaction.'

'But,' Dot was shaking her head fast now, 'but I

ordered cookies she liked. Her favourites. I made sure of the order myself. Asked the bakers to bake them in a nut-free environment and everything.'

'Can you tell me where they would have come from? You have a local distributor?'

As Dot explained about *Pearce Bakes*, Hari's mind accelerated into overdrive.

Why would anyone want to hurt Sharman? It makes no sense. Even Frank got on okay with her – relatively speaking.

Taking a steadying breath, she asked, 'Inspector, you said the pathologist still has work to do. Does that mean that it could be accidental death and that, perhaps, the wrong cookies were delivered? Or the wrong ones were put in the right box, or even the right label put on the wrong box?'

'All of those possibilities are out there.'

'So, you are not accusing my friend of killing Sharman?'

'I am not. But you can appreciate that many questions need asking.'

Dot blurted out, 'But if there were obviously nuts in the cookie, she would never have touched it. She was very sensible about her allergy.'

'The cookie looked like a chocolate biscuit, with a dark chocolate melted centre. No sign of nuts to the naked eye. It was the pathologist who detected them in her vomit.'

'Oh God!'

'The label I mentioned stated the cookies were caramel and dark chocolate flavour and had no nuts included.'

'Yes, as I said, that's what I ordered – caramel cookies with a melted dark chocolate centre.'

As Dot sank into a shocked silence, Hari said,

'Sounds like the correct label. You think that someone swapped the cookies on purpose?'

Inspector Shaw played his pen between his fingers. 'It is a possibility, but it's more likely to have been a mix up. A horrible accident.'

Hari frowned. 'A mistake at the bakery, you mean?'

The detective tapped his tablet a few times before asking, 'Have you ever been in Sharman's room? Either of you?'

'No.' Hari kept hold of Dot, shaking her head. 'Why?'

'It appears to have been searched.' Shaw gave a half smile. 'Or she could have been incredibly untidy. As yet we have not discounted that possibility.'

Hari frowned. 'Is there anyone here who knows her well enough to know if she's a tidy person?'

'I will be endeavouring to find out.'

Blushing, Hari mumbled, 'Sorry, yes, of course you will.'

Before the detective could comment, Dot clutched Hari's arm. 'People are going to blame me, aren't they?' Her voice became small. 'It was one of *my* cookies. No one will ever buy one again…'

Inspector Shaw gave Dot a sympathetic grimace. 'We will do our best to keep the cause of death vague, but—'

'You can't promise.' Dot wiped the back of a hand over her eyes. 'Poor Sharman.'

'When did you last see her?'

Dot and Hari looked at each other, before Hari spoke. 'We assumed we'd see her at the disco last night, or at least in the bar while it was going on. Neither Dot nor I are dancers. She'd said she fancied trying to dance with Lee.'

'Lee Stoneman?'

'Yes.'

Jez chipped in, 'Lee's good like that. Dances with the fans, whether he feels like it or not.'

'But she wasn't there?'

'I saw Lee at breakfast – he said he didn't dance with her.'

The inspector's eyes narrowed. 'Why did he mention that? How did Shaman come up in the conversation?'

Hari paused. 'I'm not sure now. He was asking why I hadn't been in the disco… Sharman just came up.'

'Okay.' He tapped his finger against the table. 'So you actually last saw Sharman, when?'

Chapter Seventeen

'Wasn't it yesterday afternoon?' Hari turned to Dot. 'Didn't Sharman leave us at about four o'clock? Just after maybe?'

'About then. She was…' Dot gulped, and gathered herself before continuing, 'She was looking forward to eating the cookies she'd received.'

Danny sat up straighter. 'So, she'd already got the cookies then?'

'Yes. She said she'd found them outside her door when she'd nipped back to put her signed photos in her room before she came to help us.'

'The cookies arrived quicker than you expected?'

'Well, I… I don't know.' Perspiration dotted the back of Dot's neck. 'I ordered them around midday yesterday.'

'And the turnaround time is usually, what?'

'Usually within half an hour – plus delivery, which depends on distance. It's not far from here to Bakewell – but I suppose I'd expect a longer turnaround time as I asked for extra care due to the nut allergy issue.'

'How do they get to the customer? Courier?'

'Usually a cyclist or motorbike courier. Each bakery is free to choose their own delivery method.'

'Okay, I'll ask at Reception to see who came, and then I'll be on to Pearce's.' Shaw made some more notes. 'And Sharman arrived at your stall yesterday afternoon, when?'

'Around two o'clock.'

'And she'd just found the box of biscuits?'

Dot nodded. 'That's what she said.'

Hari regarded the detective carefully. 'When do you think Sharman ate the suspect cookie?'

'Time of death has not yet been determined, but

obviously after four o'clock. If she intended to go to the disco, then I'd say it was before that began. I understand from the events schedule, the disco was due to kick off at eight.'

'That's correct.' Jez sat back in his chair. 'So, what happens now, Inspector? Does the event continue for the remainder of today, or do I wrap it up early?'

'Is there much left talk-wise? Or is it just social stuff now?'

'Just one more feature. An unexpected extra. Christine Spencer from the local archive is due to come in as soon as she's heard if the ballad found in the local archive is fake or not.'

Daniel Shaw's eyes lit up. '*Robin Hood and the Carter*? I wondered if you'd know about that. So exciting! Wouldn't it be wonderful if it was real?'

Jez's eyebrows rose. 'You really are a Hood fan, Inspector?'

'Absolutely.'

'What a coincidence.'

Shaw returned to the matter at hand. 'One more question for now. Can any of you think of any reason why anyone would want to hurt Sharman?'

'None.' Jez spoke at the same time as Hari, while Dot simply shook her head.

'Thank you all for your time.' As the inspector got to his feet, his mobile rang. 'Excuse me one moment.'

As the detective moved away, Dot burst into tears. 'Sharman was so lovely, and I killed her. At least I might have. I…'

Hari slipped an arm around Dot's shoulders. 'You did no such thing.'

'But my business… it was so much hard work to set up. This will be the end of it.'

'No reason to think that, lass.' Jez tried to be

reassuring, but Hari could see the effort he was putting into his words.

'Let's see what the pathologist says before we jump to conclusions.' Hari watched the inspector as he spoke into his mobile. 'A Robin Hood fan.'

'Sorry?' Dot blew her nose noisily on a tissue.

'Inspector Shaw — he's a fan.'

'Not so unusual. You have lots of fans, Hari.' Jez pushed his fedora back in place.

'Maybe… but a policeman at a Robin Hood Club event when a lost ballad happens to have been found, and now a fan has died…'

Dot paused in the act of taking a drink of water. 'What are you saying, Hari?'

'I'm saying I have never liked coincidences, and we don't seem to be able to move for them at the moment.'

I knew that ballad was going to cause trouble, but I never imagined this…

With permission from Inspector Shaw, Dot had retired to her bedroom, having promised Hari she'd relax in a hot bath and worry as little as possible until they had some concrete news.

Jez was busy retrieving Sharman's booking details to pass onto the authorities, leaving Hari alone at the table. Unsure what she should do, she found herself pulling her notebook from her bag.

Sharman didn't say much about the ballad – beyond the fact she was curious about it as much as anyone else was. Whether I believe in coincidences or not, her death, now, just as the ballad has been found, must be a genuine coincidence…

A hushed voice drew Hari out of her ponderings.

'At times like this I find myself asking "What

would Robin Hood do?"'

Surprised by the inspector's opening line, Hari found herself smiling, despite the circumstances. 'I think that a lot.'

'I bet. All in a day's work for you.' The policeman sat himself down opposite Hari. 'So, what would Mathilda do in this situation, Dr Danby?'

'Please, it's Hari – Harriet – whichever you prefer.'

'I like both.' He stretched his hand across the table. 'I'm Danny – or Daniel – whichever you prefer.'

Hari shook his hand. 'I like both.'

'How about I go with Hari, and you go with Danny?'

'Deal.' Hari regarded her companion carefully. 'You really have read my books?'

'All of them.' The inspector gave an unexpectedly shy smile. 'I had hoped to meet you in rather better circumstances.'

'Any news?'

'I can't say much, but the call I took just now is hopeful – if that's the right word. The pathologist has confirmed death was caused by a fatal allergic reaction. It'll be a while before we have the full postmortem results, but it could well be accidental death, so the remainder of the weekend can continue, although I'd rather no one left the hotel for the time being.'

Exhaling a rush of air she hadn't realised she'd been holding in, Hari asked, 'Can I let Dot know?'

'Soon.' Danny checked the tablet before him. 'I'm waiting for the word from forensics to let me know when Sharman's room has been thoroughly checked over. Once it is, I can let the hotel manager reopen the corridor her room was on.'

'Is that why you wanted to keep everyone in the main conference hall?'

'It's more that I wanted to make sure I knew where everyone was. The manager told me that only event guests are roomed on the same floor as Sharman, and as everyone was at your talk…'

'Not everyone.'

Danny sat up straighter. 'Jez said all the attendees but Sharman…'

'And he's probably right, but not all the invited guests were there. If we're being pedantic, then two people were missing.'

'Tell me.' Danny's finger tapped a few places on his tablet screen.

'My leading man, Lee Stoneman, and the actor who played the potter, Roger—'

'Striver. I watch regularly.'

'Oh. Right. Thanks.' Hari suddenly didn't know where to look and found herself flicking through her notebook.

'Did the celebs stay on the same floors as the fans?'

'No. Scarlett and Lee have the suites on the sixth floor so they can get a bit of downtime in the evenings, without overeager or drunk fans banging on their doors. Jez, Neil – that's Professor Frampton – me, and Roger have rooms on floor five. Dot's on the ground floor.'

Danny jotted some notes into his tablet. 'While the fans are on floors one to four, and the few everyday guests who have accidentally walked in on a Robin Hood Club event are at the far end of floor five?'

'I believe so.' Hari shrugged. 'I'll admit, when Jez was telling me about such things on our arrival, I wasn't paying full attention. I was a bit overwhelmed by all this, if I'm honest – the whole weekend, I mean.'

'I can imagine.'

'If you'd told me, back when I was marking mountains of history exam scripts or teaching medieval economy to university students, that one day I'd be here, surrounded by people who love my imagination and share my passion for all things outlaw, I'd have laughed.'

'And yet, here you are.' Danny's eyes flicked up from his tablet.

'And right now, I wish I wasn't. At least, I wish I hadn't brought Dot with me. If I hadn't, then—'

'No.' Danny reached a hand towards Hari, but then withdrew it. 'This is not your fault. It could easily have been an accident.'

'But how?' She leant forward. 'I can see it's technically possible that the bakery may have accidentally sent the wrong cookies in the wrong box; we're only human, after all, and wires could have got crossed…'

'But?'

'But Sharman was far from stupid. Dot said she was also extra careful around anything that might potentially contain nuts. Sharman spoke about it when she was offered some biscuits the other day. She couldn't have them because they had nuts in them.'

Danny's freckled forehead creased. 'You're saying you don't think she'd have eaten the cookie if she thought it *might* contain nuts?'

'Even if the box was labelled as a nut-free biscuit, I reckon she'd still have read the ingredients list.'

'I see.' He ran a hand through his cropped hair. 'But if there was no aroma of nuts, and there were no nuts listed in the ingredients, then she'd happily take a bite.'

'Yes. Dot ordered her the caramel and dark melted chocolate cookies – and she trusted Dot.'

'And, as I said, that's what flavour it said on the label. But it might not have been what was in the biscuit.'

'Obviously it wasn't, because there *were* nuts. Would the liquid dark chocolate that was in the biscuit Sharman had – whether it had caramel in it or not – disguise a nutty scent or taste, do you think? The melted chocolate Dot uses is high grade – so a little bitter. I bet it could hide mild nut scents or flavours. Almond, maybe?'

'I don't know.' Tapping into his tablet, Danny confided, 'Only one bite was taken. A biggish one.'

'Suggesting that she assumed all was well before she ate.' Hari took up her pen, doodling as she thought. 'Did she spit any of it out?'

'We think so. Hard to tell. As I said, she was sick, though.'

'Didn't she have an EpiPen in case of accidental nut eating?'

'We didn't find one.' Danny pushed his chair back. 'I need to talk to her friends to see if she was in the habit of carrying one. Jez said I should speak to a Penny Forbes and a Clara Letterman.'

'They're in the conference room. They were obviously expecting Sharman, as they'd saved a chair for her between them. I bet they're worried sick that she's…'

'Indeed.' The inspector stood up. 'This is the bit of my job I dislike the most.'

Hari chewed her bottom lip. 'What if this wasn't an accident?'

'Then I'm going to be very busy.'

Chapter Eighteen

Hari watched as Danny Shaw headed towards Jez, then uttered a few words in his ear before leading him back to the conference room. For a split second, she was tempted to follow them, but instead, she sat back down.

With a shaky hand, she reopened her notebook.

Should I have told Danny about my suspicions about the ballad?

Needing to clear her head, Hari slipped her book back into her bag and made her way to the hotel's main doors.

'I'm sorry, madam.' A young police constable gave Hari an apologetic shrug. 'I can't let anyone out for a while.'

'Of course. I wasn't thinking.'

Retreating quickly, Hari wasn't sure where she could go. Then she remembered the Green Room. Spinning around on the soles of her trainers, she decided to avoid the lift, making her way instead to the stairwell.

The inspector's a nice man. Clever. Nice eyes and...

Hari paused mid-step.

You like him because he likes your work and respected your opinion. Nothing else. He's a policeman investigating a death.

Hari restarted her climb to the next floor, trying to remember the last time that she'd found anyone attractive beyond them being a nice human being. It was over a decade, if not longer.

Get a grip. Dot'll have a field day if I tell her I think Danny's cute. Men make life complicated, and I do not like complicated.

She stopped dead for a second time as she realised

what she'd thought.

I think he's cute! Damn. I don't have time in my life for thinking anyone is cute. Stop it!

Moving forward again, Hari reached the fire door that separated the stairwell from the second floor of the hotel and strode towards the Green Room.

Seconds later, the distinctive sound of Roger Striver's voice leaked through the Green Room's semi-open door and along the corridor. The slight whine to his tone made Hari feel sorry for whoever he was with. *It has to be Lee – poor man!*

Hari slowed her approach as it occurred to her that neither Lee nor Roger might know about Sharman. She was about to go in, when a placating female voice responded to whatever Roger had said.

'I know you like to parade your life to all and sundry, Roger darling, but this time mum is absolutely the word, yes?'

'Yes, Mum!'

Darling? Doesn't sound like Elizabeth's voice, though... Hari hung back from the door, a hand over her mouth as she listened.

'I mean it, Roger. If we are to have any chance of this coming off, I need you to be on your *best* behaviour. No indiscretions, no showing off.'

'As if I'd—'

The female's voice became stern. 'You would, and please don't pretend otherwise. I've worked damn hard for you over the years, Roger, and every time you get close to the top, something happens, and it falls apart. I haven't put a foot wrong, so it *has* to be you. While your confidence is a good thing, you're often seen as a show off or an arrogant sod, and quite frankly, it puts people off!'

Embarrassed to have overheard Roger being told

off, Hari took a step back, only to stop dead again as the woman continued. Her voice was lower this time, and more earnest. Hari imagined her leaning forward as she spoke, entreating her companion to heed her warning.

'I have pulled every trick in the book to get this sorted for you. Nothing is on paper yet, so…'

'I know. You're telling me to behave.'

'No need to sulk, darling.'

'If it hadn't been for *her*, then we wouldn't have needed to skulk around like this!'

The woman gave an audible sigh. 'You did okay out of her. Be patient. You're still only twenty-nine — there's plenty of roles out there for you yet.'

Hari's pulse thumped in her ears as she listened, hoping no one would come along the corridor and see her hiding by the door.

'I'm bored of being patient!'

'Nonetheless.'

The sound of a chair being moved sent Hari's heart racing faster. She spun around and walked quickly back to the stairwell, tripping down to the reception and bar fast, in the hope that neither Roger, nor whoever he was talking to, would know she'd ever been there.

Who were they talking about? Which woman did Roger do alright out of? Was it Sharman?

'Jez?'

Hari was surprised to see the event organiser back in the bar, a large whisky in his hand.

'Oh, hi, Hari. Dot okay?'

'I've not seen her yet. I thought I'd wait until Danny had spoken to the group, so I have something to report to her.'

Jez's eyebrows rose. 'Danny?'

Colouring, Hari sat on the stool next to Jez.

'Inspector Shaw. We got talking about the series, and he introduced himself.'

'Makes sense.' Oblivious to her blushes, Jez took a swig of his drink, wincing as the liquid burnt its way down his throat. He held the glass out before him. 'I can't remember the last time I touched alcohol.'

'Forgive me, but is it a good idea to have one now?'

'It's a terrible idea.' Jez took another sip. 'You know, I love this club. It's taken every ounce of my energy for six years, and I don't begrudge it. I only have to look at the happy faces of the attendees. But now…'

'No one will blame you.'

'*I* blame me. I should have had a strict no-nut policy across the whole premises, not just in the kitchens.'

Hari felt an urge to hug her companion. 'You know that would have been totally impossible to enforce, don't you?'

'I suppose so.'

Pulling her mobile from her pocket, Hari placed it on the bar. 'I think I'll text Dot anyway.'

Hope you okay. Appears as accidental death. Will let you know for sure when I know more. H xx

Taking another mouthful of whisky, Jez gulped. 'I'm going to miss Sharman. She was such a constant in the club; someone you could really rely on.'

'Dot and I realised that very quickly. And—' The beep of her phone broke through Hari's sentence. 'Sorry, Jez, it's Dot.'

Poor Sharman. I feel horrible. I'm in the bath. X

Hari tapped out a quick reply: Not your fault. I'll come and see you as soon as I've spoken to the inspector again.

She looked back at Jez. 'Sorry about that.'

'Is Dot okay?'

'Not really.' Hari began to wish she'd ordered a whisky, too. 'You were saying about Sharman?'

Jez swivelled the glass between his fingers. 'She was always upbeat. I know she had money worries, but her smile never faltered. Last year, there was a chance she could lose her beloved shop, yet she kept positive.'

'I had no idea. She talks — talked — so passionately about *Parchment and Paper*.'

'She loved that shop. Inherited it from her father, whom she adored. I got the impression that she'd found funding from somewhere and that all was well now.' Jez pushed his fedora to the back of his head in a cowboy-at-the-bar type way. 'I suggested she applied for an Arts Council grant; perhaps she got it. I only know I didn't get mine.'

'You applied for a grant to help fund the Robin Hood Club?'

With a silent nod, Jez knocked back the remaining whisky.

'Doesn't the ticket price cover everything?'

'Nope.' Jez grinned. 'If I charged enough to cover everything, no one could possibly afford to come. Don't worry.' He sat up straighter. 'I'm just having a moment's self-pity. I should be ashamed of myself, especially with Sharman lying in a mortuary.'

Feeling bad for the fee she'd been paid for appearing at the event, Hari laid a hand on Jez's arm. 'Do you mind me asking, do you earn a wage from this? I assumed this was your business, that you got paid. You do, don't you?'

'Not a penny. I just get the satisfaction of making people happy.'

'But that won't pay the bills.'

'It won't.' Jez laid his large palms on the bar. 'Between us, this was likely to be the last Robin Hood Club event even before this happened. I only managed to get the number of guests I have here due to one of the cast kindly not accepting a fee. Now, after this, I think we can say I'll have to call it a day.'

'I'm so sorry.' Hari could see the sorrow in her companion's eyes. She wondered who'd agreed not to be paid, but didn't feel she could ask.

'Thank you. But please, whatever you do, keep that under your hat. The last thing I need is Frank finding out. He asks every year if he can headline again. If he knew there was no chance…'

'My lips are sealed.' Hari saw the conference room doors open and stood up. 'I think the inspector has finished speaking to everyone. Will you be alright if I go and find out what he said?'

'I'll be fine.' Jez reached out a hand and held Hari's palm for a second. 'Thanks for letting me moan.'

'You didn't moan.' She signalled to the barman. 'A coffee here for my friend, please. Strong. Black. Extra sugar. Charge it to room 34. Thank you.'

As the subdued event guests filed quietly from the conference room, Hari watched out for Neil. She was glad his height made him easy to spot.

She'd just seen him emerge, a grave expression on his face, when Hari spotted Danny with Penny and Clara. It was obvious that the women had been crying.

Frank Lister and Scarlett were the last to come out. Frank's expression was etched with anger, whereas Scarlett was pale and clearly shaken.

Engulfing Hari in a hug, Neil drew her to one side. 'You okay? How's Dot?'

'I'm okay. Dot's keeping to her room for a bit.'

Hari looked towards where Danny was settling Penny and Clara at the table she'd been sat at with him earlier. 'What did Inspector Shaw say to everyone?'

'That it appeared to be an accidental death, but until he had an official word on that, everyone had to stay in the hotel.'

Hari whispered, 'He didn't mention nuts or Dot or cookies?'

'No. Why?'

'It was her nut allergy that killed her – via a cookie.'

'Oh my God.'

'Exactly.' Hari sighed. 'Not everyone was in the conference room. So Roger and Lee won't know not to leave the hotel – although there is a constable on the door, so if they did try to leave, they'd find out what was going on fairly fast.' She paused before adding, 'I went up to the Green Room, but I didn't go in because I overheard Roger talking to a woman. Whoever she was, she won't know to stay inside, either. I don't know if she's a hotel guest, or someone who'd come by to see Roger for a meeting.'

'You'd better tell Inspector Shaw.'

Hari looked over to where Danny was consoling Sharman's friends. 'I will. But not for a moment.'

Chapter Nineteen

'And Mr Striver was definitely talking to a woman?' Inspector Danny Shaw raised a cup to his lips.

'Yes.'

'Ummm.' Danny took a sip of tea. 'My colleagues have been all over the hotel, and they did find Roger Striver in the Green Room, but he was on his own. When asked, he said he hadn't seen anyone from outside the hotel. In fact, he claimed he'd been alone in there all morning.'

Hari felt her cheeks redden. 'I'm not making it up.'

Danny leant forward. 'Of course you're not. I didn't mean to imply…' He paused. 'I'm sorry, but I'm sure you can see why I needed to ask.'

'Yes.'

'You've no idea who this woman was?'

'Sorry, no.' Hari hugged her arms around herself as she sat on the opposite side of the table to the inspector, in the hotel manager's office, which he'd given over to the police for their use. 'There was something about the tone of their conversation that felt—'

'Private?'

'Sort of... actually, it was more that it felt secretive. Roger was being warned not to screw something up.' She shifted uncomfortably on the plastic seat. 'I shouldn't have listened in. I'm not sure why I did.'

'Because you have good instincts.' Danny glanced around. 'And so do I, otherwise I wouldn't be sharing information with you of this nature.'

Hari blushed. 'I'm not going to get you into trouble, am I?'

'Not at all.' Danny smiled. 'I'm merely taking advice from an excellent intelligence.'

'Oh.' Rather taken aback, Hari found she couldn't

meet his gaze for a moment. Instead she burbled, 'I heard Roger say, "If it hadn't been for *her*, then we wouldn't have needed to skulk around like this!" Then the woman he was with replied, "You did okay out of her. Be patient."'

'The use of the word *skulk* underlines the sense of secrecy you mentioned.' Danny frowned in concentration as he recorded what Hari had told him into his tablet. 'And Roger definitely said, "If it hadn't been for her"?'

'Uh huh. He underlined the word *her*, if you see what I mean.' Hari felt herself go cold. 'But, as I say, I can't say who "her" was. It could have been anyone – apart from whoever it was he was speaking to, obviously.'

'True, but only one "her" is unexpectedly dead.'

Hari nodded. 'Sharman knew Roger, but not beyond the confines of the Robin Hood Club meetups. At least, that's the impression I got. She called him Frank's lapdog, but in a jokey way. Not cruelly.'

'And you've no idea who the woman Mr Striver was talking to in the Green Room was?'

'No. All I can be sure of is that it wasn't Elizabeth. That's the woman Frank Lister was with last night in the bar. She, Elizabeth, wasn't at my talk this morning, either, but I don't think she's staying in the hotel. I know she doesn't have a ticket for the event.'

'Interesting. Thank you.'

Hari closed her eyes, trying to cast her mind back to the conversation she'd overheard. 'Whomever it was, they were basically telling Roger off for being such an egomaniac. I was a bit embarrassed on his behalf, to be honest.'

'You didn't recognise her voice from anyone who visited your book stall, Hari?'

'I've thought and thought – but I've signed so many books, spoken to many people…'

'I understand. Don't worry.' Danny spoke gently. 'I had to ask.'

Hari felt frustrated with herself. 'I keep thinking there must be something I heard that could point me in the right direction as to whom she was, but I don't think I'd heard that voice before.'

'That in itself is worth knowing.' He flicked off his tablet. 'But if it does come to you, let me know.'

'I will.' Hari swallowed. 'I hate to ask, but do you know how long it'll be before Sharman's death is reported as officially accidental? Dot's really worried about her business. That sounds callous, but—'

'Not at all. I understand completely.' Danny checked his phone. 'I've not heard, but as there's no evidence to the contrary, I think it's likely that's what the pathologist will rule.'

Hari blew out a long exhalation of air. 'I had no idea what to envisage when I agreed to come along to the Robin Hood Club. A ballad mystery was unexpected enough, but honestly…'

'No one could have guessed there'd be a death on the premises.'

'And, as I said, what with that and this ballad business….' Hari shook her head.

Danny lay down his phone. 'Does that doubting expression mean you think it's fake?'

'I'd be very surprised if it wasn't.'

'You want to tell me about your thoughts on the ballad – in private?'

Hari sat up straighter, before blurting out, 'I think it's connected to Sharman's death.'

Danny tilted his head to one side. 'Go on.'

Wondering if she should have said anything, Hari

mumbled, 'Well, I can't be sure, and I know it's not my place. I mean, I wasn't saying that…'

He held up his hands. 'Either way, I'd be interested in your theory.'

'Okay. I'd quite like to talk it through with someone, and Dot's got enough on her plate to have to listen to me witter on.'

Danny hid his face in his cup as he suggested, 'After work?'

'After work?' Hari was taken aback.

'Yeah. We could have dinner – if you'd like to. Assuming that you're staying in the hotel tonight; or were you planning on going home to…'

'Salisbury. No, Dot and I are booked in until after breakfast tomorrow.'

'So, dinner?'

'Well, umm. Yes. Thanks.'

Danny stood up. 'Good. Nice to have something to look forward to.' His smile morphed into a grimace. 'Now, however, I have to go and interview everyone at *Pearce Bakes*, to try and get to the bottom of what happened with these cookies.'

'I don't know if I hope you find that someone accidentally mixed up the orders or not.'

'Quite.' Danny's mobile burst into life again. 'I must take this. I'll see you later. We could go to the pub around the corner from here? Six o'clock?'

'But I can't leave the hotel. No one can.'

'You can if you leave with me.'

Chapter Twenty

'A date!' Dot leapt out of bed, her washed-out pallor flushing with colour.

Hari rolled her eyes. 'Don't be silly! It's not a date. He's a detective who just happens to be interested in Robin Hood. He wants to know about the ballad.'

'He could get that information from the Internet.'

Hari sighed. 'I might have told him that I had a feeling something wasn't right about it.'

'And he's going to help you sleuth?' Dot pulled on a jumper.

'I wouldn't put it quite like that.'

'So, it *is* a date then?'

'Dot!'

'Let me think it's a date. *Please!* It'll give me something else to focus on.'

Sitting on the side of Dot's bed, Hari beckoned for her friend to join her. 'Why don't you come to the pub with us? You know as much about what's going on as I do.'

'No way. I'm not playing gooseberry.'

'I've told you. It's not—'

'A date. Yeah, I get it. But he's cute, and clever, and he likes Robin Hood.'

Hari shifted uncomfortably. 'Suppose so.'

Dot sat down with a thump. 'Wow! You didn't say "Don't be daft, Dot, he's not cute!"'

Wiping her fringe from her eyes, Hari felt flustered. 'I'm only sharing my thoughts on the ballad. Danny'll probably think I'm letting my imagination run away with me.'

'Danny?' Dot's eyes widened. 'On first name terms then.'

'Oh, shut up!' Hari got up and threw a pillow at her

friend. 'Come on, you can't hide in here until the event is over, and as we aren't allowed to leave the hotel yet, it's a choice of back to the book stall or the bar.'

Dot's positivity evaporated. 'I'm not sure I can. What if everyone blames me?'

'They won't.'

'How can you be so sure?' Dot sank back onto the bed.

'Because not one person has said anything other than how shaken you must be as you and Sharman had become friends. Only Danny, Neil, Jez and us know that it was probably her allergy that killed her.'

'No one knows?' Hopeful relief rang through her voice.

'It's confidential information. Plus, remember, we don't know that it *was* the cookie yet. The police suspect it was, but until all the tests are done, we can't be totally sure.' Hari paused. 'I suppose Penny and Clara might have been told about the allergy connection, but in all honesty, I doubt it.'

'But if they *do* know—'

'They won't blame you.'

'But—'

'They *won't*.'

'But—'

'Jez and I will look after you, Dot.' Hari gave another heavy sigh. 'And maybe we should look after him. He's in quite a state.'

'I bet he can't believe this has happened at his event.'

Hari pulled a face as she recalled Jez sipping at a tumbler of whisky. 'He's a man with a lot on his mind. We can take care of each other.'

'Okay, but promise me, if it gets hostile, we can go home.'

Shaken to see her friend so unsure of herself, Hari placed a hand over hers. 'I promise, if that happens, I'll ask Danny if we can leave the hotel to find another local one. I can't do any more than that.'

'Okay.' Dot stood up again. 'Let's go back to the stall. Best to be busy, and if people are at a loose end, they might well want to buy more books to read.'

Hari smiled. 'That's better.'

'How do you mean?'

'I was worried that I'd lost the real Dot for a minute. But if you're thinking marketing, then I know you're alright underneath.'

Dot stuck out her tongue. 'You will stay with me until you go out this evening, won't you, Hari?'

'Promise.'

Having persuaded Dot to leave her room, Hari felt a strange reversal of their usual roles as her best friend stuck to her side like a limpet. Normally she was the anxious one, with Dot chivvying her along. Now Dot was keeping her eyes on the randomly patterned carpet, while Hari kept hers open for trouble while a steady stream of encouragement flowed from her lips.

'Okay, so most people were in the bar when I came up. We have to go through that way to get to the trading area, but it's going to be fine. Ready?'

Linking her arm through Hari's, Dot pulled a face. 'Not really. Are you sure that—?'

'I'm positive. And the sooner you go back in there, the better.'

'Pulling the plaster off in one movement, you mean.'

'Better than easing it off so it catches on all the little hairs.'

Dot found her smile reappeared despite herself. 'I

bet you do that.'

Hari chuckled. 'I do. I'm hopeless. Always hurts way more than if I just ripped plasters off, but I never can quite bring myself to do it fast.'

Exhaling as the double door to the bar area came into view, Dot murmured, 'Hari, what if…?'

'I'm sure that it was a horrid accident, but if — just *if* — it wasn't, then it will soon come to light that someone else was responsible and not you.' Hari pushed her shoulders back and walked faster, towing Dot in her wake.

Jez was by Dot and Hari's side in seconds.

'Thank goodness you're here, Dot. I was so worried. What a shock all round.'

'Just a bit.' Dot chewed on her bottom lip. 'I can't believe it.'

'Nor me.' Jez drew a hand across his pale face. 'I've just announced that, as obviously we can't go anywhere for a while, we will keep the stalls open for a few more hours, if that's okay with you two?'

Hari nodded. 'We rather assumed you would. We're on our way there now.'

'Good. Thank you.' Jez surveyed the huddled groups of friends, all engrossed in muted conversations. The blanket smiles that the weekend had engendered were gone as the loss of one of the Robin Hood Club's staunchest members sank in. Jez lowered his voice. 'I know I mentioned I wasn't sure about running another event, Hari, but now I really can't. How could I without Sharman? Everyone knew her. She was a force of nature. This is so unfair.'

'I really liked her.' Dot gulped. 'She was so positive. Hoping to do a PhD soon. On Robin Hood, I assumed, although she never said it would be specifically on him.'

Jez played his hat brim through his hands. 'It would have been. She was so knowledgeable about the legend. I had no idea she was actually going to get the chance to study, though. Since the first meeting six years ago, she'd talked about doing one, but as she had no money…'

Hari felt a quiver of cold run down her spine. 'She was coming into money… or, she said she expected to.'

Dot took a tissue from her pocket and blew her nose. 'She said as much to me during the banquet. That she expected funding soon.'

'Did she say where from?' Hari asked.

'I didn't like to pry.' Dot's eyes narrowed. 'You've got your historian on the trail face on again.'

'What? Oh, no…' Hari swapped her long, black ponytail from one shoulder to the other. 'I was just thinking… it's nothing.'

Not noticing the disbelieving expression on Dot's face as she regarded Hari, Jez said, 'I'm rather hoping to get another talk organised. While you two were in Dot's room, I had a text from Christine. The initial information about the ballad's authenticity won't be with her until at least six – maybe later – or not at all, perhaps. Either way, she'll come over at eight.'

'Assuming the police have finished, and she can come into the hotel.' Hari immediately regretted being the voice of reason as she saw the worried expression on Jez's face furrow further. 'I'm sure they will have, though.'

'Hope so. Speculation about the ballad is pretty much the only other topic of conversation in here apart from poor Sharman. That's why I thought I'd rustle up an additional talk. Keep people's minds occupied until we know if we can leave or not.'

'Sounds like a good idea.' Hari kept her eyes on the people milling around the bar. No one was paying attention to either her or Dot.

'So, this talk. Hari, I don't suppose—'

Guessing what Jez was about to ask her, Hari spoke fast. 'I can't imagine anyone would be in the mood to listen to me droning on again in the circumstances.'

'But we didn't finish your interview. A lot of people came to listen to you. To talk to *you*.'

'And they have, Jez. Nonstop.' Hari smiled. 'Most people came to see Lee and Scarlett and Roger. Not me.'

'Maybe.' Jez looked about him. Scarlett was surrounded by fans in the corner of the bar. There was no sign of Lee or Roger. 'I just don't like not delivering on what I've promised.'

Suddenly feeling as if she was the one letting everyone down in the face of Jez's worry, Hari found herself muttering, 'I don't want to leave Dot on her own, Jez. If you wouldn't mind staying with her, I'm happy to do an informal chat in the hall about writing the series – *if* it's wanted.'

Jez plonked his hat back on his head. 'I'll happily sit with Dot. In fact, the prospect of sitting still in such good company is more than appealing. Shall we say you'll be in the hall in half an hour?'

Hari gave an internal groan; she'd rather hoped to have time to sit and think about the puzzle of the ballad before seeing Danny later. 'Sure. But if no one shows up, I'll not mind one bit.'

Glad to see Dot fussing over piles of books; knocking them into regimented order on the table, Hari looked up as Jez approached the stall with three takeout coffees in a cardboard carrier.

'Might as well have a caffeine shot.' He passed a cup to Hari. 'It's going to be a long afternoon, I think.'

'Thanks, Jez.' Hari took her cup, holding it to her chest, part for the warmth, and part for the sheer comfort that came with holding a cup of coffee. 'It'll help keep the throat lubricated if I've got to keep talking. Although, I've no idea what else there is for me to say.'

'Just chat. Ask for questions.' Jez sighed. 'I'd come and host but—'

'It's okay. It would appear a bit heartless if we just picked up where we left off.'

'Exactly. I announced it as an informal chat with the focus on the actual writing process rather than the show. Thought that would be easier for you.'

Hari felt some of the tension in her shoulders dissipate. 'Thanks. That's certainly easier.'

As Dot finally sat down, the table before her tidied to within an inch of its life, she whispered, 'Frank's very quiet.'

Hari observed the stall opposite. 'I hadn't even noticed him come in.'

Her fellow author was sat on his own behind his stall. His expression solemn, his eyes closed.

Jez took the lid off his Americano. 'Frank knew Sharman for a long time. Maybe I should see if he's okay.'

'Drink your coffee first,' Dot said. 'He doesn't look like he wants to be disturbed for a minute. And umm... if Hari has to go, I don't really—'

'Don't worry, Dot. I'll not abandon you to face the fans on your own.' Jez gave her his best bolstering smile. 'Not that there are any just now. Seems the bar is the place for the moment.'

'Good.'

Dot had no sooner spoken, when the door opened, and Penny and Clara came in. Hari saw the colour drain from her friend's face as they approached the stall.

Jez was on his feet before Hari was. 'Penny, Clara, I'm so, *so* sorry.'

Penny's eyelids were puffy and her voice hoarse from crying. 'We thought she'd fallen asleep. She'd been so tired lately from stressing about keeping her business going. We were sorry she missed the dance, but thought we were doing the right thing leaving her to rest.'

Hari felt a lump come to her throat. 'I've no idea what to say. I'm so sorry.'

'There isn't anything anyone can say. I don't suppose either of you have seen Inspector Shaw?'

As everyone shook their heads, Hari, not wanting to implicate Dot by letting on she knew he'd gone to the bakery, asked, 'Why did you want him?'

'This.' Clara hooked the shoulder bag she'd been carrying off her arm. 'It's Sharman's. She left it in our room by mistake. We'd been messing around, trying on outfits before the disco. It got lost under a heap of dressing up clothes. I found it just now. I bet she'd have come back for it, but…'

Seeing tears well up in Clara's eyes, Hari simply said, 'I'm sure she'd have missed it eventually. The inspector gave me a card in case I remembered anything. I'll call him.'

On instructions from Danny Shaw, via Hari's phone, Clara and Penny gave the bag to Hari. Taking it carefully, she headed out of the trading area, towards the hotel's main door, where Danny had asked for the bag to be handed to the constable on duty.

Stopping on the way to answer a call of nature,

Hari hung the bag on a hook on the inside of the toilet cubicle door.

I must not look inside. It is none of my business what's in there.

Hari had washed her hands and was about to head back into the hotel foyer and to the constable, when a nagging thought arrived in her head.

I wonder...

Glad there was no one else currently in the washroom, Hari went back into the toilet cubicle and rested Sharman's bag on the closed loo seat. Wrapping some tissue paper around her hand in an attempt not to get fingerprints inside the bag, Hari emptied out the contents, one item at a time.

After the usual predictable contents of paracetamol, a sanitary towel, a pen, several random boiled sweets, a pack of travel tissues and some old receipts, Hari found a notebook and, right at the bottom, safe in its own black drawstring bag, was Sharman's EpiPen.

No wonder the police couldn't find it in her room. Poor Sharman.

Hari tried to quiet the image that instantly entered her head of Sharman, knowing something was wrong, hunting around her room for her bag and her life-saving pen, only to realise she'd left it in her friends' room; far too far away to get to.

Picking up Sharman's notebook, Hari put everything else back in the bag before sitting on the closed seat and flicking through the book.

Having left the bag, complete with notebook, in the care of the police constable watching the hotel door, Hari hurried back to the trading area. Her head spun.

I need to speak to Danny – but what do I say? That I've been snooping in Sharman's private property?

Messing with evidence?

Pushing open the double doors that divided the hotel bar from the trading area, Hari was surprised to see a large group of people making their way into the hall. She dashed to her stall.

'They can't all want to talk about my books *now*, surely?'

'I told you,' Jez adopted a reassuring tone. 'The guests came to see you this weekend. As no one can leave until Inspector Shaw gives the okay, and there's only so much else to do here, you were bound to have a well-attended session.'

'Oh.' Hari's hopes that no one would be in the mood to talk to her so she could call Danny with her new information were further dashed as Neil came into view. 'Hello. I thought you'd escaped into your room for a bit to work?'

'I couldn't concentrate. Came out for a drink and heard you were going to talk about Mathilda.' Neil picked up a copy of Hari's first novel. 'You want me to bring in one of each of your books, to hold up as you talk about them?'

'Well…'

Dot started to collect the six titles together. 'That is a great idea. Save you having to worry about what to say, Hari. You can give a potted history of the writing of each book.'

'I can't remember what I wrote in each one, let alone the circumstances around which I wrote them! Especially the early ones! I've written hundreds of thousands of words since Mathilda's first adventure.'

'A quick read of each blurb will jog your memory.' Neil took the pile of books from Dot.

'I wouldn't worry.' Jez beamed at Hari. 'Your fans will know your books inside out. They'll happily tell you what happened in them.'

Hari had been so engrossed in a conversation between one of the convention guests and the challenge of getting enough historical detail in a novel, without it being too textbook-ish, that she hadn't noticed Roger join the audience.

Seeing him sat near the back, a subdued expression on his face, brought her up with a jolt. The fact he'd silently snuck in without making sure that everyone knew he was in the room felt very out of character.

The woman I heard him talking to ordered Roger to keep his ego on hold...

The group were all sitting in the middle of the seating area, with Hari among them, rather than up on the stage with a microphone. It was more friendly and relaxed that way. Hari had begun by saying that she was merely there to help keep minds occupied after the awful events of the day, and that if people felt they needed to leave, or wanted to talk about other things than her books, they could. So far, however, the focus had been on her work, and she was becoming increasingly surprised by the number of budding historical fiction writers present.

Jez told you there'd be folk hoping the writing magic would rub off on them.

Having explained, again, why there was no Robin in her stories, Hari was just wondering how to wrap things up so she could go and see how Dot was, and to make a call to Danny about the contents of Sharman's bag, when Roger suddenly spoke.

'You know, Hari, your Mathilda really is a fabulous invention. It's no wonder that Frank's series was cancelled before it saw the light of day.'

Feeling rather wrongfooted, but saved from having

to respond by a chorus of agreement from the fans present, Hari was relieved when the door to the hall opened, and Inspector Shaw put his head round.

'I'm sorry to interrupt, but Roger Striver, could I have a word, please?'

Chapter Twenty-one

Having brought the conversation with her fans to an end, Hari rejoined Dot and Jez, with Neil at her side.

'Any idea why Shaw wants to talk to Roger?' Neil asked as he replaced the books on the stand.

'Not really.' Afraid that her expression would give her away, convinced it was to do with the conversation she'd overheard, Hari focused on her novels.

Meanwhile, exchanging an anxious glance with Jez, Dot said, 'We saw Danny go into the hall, and then come out with Roger. He didn't say anything about Sharman while he was in there, did he?'

'He said nothing beyond that he wanted to talk to Roger.'

Jez nodded. 'I can't imagine what Roger might have to say about Sharman.'

'The police will need to talk to everyone before we can leave the hotel, I suppose.' Feeling a patina of perspiration mottle her neck, Hari fussed over her books. 'I wondered; would you be alright if I went up to the Green Room to fetch us some sandwiches? Lunch time came and went and suddenly my appetite has come back.'

'Absolutely.' Jez rubbed his stomach. 'Now you've mentioned food, I could probably do with something myself. Would you mind bringing a selection down?'

'No problem. Neil, Dot, do you want some too?'

As Dot gave a thumbs up, Neil said, 'I'm okay, thanks. I'll head back to my room for a bit. I brought supplies from home.'

Hari was about to follow Neil from the trading zone when a couple of the guests who'd been at her informal chat arrived, requesting signatures on books they'd already purchased. 'I'll just help these folk, then I'll grab us some food.'

Feeling bad for privately cursing the fans who'd held up her departure, Hari hoped that her hunch that Danny would take Roger to the Green Room to talk to him was correct.

Hurrying up the back stairs, Hari didn't allow herself to contemplate whether she was following Danny and Roger because she wanted to find out what Roger would say about the conversation he'd previously denied having, or if she just wanted to see Danny again.

Don't be ridiculous.

Slowing her pace as she reached the Green Room, Hari saw no one in the corridor ahead, nor could she hear any conversation coming from within.

She hadn't been sure what she intended to do – listen at the door, perhaps. Now there was nothing obvious to overhear, she took a deep breath and went inside and headed to an array of clingfilm-wrapped sandwiches.

'Hi, Harriet.'

Her hand flung to her chest as she leapt in surprise. 'Oh my God, Lee! You scared the life out of me.'

'Sorry.' He gave a sad shrug. 'Seems I'm destined to upset you whenever we meet.'

'Not at all. I guess we're all a bit jumpy right now.'

Lee patted the chair next to him. 'Fancy a chat?'

'Sure.' Surprised by the invitation, Hari sat down. 'Are you alright? Hope you don't mind my saying, but you're looking a bit—'

'Floored?'

'Well, yes, now you mention it.' Hari paused. 'Sharman?'

'I liked her. We got on. She was so…'

'Jez described her as a force of nature.'

'And he was right.' Lee picked up a tumbler of whisky Hari hadn't previously noticed and swirled its contents around the curved glass. 'This is my second convention, and she was there last time, too. Always smiling. She was a person you could really talk to. Although she was a fan, Sharman never lost sight of the fact that the stories are just that – stories.'

'You mean, she never mixed Lee Stoneman up with Will Scathlock.'

'Precisely.' He took a sip of his whisky. 'She was clever, too.'

Wondering how many more times her leading man would take her by surprise, Hari found herself asking, 'Forgive me, but you and Sharman… you weren't…'

He gave a sad smile.

'Sorry. I should never have asked.'

Lee shrugged. 'Neither should I.'

'What?'

'I should never have asked her out.' Downing the rest of his whisky in one, Lee stood up. 'She actually laughed, you know, when I asked her. Doesn't make a boy feel good.'

'Sharman laughed at you? That doesn't sound like her.' Hari bit her lip. 'Although, I didn't know her, really.'

'At the time it felt like I was being laughed at. Now, I'm wondering if she thought I was joking; if she laughed because she felt awkward.'

'Maybe she wanted to say yes, but she couldn't believe that you'd want to be with her because she isn't famous like you?'

'Maybe.' Lee shrugged. 'But why wouldn't she think I was serious? We spoke often. We got on. She actually *got* me. At least, I thought she did.'

'Often?'

'Sorry?'

'You said you spoke to her often, but the Robin Hood Club meets once a year, and you've only been to two – including this one. I know she went to all six…' A new thought came to Hari. 'Why were you at the other one anyway?'

'Jez invited me. Even without *Return to Sherwood* being the featured show, the fans still came to see me. Any Robin Hood connection is better than no Robin Hood connection to most of these guys. And good on 'em. Seeing so much passion for a subject in one place is wonderful.'

'I couldn't agree more.'

A gentle smile of remembrance crossed Lee's face. 'Sharman and I hit it off at once. She had purple hair the first time we met – in Oxford this time last year. We got chatting in the hotel bar after a talk on the Errol Flynn movie. There was something about her.'

An image of Inspector Danny Shaw flashed through Hari's mind. *There's something about him, too…*

'Did anyone else know you liked Sharman in that way?'

'No. Seems she didn't believe it herself. Although, as I said, I saw her often enough; I'm sure the penny must have dropped.'

'How often did you see her outside of the RHC?'

'She came to see me at different locations around the UK when I was filming four times since last May, and then, we had more regular meetings when I was in the north of England working at the end of last year. And we've chatted on WhatsApp at least once a week since.' He stared into his empty glass. 'I should have gone to find her when she didn't show at the disco…

but there were so many other people. I couldn't get away. If I had, then perhaps…'

Hari sighed. 'It's no good thinking like that. I'm so sorry, Lee, I had no idea.'

'It took me ages to decide to go for it with her. Sharman isn't – wasn't – the usual sort of partner for an actor to walk up the occasional red carpet with, but I finally realised I'd fallen in love with her, and I didn't care what others thought. And now…'

'Did you give her any clue that you saw her as more than a friend before this weekend?'

'I'd hinted at it, but when I told her how much I wanted to be with her, she didn't believe me. Perhaps I read all the signs wrong. Perhaps…' Lee's words faded into silence. 'Makes no difference now, does it.'

'Sadly not.' Hari wasn't sure what to say. 'I wish I could help you feel better.'

'It's nice to just say it out loud.' Lee looked up at his script writer. 'You won't tell anyone, will you? It isn't that I'm ashamed of her, but I can't face all the sympathy or the inevitable media interest that would follow.'

'My lips are sealed.' Hari ran a hand through her sleek, black hair. 'When did you tell her how you felt? Yesterday?'

'In the afternoon – before we all went to get ready for the disco. She'd just left your stall, and was on her way to her room. I pulled her to one side in the bar and told her how I felt.' Lee blew out a heavy breath. 'The more I think about it, the more I wonder if, for a split second, she was going to say that she loved me too – but I'm probably just being fanciful.'

'That was the last time you saw her?'

'Yes. The very last time.'

***

The remainder of the afternoon seemed to last forever, while at the same time, it passed in a flash. Once Hari had returned to Dot, Jez had taken his leave to check on all his guests. Then, between signing books and reassuring Dot that her cookie empire would survive, Hari had spent a lot of time thinking. The first thought being that she'd leave telling Danny about Sharman's bag until she saw him in the pub.

There had been no sign of either Roger or Danny all afternoon, leading her – and several others – to wonder if their chat had taken place at the police station rather than in the hotel. Hari had expected Frank to have something to say about the situation, but Frank was no longer in the trading area. Jez had told her Frank had closed his stall during her talk and was working in his room until they had word they could leave the hotel.

Now, taking her notebook from her handbag, Hari flicked through the pages as she reflected on her encounter with Lee in the Green Room. She had not seen that conversation coming. Nor, thinking back over the past few days, had she noticed any sign that he'd liked Sharman beyond her being a friendly face at an annual event. In turn, Sharman had shown no indication that she had a crush – or more – on Lee.

I promised not to tell anyone about Lee liking Sharman, but should I tell Danny? Being rejected by Sharman gives Lee a motive to kill her – if it wasn't an accident...

Lee was incredibly handsome; an actor with a glittering career ahead of him, and if the celebrity magazines could be believed, he'd had numerous relationships with equally attractive models and fellow actresses.

Why wouldn't he want someone like Sharman,

though? As he said, she was easy to talk to, clever, and it was obvious she had a lot of fun in her. Am I dismissing the idea simply because she wasn't conventionally attractive in an "as seen on TV" sort of a way? Hari muttered thoughtfully, 'She was striking, though – stunning even…'

Dot frowned. 'You okay, Hari?'

'Sorry, I was thinking aloud.' She stuffed her notebook back into her bag and checked her watch. 'Should we pack up? It's almost four-thirty and I can't imagine anyone buying anything else now.'

Dot looked at their table display, which now held only a dozen or so books, no mugs and one t-shirt. 'Can't argue with your level of sales.'

'Thanks to you.' Hari gave her friend a hug. 'I'm so glad you came.'

'I wish I hadn't. Then Sharman—'

Holding up a hand, Hari stopped the words that were forming on Dot's lips. 'No. If someone meant to do Sharman wrong, then they would have, cookie or no cookie. And if it was an accident, it was one not of your making. This is *not* your fault.'

'Okay.'

'Good.' Hari lifted an empty cardboard box out from under the table. 'Let's get packed up.'

'I could do it on my own if you want to go and get ready for your date.' Dot gave an impish grin.

'Still got it in you to tease me, then?'

'Yup.'

Rolling her eyes, Hari was about to fish under the table for a roll of bubble wrap when an idea struck her. 'Actually, would you be alright on your own for a minute, Dot? I need to ask someone something.'

'That sounds mysterious.'

'I'll tell you later.'

'Go on then. Seems that you were right about no one knowing about the cookie situation. I'll get this all packed and then we can go and beautify you.'

'Don't even think about it!'

Hari knocked on Lee's hotel room door, her heart thudding rather faster than usual. She wasn't sure how he'd take the question she wanted to ask him.

Having waited twenty seconds, and hearing no footsteps heading towards her, she was just contemplating whether she should knock again or give up and try later, when a shuffling sound from within led to the door swinging open.

'Oh, hello, Harriet.' Lee stood, wrapped in a towel, his short hair dripping around his shoulders. 'I was grabbing a shower.'

Not sure where to look, Hari gabbled an apology for disturbing him. 'I'm sorry to ask this, and I'm not sure if it's important or not, but did you ever lend Sharman money?'

'What?' A cloud crossed Lee's face.

'I'm sorry – of course you don't have to tell me. I know it's a personal question, and I would never ask, but—'

'You think money is behind her death, Hari? You don't think it was an accident?'

'I'm not sure what I think, really – but there's this niggle at the back of my mind that all isn't as it appears to be, and—'

'It might help find out what happened to Sharman?'

'It might.' The expression on Lee's face extinguished any notion she'd had about him not being sincere about his feelings for her. 'Although, I could be well off beam, so I'd rather you didn't tell anyone of my doubts.'

'If you keep my secret, then I'll keep yours.'

'Deal.' Hari hoped she wouldn't have to break that promise as she prompted, 'So, did you lend her money?'

'A little, yes.' Lee checked left and right along the corridor, making sure that there was still no one around to overhear them. 'I offered to loan her enough to secure the business, but she wouldn't have that. Said that was money she needed to earn herself. She was quite a proud person.'

'It was her father's business. I got the impression from her friends that it was important to her.'

'It was. I never got to see it in person – although I did via WhatsApp, of course. I'd have liked to, though.' Lee pulled the towel more firmly around his waist. 'Anyway, the money I gave her – she insisted it was a loan, even though I saw it as a present. Either way, it was so she could do the PhD she always wanted to do.'

'Ah. I see.' Hari felt a weight lift from her shoulders. 'That makes perfect sense. Thank you.'

'Does it help?'

'It does.' Hari took a step backwards. 'Thanks. I'd better let you get dry before you catch your death… Oh. Sorry!'

'It's okay, Harriet. Sharman had a decent sense of humour. She'd probably have smiled at that.'

Sitting in her hotel room, having promised Dot she'd make at least a little bit of an effort before she saw Danny, Hari sighed. She wasn't at all sure their dinner would happen, as no official word had come to say the guests could leave the hotel yet.

I know he said I could leave if I was with him, but that hardly seems fair on everyone else.

Instead of following Dot's wishes, apart from a

token effort of brushing out her ponytail, letting her jet-black hair fall over her shoulders, she decided to stay dressed exactly as she was.

If black jeans and a white shirt don't work for him, he'd never have asked me out in the first place.

Her thought brought her up short.

Anyway, it isn't a date.

Sitting on the edge of her bed, she pulled her notebook from her bag again and scribbled *Sharman had money from L for PhD* before jumping up as the ring of her mobile broke the silence of the room.

Chapter Twenty-two

Back in the same cheap and cheerful Wetherspoons pub restaurant where she'd first discussed the ballad with Neil, Hari felt decidedly less relaxed this time around.

It had been one thing talking to Danny in the hotel, while he was there in his official capacity, but here, they were in the wild, and she wasn't sure who she was supposed to be. Dr Harriet Danby, the writer, or just Hari, the thirty-something with very little dating experience and an inability to do small talk.

'Are you alright?' Danny opened one of the menus that had been propped between the salt and pepper shakers. 'You look edgy.'

Hari grabbed the other menu, glad to have something in her hands. For a moment, she hadn't known what to do with them. 'Sorry, it's been quite a day and, if I'm honest, I'm not used to having meals out with people I don't know.'

'Nor am I.' Danny scanned his menu as he spoke. 'The only people I get to meet are suspects, although the majority are innocent. But once you've given them the fourth degree about something or other, they are less inclined to come out with you.'

'Makes sense.' Hari looked at the menu, even though she already knew she'd have the same meal she'd had when she'd been before. 'I'm know I'm only here because of poor Sharman and the fact you like Robin Hood.'

'Not only because of that, I hope.' Danny tilted his head to one side. 'Tell me about yourself.'

Hari, who was already nervous, felt a wave of anxiety start to do breaststroke around her stomach. 'There's not much to know about me, really. I'd rather know about you and your work because…'

Danny laughed as he put down his menu. 'How about we leave work for a little while and both accept that we don't particularly like talking about ourselves? We could allow each other five personal questions, then we'll move onto safer things, like Robin Hood.'

'Five personal questions?'

'Yup.'

'Okay.' Hari held up her menu. 'But let's order food first. I'm famished.'

'Sure.' Danny waved his phone. 'I've got the app, so we shouldn't have to move. I'm up for a jacket spud and tuna. You?'

'Snap.'

'Seriously?'

'Yup. It's what I always have at a Wetherspoons,' Hari smiled, 'but if it makes you uncomfortable to have the same meal as me, I can swap the tuna for chilli.'

'Not at all.' Danny pressed a few buttons on his phone. 'Just means we've both got good taste. I'm sticking to coffee as I'm on call. You want a glass of wine or something?'

'I'll go with coffee too, please. Black. No sugar. And some tap water, if that's okay?'

'Done.' Danny sat back in his seat. 'All ordered.'

'How much do I owe you?'

'Nothing.'

'Now, come on. I should pay for—'

Danny shuffled his chair closer to the table. 'I asked you out. If you decide that you can stand to accompany me on another occasion, then it'll be your turn to foot the bill. Sound okay?'

'Sounds okay.' Suddenly thirsty, and hoping their order was processed quickly, Hari bit back her desire to ask how his interview with Roger went, instead saying, 'I'm so glad the hotel was opened up again. Thanks for calling to let me know. No one felt like leaving while they could, but the minute we were told we were confined to quarters, suddenly everyone was keen to get outside as fast as possible.'

'Fairly standard reaction.' Danny nodded. 'As I said on the phone, nothing suggests it being more than accidental death at this time. How's Dot?'

'Shaky, but better now she has spent an afternoon in the hotel without a single person knowing Sharman died via cookie consumption.'

'I'm sure she is.' Danny leant back to let the waitress deliver their drinks and cutlery. 'We seem to be avoiding the five questions.'

'It was worth a try.' Hari chuckled. 'How about keeping them easy? I'll kick off with, I know you are Inspector Danny Shaw, but how old are you?'

'I'm thirty-two.' He blew across his coffee before taking a sip. 'And you are Dr Harriet – Hari – Danby, and you are an author and script writer, who is, how old?'

'Thirty.'

'You are very young to have so many books and a TV series.'

'You are very young to be a Detective Inspector.'

'Fast track – university graduate and all that.'

'Which subject?'

'History, naturally.' Danny marked the questions off on his fingers. 'That counts as your second question.'

Hari placed her cup in her saucer. 'Damn, I wasn't thinking, but I suspect it would have been a question I asked.'

'So, I'll ask, assuming you also did history, where did you study?'

'Bristol. That's where I met Neil. Professor

Frampton, who you met earlier. He was my dissertation supervisor during my third year, and then my PhD supervisor.'

'He seemed a nice chap.'

'He is. We've been friends ever since. He saw the ballad with me on Saturday before it went off for analysis.'

'You're both so lucky. I'd have loved to have seen it.'

'You are that interested, then? In Robin Hood, I mean?'

'Always have been. My grandmother gave me the *Legends of Robin Hood* when I was about seven. I've been a fan ever since.'

Hari counted on her fingers. 'I make it that I've got two questions left to ask you.'

Danny wrapped his hands around his coffee cup. 'And I still have three to go. So, I know you live in Salisbury now, and you went to Bristol University, but where are you originally from?'

'Leicester. A suburb called Knighton, to be precise. You?'

'I'm from here.' Danny raised his arms, gesturing around him. 'If you were born and bred in the Peak District, why would you ever leave?'

'Can't argue with that. It's beautiful. I love to go walking, and the Peaks is a favourite place to do that.'

Danny opened his mouth and then shut it abruptly.

'Are you okay?' Hari quickly added, 'That wasn't an official question, by the way.'

'Fair enough. I'm okay. It's just, I was about to ask you something walking related, but I didn't want to use up a precious question, so I will refrain, and instead ask you, what's your family like?'

'Oh, well, there's Mum and Dad. They still live in

Leicester. I'm their only child. My mum's parents are around, but Dad's passed away some time ago, sadly. I have a million cousins in India, but in truth, I struggle to keep track.'

'India?'

'Mum is from the Punjab, met Dad while he was over there doing some voluntary work between school and university. They fell in love and, after a lot of what they only refer to as "issues" which they will not be drawn on, Mum came over and settled with Dad in Leicester. He went to the university there, and she got a job in the local library. I came along, and now it's now.'

'I hope it isn't too much of a stereotypical assumption to say you clearly inherited your mother's hair. It's beautiful.'

'Oh… umm, thanks – and yes, I did. My mum has lovely hair.' Talking quickly, Hari returned the question. 'And your family?'

'Just Mum now. Dad died of cancer two years ago.'

'I'm so sorry.'

'Thanks.' Danny's eyes fixed on the remainder of his coffee. 'Then there is my brother David and my sister Pippa. They also live locally. With Dad gone, none of us felt we could leave Mum isolated – not that we mind being here.'

Unsure what to say, Hari was glad that the waitress chose that moment to bring their baked potatoes. 'We've had five questions each now – with add ons.'

'I'm glad you were paying attention. I'd lost count.' Danny pulled his dinner closer. 'Shall we give up and talk about the ballad now? After all, we've only got an hour and a half before the archivist is due at the hotel with the verdict!'

'Hopefully.'

'Hopefully.' Danny thrust his fork into a mound of tuna. 'So then, what do you think, fake or real?'

All that remained of Hari's jacket potato was a small area of skin that was just that little bit too crispy to eat. She lay down her cutlery as she finished describing her visit to the Buxton Archive and her sighting of the discovered ballad.

'You're so lucky to have seen it.'

'I am.' Hari bit her bottom lip. 'Forgery or not, it is a work of art.'

Danny put down his fork. 'Everything you've said as we ate makes me think that you believe it to be an invention.'

'A good one, but yes. Although, I'd love to be wrong.' Hari took a sip from her glass of water. 'What I can't work out is why.'

'People forge things all the time.'

'They do, but not like this. Not in this way. This is all so... so stage managed.'

'The fact that it was found here, you mean. Here and now; this weekend. The Robin Hood Club weekend.'

'Exactly. As I keep telling Dot, I do not like coincidences, but this time especially. It all seems too good to be true. Here we are, ballad experts like me, Neil, and Frank, literally on the doorstep just a week or so after the ballad was found. Not to mention Lee and Scarlett – who would both benefit in some way from the positive publicity it would bring – is bringing – to the world of all things Robin Hood. And that could help Roger, too, I suppose – although his role in the show isn't so big.'

'It's a mercy the press hasn't been sniffing around – in fact, it's odd they haven't.'

'The press has been interested, but the ballad was found just long enough before the convention for them to have come and gone prior to our arrival. There was no big announcement about the Robin Hood Club being in town. Tickets sell out instantly within the circle of fans the club was designed for. No need to advertise, so the press probably doesn't know it's happening.' Hari paused. 'You don't think… I wonder… perhaps it was found earlier than expected. Perhaps the ballad was *meant* to be found during the convention?'

'How could that be guaranteed?'

'I've no idea. In fact, I've no idea about any of this, really, except that it's all rather too good to be true.'

Picking up his glass, Danny said, 'If it had been found this weekend, then there wouldn't have been time to have it analysed until you'd all gone again. The checks to see if it's real wouldn't have happened yet.'

'Analysis is only happening this fast because such a document hasn't been discovered in a very long time – and, if it is a fake, it is exceptionally good.'

'It is only a matter of time before the press pop up again to find out the results.' Danny wrinkled his nose. 'When word gets out that there's been a death at the hotel that has people associated to the ballad, accident or not, they'll circle like vultures.'

Hari looked quizzically in his direction. 'The way you said that… you aren't convinced, are you? That it was an accident, I mean.'

Danny pulled a face. 'Gut feeling. I'm probably wrong.'

'Either way, I've something to tell you. I was going to before we ate, but with you saying it was being ruled an accident and—'

'Woah!' Danny held up a hand. 'Slow down. If you have stuff that might help, then I'm all ears.'

Glancing around, glad to see all the other diners were too intent upon their own conversations to pay any heed to their conversation, Hari asked, 'Can I ask what Roger said?'

'Ahh... not really.'

'Okay. So, can I take a guess, then?'

'Be my guest.'

'I'm assuming you took him to the station for the interview?'

'Because he had previously said he was alone in the Green Room when we found Sharman, and you – a witness – said he was with someone. Yes.'

'He continued to maintain he was alone?'

Danny paused. 'I can neither confirm nor deny that you are completely correct in that assumption.'

'Thank you.'

'And, as we know Sharman died just prior to the start of the disco, and Roger was seen in the bar for a couple of hours before it began, and then was dancing at the disco all evening, we had no reason to hold onto him. A fact he was at pains to point out.'

'I'm sure.'

'Plus, we are thinking accident. Officially.' Danny glanced around them before going on, 'Roger went on about how much hard work he'd spent getting this far in his career and how being dragged into a police station wasn't going to help.'

Hari suddenly sat very still. 'Hard work.'

'Sorry?'

'Oh my God! That's what it was! I've been racking my brain trying to remember.'

'Remember what?'

'More of what I overheard between Roger and the mystery woman when she was with Roger.'

'Go on.'

'She said, "I've worked damn hard for you over the years, Roger, and every time you get close to the top, something happens, and it falls apart."' Hari picked her glass of water back up. 'It must have been his agent he was talking to. That is a totally *agent* thing to say. I should have realised before! Jez told me about her... she's called Maisie.'

'Do you have a surname?'

'No, sorry. Jez did tell me, but I can't remember what it was.'

Danny scrubbed a hand through his short brown hair. 'Roger was adamant he wasn't talking to anyone.'

'And it's just my word against his.'

'I think I trust your word over his.'

Hari laughed. 'You barely know me. I could be making it all up. I'm a fiction writer, after all.'

'And he's an actor.' Danny grinned. 'Professional liars both!'

'I'm rubbish at lying, to be honest. Unless it's on paper.'

'Like the ballad.'

Hari's smile vanished. 'You don't think I'd forge–'

'No. No, of course not. I didn't mean that at all.'

'Sorry.' Hari sighed. 'It's just, when Christine Spencer came to talk about the ballad – she's the archivist who found it – Roger suggested I was the one most able to fake it. Something Frank Lister was more than happy to back up.'

'Nice.'

'Roger claimed he was joking, but it didn't feel like a joke. Especially as I could technically do something like that. I just wouldn't.'

'Of course you wouldn't.' Danny raised his glass to his lips. 'But you have theories on who could and would, don't you?'

Chapter Twenty-three

'I have several theories. But as they are just that, theories, with no evidence to back them up whatsoever, I should probably keep them to myself.' Hari leant forward. 'There is something more important I need to ask you, though. A couple of somethings, actually.'

'Fire away.'

'Have you had the chance to see inside Sharman's bag?'

'Not yet.' Danny picked up his cup, swilling the remaining contents around, creating a small whirlpool of caffeine. 'It's back at the station. As the pathologist's found nothing to suggest it wasn't an accident, I thought it could wait until tomorrow.'

'Despite your gut instinct to the contrary?'

'My instinct means nothing if there's no evidence to back it up. Why do you ask about the bag?'

A pink blush came to Hari's cheeks. 'I might have had a peep at the contents.'

'I see.'

'I had this feeling and—'

He brushed the explanation aside. 'Never mind that, what did you find?'

'Her EpiPen.'

Danny's mobile phone was open and he'd placed a call before Hari had the chance to say anything else.

'The coroner will need to know. Poor lass, I imagine she…' He broke off suddenly as his call connected. 'Dawson, a bag was handed in earlier connected to the death at the Harmen Hotel. I've just learnt that Miss Peterson's EpiPen might be inside. I know I said it could wait until the morning, but can you get the contents logged and inform the coroner A.S.A.P? Thanks. I'm just grabbing some food, then

I'll go back to the hotel… I know it's not *officially* a crime scene, but I just want to dot a few more I's and cross some T's… I'll see you later.'

The comfortable atmosphere that had existed between them wavered as Hari watched Danny in full inspector mode. 'I should have called you right away. I'm sorry.'

'We know now, that's all that matters.' Danny pulled his tablet from his jacket pocket and scrolled through his notes. 'So, we found a bag in her room which we took to be her handbag. I hadn't considered that she might have two.'

'The bag Penny and Clara found is not a handbag. It's a small rucksack containing some dresses. She'd been in their room trying things on for the dancing later.'

Maybe she'd wanted to look her best for Lee… Maybe Sharman did feel the same about him…

Rather than breaking her confidence to Lee, Hari said, 'I bet she put her EpiPen in there in case she had snacks while they chatted about what to wear.'

'But then she forgot to take it away with her.'

'Perhaps she wasn't intending to be gone long.'

'If that was the case, why didn't Penny and Clara search for her earlier? Raise the alarm?'

'They assumed she'd fallen asleep. There's something else.'

Danny checked his watch. 'Is this a big something? Would it be better tackled with a side order of pudding?'

Relieved he wasn't cross with her, Hari said, 'Biggish – but I find searching for solutions to sizable problems are often aided by the consumption of pudding.'

'You're a woman after my own heart.'

Unsure which of the two of them went redder as Danny's innocently spoken saying slipped out, Hari rushed on, 'There's a notebook in Sharman's bag, too. Whatever you or I think, Sharman had her own suspicions about something going on at the Robin Hood Club.'

'Something? The ballad?'

'She didn't say. She has literally written – *"All is not right at RHC"* – but whatever was bugging Sharman, it was causing her to keep a careful eye on Frank.'

'Frank Lister?'

'Dot and I wondered why Sharman was so willing to help us – and you yourself questioned why she would pay for an expensive weekend ticket for a convention she loved, and then spend so much time sat at my book stall, helping me and Dot out.'

'You think she volunteered to help you so she could sit and watch Frank?'

'In her notebook she writes about him being *"up to something"* – but she wrote no more than that. Frank's stall is directly opposite mine. What better place to keep an eye on him without arousing suspicion?'

Danny got up. 'I'm sorry. We're going to have to take a rain check on pudding. I must see that notebook.'

'I totally understand.' Getting up too, Hari shrugged her jacket back on. 'She hadn't written anything else – I wonder if she might have done, though. She referred to him as positively medieval in his attitude when I first met her, but she did give him credit for coming back to the RHC every year and making sure he remembered everyone's names. I could understand her not liking or trusting Frank, though. In all honesty, few people do, and he brings a lot of that on himself.'

'In what way?'

'Little things. He was horribly rude about Sharman's hair colour, for a start.'

'Green hair is not everyone's thing.'

'True, but it was *her* hair. He could have kept his opinion to himself.'

'Did you notice anything about Roger in her notebook?' Danny wove his way towards the pub door, holding it open for Hari as they headed into the early evening light.

'No, but I was conscious of doing something I shouldn't have been, and I was in a hurry.'

Danny chuckled. 'If you ever decide to become a private detective, always check the evidence out fully before worrying about the time it takes.'

'An unlikely career calling for me, but I'll remember that tip, just in case.'

'I must go.' Danny extracted his car keys from his pocket. 'Hopefully I'll see you at the hotel later.'

'You will?' Hari was aware of the hope in her voice and felt a new blossom of pink flush her cheeks.

'I want to hear what Christine Spencer has to say.'

'Of course.'

'And I'd like to see you, too… if that's okay?'

Hari smiled. 'That would be okay. Oh…'

'Oh?'

'I meant to ask, the bakery – did Dot make a mistake when she placed her order? She's beating herself up big time, and I'd love to be able to put her mind at rest, but if you need to go, you can tell me later. If you're allowed to tell me, of course.'

Danny walked to the side of the pavement, sheltering under the awning that ran along the front of the pub, keeping out of the way of the passing pedestrians. 'I was going to tell Dot later, but I'm sure she won't mind you knowing first. But I really need to get back to the station.'

'Fair enough.'

Danny had taken two paces away from Hari when he stopped and asked, 'Ride with me?'

'Really?'

'Really.'

They were no sooner in Danny's pristinely clean, black Polo, when he started to describe his visit to Dot's local Cookie Creations bakery.

'The folk at *Pearce Bakes* were devastated to think something they may have done had accidentally caused a death.'

'And?'

'A great many cookies were ordered yesterday via Cookie Creations. There was also one batch of cookies made up – a direct order from Dot herself – rather than one that went through the usual ordering website. It was for caramel cookies with a dark chocolate melted centre, just as Dot said.'

'Sharman's favourites.'

'There *were* nut cookies being made on the premises at the same time, including Dot's new almond and pistachio cookies and some dark chocolate peanut cookies, but all that took place in a different part of the bakery. The nut area is well away from the rest of the bakery, for obvious reasons. No one at *Pearce Bakes* can see how the mix up occurred, but somehow the wrong box *must* have been labelled up for Sharman – hence her getting nutty cookies. Although I can't quite see how it happened yet, human error does seem the logical answer. No blame to anyone, although that won't stop the poor folk at the bakery feeling bad.'

'I'm sure.'

'A motorcycle courier took them, as an individual special order, to the hotel. I have spoken to him, and he swears he delivered it to Reception and that the box was unopened. Constable Harker — he's the chap on the door at the hotel — has seen the hotel's CCTV confirming the courier's arrival and departure from the hotel.'

'And the receptionist had the cookie box delivered to Sharman's room?'

'Yes. Unopened and taken to her room within ten minutes of delivery. The box was never out of sight.'

Hari gnawed on her bottom lip. 'I'm sorry, Danny, but it must have been out of sight at some point.'

'How do you mean?'

'The cookie found with Sharman was a chocolate cookie with a dark chocolate melted centre with nuts in it. Presumably powdered so there was nothing visible and not enough nuts to give off a telltale aroma.'

'And?'

'Well, does Pearce's bake cookies exactly like that?'

Danny suddenly swung the car left at the next junction. 'I need to get back to Pearce's.'

As she waited in the car for Danny to re-emerge from the bakery, Hari ran over every conversation she'd had with Sharman.

An anxious ten minutes later, Danny rejoined her in the car. She looked him in the eye. 'Were our instincts right all along? Not an accident?'

'I hate my gut sometimes. I'd have loved to have been wrong.' Danny blew out a ragged breath. 'You were right. They *don't* make any biscuits here beyond those ordered from Cookie Creations, or anything at all containing ground nuts or even flaked nuts. Just halved or whole nuts, depending on the recipe in question.'

'So there was no mix up this end.' Hari exhaled slowly. 'I bet they're relieved.'

'You could say that. The wrong cookie type was *not* boxed up by mistake. It's as you were implying. The right type was made and sent, but—'

'Those weren't the cookies in situ when Sharman opened the box.' Hari gulped as Danny fired the car's engine back into life. 'Someone used the right box and the note from Dot, but swapped the cookies.'

'It's looking very much like it.'

Chapter Twenty-four

Hari's mobile rang as Danny's car pulled out of the bakery car park.

'It's Dot.'

'You can't tell her anything.'

'But—'

'No. I'm sorry, Hari, but the game has changed. I should never have spoken to you, let alone anyone else.'

'If you hadn't, you would still think it was an accident.'

'Ummm.'

Hari's phone was still ringing. 'If I don't answer, she'll worry.'

'Go on, but say nothing about our suspicions.'

'Hi, Dot.' Hari could feel the strain in her voice. 'You okay?'

'I don't know. The police are here again. We're back to no one being allowed in or out of the hotel.'

'Oh God, really?' Hari hoped she sounded surprised enough. 'Does that mean no talk from Christine?'

'Luckily she got here early. As did Elizabeth.'

'Did she?'

'Yeah. Moral support for Frank, apparently. Although, I've no idea why. He is clearly besotted with her, but it's obviously not mutual.'

'Where are you?'

'In the trading area. I'm the only one in here. Told Jez I wanted to double check I'd taped up the boxes of remaining stock so that I could call you in private. Everyone's in the bar or their rooms – if they've still got them. Loads of folk had to check out this morning as they expected to go home today.' Dot's voice was laced with panic. 'They've changed their minds, haven't they? They don't think it was an accident.'

Hari turned to Danny as she replied, hoping that he'd be able to infer what Dot had asked her from her reply. '*If* they don't think it was an accident anymore, that would explain why the police are there again. I'm so sorry, Dot.'

'What if they think it was me?'

'No one will think you did this to Sharman.' Hari looked questioningly at Danny as she spoke. He shook his head.

'Danny's next to me. He's shaking his head – he doesn't think it was you.'

'You knew about this?'

'Only that we had our meal interrupted by new information. We're just outside the hotel now.'

'But it's been shut down. How are you going to get back in?'

'As I said, I'm with Danny, so I assume I'll get in with him.'

'Of course. Sorry.' Dot paused. 'I'm not thinking straight. This is so awful. Does Danny know what's going on?'

'Yes, but he's not saying anything.' Hari gave Danny an apologetic shrug as she spoke. 'I'll be there soon. Don't worry.'

'Don't worry! A very officious sergeant just gave me the third degree about my cookie ingredients in a very loud voice in front of everyone. I doubt I'll sell another cookie ever again!'

Danny was still grumbling about his overly ambitious and, frankly, cack-handed sergeant as they turned into the Harmen Hotel car park.

'Sergeant Dawson does not like the fact I'm

younger than him, of higher rank than him, and cleverer than him.'

'That's a bit cliché, isn't it?'

'You've no idea!' Danny rolled his eyes. 'He particularly dislikes that I am a local.'

'Why would he object to that?'

'Because he isn't. Folk have seen me around and about Buxton since I was a boy. They trust me.'

'Makes sense.'

Danny parked alongside a battered Ford Focus. 'Dawson's car. Right now he'll be enjoying being the senior man on the scene.'

Next to the Focus, Hari saw a single panda car. 'I was expecting loads of police cars.'

'You watch too much television. In real life there are low budgets and, in this case, zero evidence pointing to a particular criminal.'

'I'm glad about that.'

'What?'

'It means you don't see Dot as a suspect.'

As they got out of the car, Danny said, 'If anyone asks, you've been helping with our enquiries.'

'Now you're making me sound like a suspect.'

'Sorry.' Danny shrugged. 'I'd rather not be seen to have taken you out to dinner while we're in the middle of an investigation.'

'It's okay, I understand.' Hari took a deep breath. 'What will you do first?'

'I want to see what's in that notebook. Hopefully Dawson will have had the common sense to bring it with him. Plus, I want to talk to Roger's agent if she's here. Assuming your theory about this Maisie woman being the person you overheard him with in the Green Room is correct.'

'You think what I overheard is connected to

Sharman's death?'

'No idea, but I want to know who the "her" they referred to was.'

'So do I.' Hari bit her bottom lip. 'I'll keep my ears open while you're doing your thing.'

'Thanks.'

As they walked towards the hotel's entrance, Hari felt her pulse thump in her neck. 'Jez will want to let Christine share her news about the ballad findings – if she hasn't already. Will you be able to let that go ahead?'

Danny steadied his stride. 'Normally I'd call a halt to everything, but you think the two things are connected, don't you? The ballad and the death.'

'Yes, but I could be letting my imagination run away with me after spending the last few years building stories with crimes at their core.'

'Or you could be right.' Danny paused before asking, 'You think Frank is connected to this ballad business?'

'I think Sharman believed he was.'

'Then, for now, we should say nothing about Sharman's death becoming suspicious.' Danny exhaled slowly. 'Unless my trusty sergeant has already blown that possibility.'

'People aren't stupid. The fact you've closed the hotel again will tell them something has happened. Dot has already put two and two together.'

'I've had an idea about that. But first, I want a quick word with Penny and Clara.'

'Ladies and gentlemen.' Danny stood on the stage before a hall packed, not just with the Robin Hood Club attendees and guests, but also the hotel staff.

'My thanks for your cooperation and apologies

once again for the inconvenience. I've asked Mr Barnes to gather you all together in here so that I can speak to everyone at once.' He raised a hand towards Sergeant Dawson who stood by the door that connected the hall to the trading area. 'Is everyone accounted for? No one staying here or working here that's missing, Dawson?'

'All present and correct, Inspector.'

'Excellent.'

Hari, sat next to Jez, Neil, and Christine on the stage, felt incredibly self-conscious as she waited before the subdued audience. After the enthusiasm of the last two days, it was as if she was viewing a completely different group of people.

She could see Dot, Penny, and Clara on the front row to the right side of the aisle, with Lee and Scarlett sat behind them. Meanwhile, Frank, Elizabeth, and Roger were sat on the front row of the left side of the aisle. No one sat on the row behind them — the remainder of the audience taking up the seats on the third row back, and in the case of the hotel staff, sitting on random benches placed along the sides of the hall.

The atmosphere was heavy with uncertainty.

Hari watched Danny as he stood in front of her, wondering what he'd say to explain the return of the police presence.

'I can assure you we will not be keeping you here for any longer than we need to. It is now clear what happened to Miss Peterson, and before we can officially sign off on this unfortunate situation, we need to do a quick search of the hotel's communal areas. You can appreciate that this is best done when there are no people milling about. It seemed logical for me to ask for you to all meet here – especially as so many of you are anxiously awaiting news about the recently found ballad.'

A hand in the audience shot up. It was Frank's. 'Inspector Shaw, can I ask what you're searching for, just in case one of us here can be of assistance?'

'You beat me to it, Mr Lister. I was coming to that.'

As Danny surveyed the audience, Hari followed suit, trying to read anything significant from the combination of blank, worried, and restless expressions before her.

'The item we are searching for is an A5 sized notebook. Brown cover, spiral bound. We have learnt that the notebook was important to Miss Peterson. She used it as a sort of diary, recording her experiences and ideas. Her mother is keen to have it, and yet it isn't in her room.'

'You think she dropped it?' Frank's voice was perfectly calm.

'That is certainly a possibility.' Danny lifted his gaze to encompass the whole room. 'Has anyone seen it?'

Lee raised his hand. 'I saw her with it on a number of occasions.' He paused. 'I never saw inside it, but I know she tended to carry it with her.'

'I see. Thank you, Mr Stoneman. Anyone else have information on the notebook?' Danny waited, but no one spoke. 'Right then. While we wait for the officers to complete their search—'

'Inspector,' Penny called softly.

'Miss Forbes?'

'Yes. Penny Forbes.'

'Penny. Can you help with this?'

'I've not seen it lately, but I know that Sharman wrote her ideas in it. She was writing in it when we started trying on clothes for the disco. We'd,' she sniffed, gathering herself before going on, 'brought a few outfits each. The three of us are of similar size, so we planned to swap and change and… you know…'

'I understand. And you saw her writing in her book prior to that?'

'Yes. She stopped as we got the clothes out of our bags. Sharman said she'd had a few ideas about the ballad. That… well… she wasn't convinced it was real.' Penny looked towards the stage. 'Sorry Jez, Christine.'

Hari glanced to her left. Both her colleagues nodded sympathetically as Danny cut in. 'Thank you, Penny. That's very interesting. Talking of the ballad, while the search for the notebook goes on, I for one would be fascinated to hear what news Miss Spencer has on this matter.'

Standing down from the stage, Danny joined his sergeant, who, having received some whispered instructions, left the hall. Adopting the position Dawson had vacated, Danny raised a hand towards Jez, indicating he could start the talk.

He's preparing to listen. Hari felt her breathing calm a little. *He really doesn't think I'm imagining things. He thinks there's a connection between the ballad and Sharman's death, too.*

With a fraction's hesitation, Jez rose to his feet. Hari's heart went out to him. He appeared to have aged ten years since she'd last seen him.

Taking a sip of water, Jez signalled to the sound man at the back of the room to activate his microphone, and dived in.

'As Inspector Shaw has kindly allowed us to continue with this, the last event – albeit an extra and unexpected one due to the fortuitous timing of the finding of *Robin Hood and the Carter* in Buxton – I won't hold things up further by chatting, but will hand straight over to Miss Spencer – Christine – who has news for us.'

Opting to stay sitting, Christine thanked Jez before addressing the room. 'As you all know, the emergence of this ballad has caused considerable excitement in the literary world. It has been many years since a medieval work of literature has been discovered in the United Kingdom. One that features Robin Hood – a character so engrained within our culture – was bound to send the academic and antiquity associations of the nation into overdrive.'

Hari's shoulders tensed as Christine spoke. Wishing she'd just spit out whether it was fake or not, she found her eyes drifting towards Danny while her mind played through the implications should it be real after all.

Why am I so sure it's fake?

Christine's voice broke back through Hari's thoughts. 'As I explained before, the tests on the parchment and ink have been fast tracked.'

'And?' Frank's voice cut through the expectant atmosphere.

'*And*, Mr Lister,' Christine fixed her librarian's stare on the author, 'we are awaiting DNA analysis.'

'DNA?' Jez turned to their guest. 'Does that mean…?'

'Sadly, yes. The initial findings show that the ink has been faked. So the question now is, can DNA analysis tell us who the forger was?'

A hubbub of chatter broke out, mingled with sighs of disappointment as what Chirstine had said sank in.

Hari felt a cold shiver run down her back.

The ink… Roger and Frank said I could have done that. I could have… but I didn't. But what if people think I did?

'If I could continue?' Christine raised her voice as

she got to her feet. 'So, sadly, the ballad is a fake. I can confirm that the parchment itself is old – possibly sixteenth century. Tests are ongoing. If they are from the 1500s, then it means someone has done the unthinkable, and has destroyed another work of art – a real one – in order to create this fiction.'

'But why?' It was Scarlett who called out, voicing the whispered opinion that was zipping around the hall like wildfire. 'Why do something so awful?'

'An excellent question. One only the forger can answer.'

Jez stood up; his hands raised to quiet the growing volume of indignation in the room. 'I think I can echo Scarlett's outrage, and our disappointment. How wonderful it would have been if the ballad was real.'

'It would,' Christine agreed. 'It's also sad that the talent of whoever wrote it will be forever tainted. The ballad is brilliantly constructed. It shows a real skill and understanding of the art of storytelling, not just for the time it was allegedly written in, but of the historian they must be now.'

'You are saying that whoever faked this was an expert in medieval ballad literature, not just a good forger?'

Hari could feel every eye in the room land on her as Christine responded to their host.

'What I'm saying, Jez, is that whoever wrote the ballad was an expert. They could have been innocent, of course – written it and then the forger found it, saw the potential, and used it to their advantage.'

'Unlikely?'

'Highly. I would imagine it was written on purpose, but whether by the person who forged the ballad, or in collusion with them, I could not say.'

Feeling hot, Hari struggled to convince herself that

everyone wasn't staring at her in an accusing way, and that there were other ballad experts in the room.

Sharman thought she knew who forged it. I'm sure she thought it was Frank...

Suddenly, Hari found herself looking up and staring straight into Frank's eyes. His expression had accusation written all over it.

Chapter Twenty-five

An absence of sound in the hall remained as everyone took in what Christine's news meant.

Risking another glance in Frank's direction, Hari was relieved to see he'd stopped staring daggers at her.

Hari switched her attention to Elizabeth. If she noticed Hari glancing at her, she'd not registered as such. For the past few minutes, she'd been focused on her mobile.

Sending a text or email, if the movement of her hand is anything to go by.

Averting her gaze from Elizabeth's eyeline, not wanting her to see she was being watched, Hari tried to concentrate.

Sharman was sure Frank was up to something — but that doesn't mean she was right. What Danny said to everyone about the notebook was a lie. He has it safe, it's no more lost than I am, so what does he hope that will achieve?

I wish I'd spent more time talking to Sharman.

Jez, who'd let the consternation in the room rumble on for a few minutes, gave a quick clap of his hands to regain control. 'While we are obviously disappointed, like our much-missed friend, Sharman, I'm sure we all had suspicions about the ballad's credentials. It was lovely, though, just for a little while, to think the Robin Hood canon was to be enlarged.'

A murmur of acknowledgement ran through the audience.

Before anyone had the chance to speak, Jez turned to Danny. 'Inspector, may I ask, as you are here, what happens next in cases of forgery such as this?'

'An excellent question, Mr Barnes. The case will be referred to the Fraud department, probably with guidance from the Arts and Antiques squad. While it isn't technically the latter, it was presumably intended to be passed off as such, and their knowledge will be valuable. Personally, I have little experience in such matters, and will bow to my colleagues on this. I would, Miss Spencer, prepare yourself for enquiries from those quarters in the near future.'

As Christine inclined her head, Jez thanked the inspector and faced his audience. 'While we are disappointed, how lucky we are, ladies and gentlemen, to have so many modern-day writers to continue the tradition of writing outlaw tales. A tradition that this very club has been celebrating for the last six years. Two of these writers, Harriet Danby and Frank Lister,' Jez gestured to both authors, 'are here today. And while we cannot now ask their opinion of the new work with a view to how it might have influenced past stories — or indeed future stories they themselves might decide to write, we can take solace in the fact that their work will continue to entertain us for years to come.'

'Well said, Mr Barnes.' Danny stepped forward. 'I wonder if perhaps I could ask a few questions of your panel. I confess that I've been a lifelong Robin Hood fan… and as I've already mentioned to you and Dr Danby, should the circumstances have been different, I'd have rather enjoyed coming along this weekend as an attendee.

'The lack of Sergeant Dawson's presence means that, thus far, the search for Miss Peterson's notebook has not been completed, so while we wait – if you would beg my indulgence as a fan of the legends – would it be possible to ask what Dr Danby, Mr Lister and Professor Frampton think about the ballad that has been found? I'm sure we'd all be interested in their views on this forgery.'

Hari mentally applauded Danny. Hoping her face was impassive, she turned to Jez, waiting to hear his response. Frank, however, got in first.

'An excellent question, Inspector.' Already on his feet, Frank edged past Elizabeth and strode confidently to the stage. 'I trust you have no objection to me joining the panel on the stage, Jez? I know I'm not classed as an expert by yourself, but the inspector clearly thinks I'm worthy of the title.'

Hari heard Christine's sharp intake of breath to her right at the cheek of the man.

'There was never any question of excluding you, Frank.' If Jez felt slighted or annoyed, he managed to prevent his tone from giving himself away. 'Please, take my seat. Would you like a microphone, or will you manage?'

'I'll manage.' The way Frank replied made Hari wonder if he'd rather hoped Jez would object to his presence so he could argue his case.

Danny moved towards the audience. 'I'll take a seat, if I may.'

Hari watched as, rather than taking the nearest empty seat, he moved around the room and sat down in Frank's vacated chair, next to Elizabeth.

Not waiting for anyone to have the chance to comment, Danny asked, 'Dr Danby — Hari — when we spoke earlier, you admitted that Sharman Peterson had told you she had doubts about the validity of the ballad, doubts you shared. Was that for any academic reason, or just a hunch?'

Feeling everyone in the hall focus on her, Hari exhaled before saying, 'A hunch. I'd have loved it to be real, but the fact of it being found here and now – it was just too convenient.'

'The language was good, though,' Neil chipped in.

'And if the forger had decided to let his or her work be found in another place or at another time, there may have been less suspicion. Although, I imagine the same tests would have been run, so—'

'So, it would have been uncovered as a fake eventually anyway,' Danny finished the sentence for him. 'Miss Spencer, can I ask, when you first saw the ballad, what was your immediate impression? I think it can be admitted now that you are the one that personally found the piece, rather than just someone on the premises at the time. Did you know what you'd found?'

'Not at first.' Christine, her expression calm, said, 'I knew from the touch of the parchment that whatever I was holding was old.'

'Which it was.' Danny nodded.

The archivist pulled a face. 'I hate to think what works of art were destroyed to make this fake. To me, that's a bigger crime than the forging of a ballad.'

Jez's kind face creased into a frown. 'As we've heard, many of us agree with you there.'

Danny turned sharply in his chair to Elizabeth. 'How about you, Miss Jeffries? Or is it Mrs?'

'Is my marital status any of your concern, Inspector?'

Ignoring the question, he gave her a wide smile. 'Do you have an opinion on all this? The notes my sergeant made prior to my arrival tell me that you're an expert on old books.'

'Well…'

Danny raised his voice a fraction, making sure that everyone in the hall could hear him. 'How fortunate you are to be here, in this very hotel, at a time when I've instructed everyone to be in the hall, be they resident, staff, or merely passing through. Otherwise you would have missed the verdict. You have no ticket for the Robin Hood Club event; am I right?'

'I'm Frank's guest.'

'How nice.' Danny flicked his attention to Jez. 'I hadn't realised ticket holders could bring in a guest for free.'

'They can't.'

'Oh.' Danny swivelled to face Roger. 'Is that why your guest isn't here, Mr Striver? Where is your agent, by the way?'

Hari wasn't sure how she didn't clap as she witnessed Danny in action. Frank was clearly extremely uncomfortable; Elizabeth was doing an impression of a woman who'd not just sucked on a lemon but had swallowed one, while Roger was clearly trying to decide how much Danny knew. And while all this was going on, the audience was giving each other questioning looks.

'Mr Striver, I asked you a question.'

Roger's response was forming on his lips as the door to the hall opened and Sergeant Dawson stepped inside.

'If I could interrupt, sir. I've found an additional person. Would you like me to bring them in here, or would you like to speak to them separately?'

Chapter Twenty-six

Hari watched as Danny joined Sergeant Dawson at the hall door. There was a hurried, muted conversation before both detectives left the room. The second the door closed behind the policemen, the hall erupted into a wave of low mumbles and conflicting theories.

Leaving her place on the stage, Hari pulled off her microphone and joined Dot, Penny, and Clara. 'Are you three alright – well, as alright as you can be?'

'Not really.' Dot signalled towards the closed double doors. 'Any idea what's going on?'

'Not a clue.'

'Fibber.' Dot nudged her friend in the ribs.

Worried about being overheard, Hari mouthed, 'They think Sharman was murdered.'

Penny and Clara went white, while Dot, already ashen, sank back onto her chair.

'Don't say anything to the others.'

Penny wiped a silent tear from her cheek. 'I guessed as much when the inspector asked us to lie about the notebook being missing, but I wanted to be wrong.'

Clara turned to Lee behind her. 'Are you alright?'

Hari was surprised that Sharman had confided in her friends about the not-quite relationship between her and the actor. That hadn't been the impression she'd got from Lee.

'Not really. You?'

'No.'

Scarlett's flawless forehead creased as she recognised the hurt in his eyes. 'Lee?'

'Sharman and I were friends.' He checked around him to make sure no one was paying attention. 'I enjoyed her company. Met up with her whenever I was working in the north of England, that sort of thing.'

Scarlett's eyebrows raised as she regarded her co-star. 'I had no idea. Why didn't you say?'

'Because it was no one's business but ours.' Lee appeared anxious, as if half expecting a journalist to pop up in the empty row of chairs behind him. 'You know what it's like. You can't have a normal friendship or anything without someone putting their oar in.'

'True.' Putting her arm around her co-star, Scarlett gave him a hug. 'I'm so sorry, Lee.'

Hari, who'd been struggling to know what to say, was relieved when Penny beat her to it.

'This person that the inspector has disappeared to see… who do you think it is?'

'Can't be anyone from the Robin Hood Club,' Clara said as she swivelled in her seat, making no attempt to disguise the fact she was trying to work out who might be missing. 'Jez checked the attendee list as we all came in while you were arriving with the policeman, Hari.'

'Why were you with him, anyway?' Scarlett withdrew her arm from Lee's shoulders and gave her script writer an inquisitive look.

'Helping with enquiries.'

This time it was Lee's eyebrows that shot up. 'That makes it sound as if you are involved – or that they think you are.'

Hari's cheeks reddened. 'I promise I'm not. I was telling them about the time Sharman spent on my stall, that's all.'

Clara stopped her unsubtle surveillance. 'There's no one missing, I'd swear to it.'

'The inspector said it was Roger's agent that was missing,' Penny reminded her friend.

'He didn't, did he?' Clara's concern deepened. 'He

was just asking where she was and… Ah, I see.'

Scarlett groaned. 'I had rather hoped that the dreaded Maisie would not be making an appearance.'

'You've met her before then?' Hari asked.

'Yeah. She's often with Roger.' Scarlett looked at Lee as she added, 'Thinking about it, it's odd that she hasn't been hanging around here from the moment he arrived.'

'What does she look like?' Hari, who'd already assumed Maisie must be the person Dawson had found, cast a glance in Roger's direction. He was staring at the closed door. She wasn't sure whether he was praying it would reopen or was willing it to stay closed for ever.

Her thoughts were cut short by the return of the policemen. Danny wasted no time. 'Many thanks again to everyone for your patience. Our search is now complete, and we've had the chance to gather all your names and addresses from the reception computer. Those of you who are staff are now free to head back to work or go home if your shift is over. If, for any reason, you'll be leaving the area in the next few days, please let the constable on the main door know as you leave.'

This announcement was swiftly followed by a couple of dozen people leaving the room in varying states of relief – some understanding, some muttering about how late tonight's dinner in the restaurant was going to be.

As the final hotel employee left, Frank got to his feet. 'Inspector, when can we leave? I was rather hoping to catch the last train home this evening.'

Danny opened the tablet he held and scrolled through it. 'I have it here that you are booked in here for another night, Mr Lister.'

'Well, yes, I am, but after everything that has happened, I'd rather like to leave.' Frank scowled. 'I'm sure many others feel the same.'

There was some murmuring of agreement from behind Frank, but, as Hari watched, she got the impression that most people wanted to stay to see what would happen next.

This is the closest they'll ever get to being in a Poirot moment.

'I'm sure we'd all like to go home, Mr Lister. I certainly would. Sadly, I, like you, will be here a little longer.' Danny raised his voice so the whole room could hear him. 'Those of you who are staying the night here are free to depart the hall. Please do not leave the hotel without telling the constable on the main door where you are going. Those of you who were planning to go home today, please form an orderly queue to tell Sergeant Dawson if you are heading directly home or going elsewhere.' He waved his hand to where Dawson had set up a table by the edge of the stage. 'Once we have confirmed we have your correct contact details, you can leave.'

'Thank goodness for that.' Frank got up. 'Come on, Elizabeth, we can—'

Inspector Shaw, however, hadn't finished yet. 'You are all free to leave, with the exception of the following people. Harriet Danby, Dot Henderson, Lee Stoneman, Scarlett Hann, Penny Forbes, Clara Letterman, Frank Lister, Elizabeth Jeffries, Roger Striver and Jeremiah Barnes. I'd like to ask you a few more questions, if you'd be so kind.'

Frank's face turned puce. 'I'm not sure I will be so kind, Inspector. This is ridiculous. The ballad is fake, and rumour has it that the girl died by accident. That's it – end of saga.'

'Is that so?' Danny spoke with firm reassurance. 'Then I can't see that it'll take that much longer. If you wouldn't mind sitting down again. Just a few loose ends, as they say.'

As Danny went to help Dawson, Hari heard Frank grumble, 'Man thinks he's bloody Columbo.'

Fifteen minutes later, all the other occupants of the hall were gone. Dawson called out to those who were left. 'If you'd all follow us, please. We have secured a large table in the bar. It'll be much easier to talk in there.'

With a quick disconnection of microphones and some murmured wonderings as to what would happen next, the group trailed into the hotel bar. It was deserted but for a constable, who stood with a small but angular woman in stupidly high heels.

'Maisie!' Jez pulled off his hat. 'Where have you been hiding?'

'Hiding is the operative word, Mr Barnes,' Dawson said as he indicated to everyone to sit down.

Taking his seat, Jez regarded the latest member of the party as she tossed her tight, orange-tipped curls back. 'I know you weren't invited, Maisie. But as you always tend to appear when Roger's around, I've been expecting you to grace us with your presence all weekend. I was only saying to Hari the other day that where one of you goes, so does the other.'

'Roger is my responsibility. He pays me to look after him, so that is what I do.'

Hari looked up quickly. *I've heard that voice before...*

Danny tapped a few keys on his tablet before saying, 'I understand Sergeant Dawson and Constable Matthews found you in the sauna, Miss Flowers.'

'I was making the most of the facilities while it was quiet.'

'It was quiet because the police decreed everyone

should be in here.'

'I didn't know that.'

Danny's eyes widened, a visual statement of his obvious disbelief. 'And prior to taking advantage of a mysteriously empty spa room, where were you?'

'In Roger's room making some calls while he was busy here.'

'Busy *here*,' Danny repeated. 'The implication being that you *did* know everyone was requested to be in the hall.'

'All the guests, yes. But I'm not a guest.'

'You are splitting hairs, Miss Flowers.'

'And you are being pedantic, Inspector.' Maisie plonked her designer handbag onto the table in front of her. 'This is a bar — any chance of a gin and tonic?'

'None whatsoever.' Danny's hand hovered over his tablet. 'Where were you when the message to assemble in the hall came?'

'In Roger's room. Don't you listen, Inspector?'

'Not only am I listening, but I'm not liking what I am hearing.' He turned to Roger. 'Mr Striver, when the knock on your door came asking you to assemble in the hall, you were in your room.'

'Yes.'

'But you didn't think to mention that your agent was with you?'

'She wasn't officially there. She'd just come to have a chat about my audition for *Anything Goes*.'

Danny bit off each word as he spoke. 'Mr Striver, may I remind you that a woman has died in this hotel and a manuscript has been faked. If a policeman issues orders for *everyone* in the hotel to come to the hall, then that is exactly what he means.'

'Sorry, Inspector.'

'When did you arrive in the hotel, Miss Flowers?'

'Lunchtime.'

'And you were in Roger's bedroom all that time – with the exception of when you decided to take a sauna?'

'Correct.'

'And you are here in the first place because of your client's next role?'

'Correct again, Inspector. Roger has secured one role within the musical, but I've been negotiating for a better one.'

Jez rolled his eyes. 'Of course you have.'

Maisie fixed her startlingly blue eyes on Jez. 'Don't judge me for wanting the best for my client. Just because you always treat him as if he's a sub character—'

'In *Return to Sherwood* he *is* a sub character!'

Seeing how close to exhaustion Jez was, Hari cut in, 'Maybe we should get back to the point?'

'Indeed.' Danny laid both his palms on the table. 'And the points — plural — are these. The ballad is fake. Someone faked it. Sharman is dead. Someone killed her.'

Chapter Twenty-seven

Although Hari knew that Danny had changed his mind as to the manner of Sharman's death from accidental to deliberate, hearing him say it out loud in public still felt like a massive blow.

Dot looked like she was going to be sick as Penny and Clara sat in silence, tears threatening. Lee closed his eyes, his face bowed as he, too, struggled not to break down. Jez was clearly gobsmacked, while Scarlett, Frank, Elizabeth, Roger and Maisie regarded each other with a mix of shock and surprise.

Giving everyone a moment to compose themselves, Danny explained that Sharman had died from her nut allergy, but that there had been no mistakes made at the bakery, and that Dot need have no fear – she was not responsible for mis-ordering the biscuits, nor had there been any misunderstanding with the interpretation of her request for the cookies. They'd been made and sent to the hotel exactly as per her instructions.

'I can't tell you what a relief that is.' Dot's usually confident voice was shaky as she added, 'I've used *Pearce Bakes* as my supplier in this region for almost a year now. I'd hate for them to have lived with such a mistake.' She paused. 'Although, I'd still rather that it had been an accident.'

Aware of everyone giving her friend suspicious looks, despite what Danny had said, Hari took hold of Dot's hand and gave it a squeeze. 'What you are saying, Inspector, if I'm understanding the implication, is that, between the thank you cookies Dot ordered for Sharman arriving at the hotel, and Sharman taking a bite of one of them, someone swapped the original biscuits for the ones found in her room. Chocolate with a dark melted chocolate centre – with hidden nuts inside them.'

'Exactly that,' Danny confirmed.

'I don't do that flavour combination!' Dot sat up straighter.

'So I understand.' Danny smiled. 'We should have confirmation from the lab tomorrow, but it seems that powdered nuts of some sort – probably almond – were in the melted middle. The scent would have easily been disguised by the richness of the melted dark chocolate.'

Penny wiped a hand over her eyes. 'It wouldn't have taken much. She was severely allergic.'

Jez nodded. 'She isn't the only one in the Robin Hood Club with a nut allergy, but hers is the worst. One of the reasons I picked this hotel, as with the others I've chosen over the years, is that it claims a nut-free kitchen.'

Danny scribbled a note on his tablet, and a second later Dawson left the room.

'While Dawson goes to talk to the kitchen staff, can I ask you, Miss Jeffries, to confirm what time you arrived in the hotel today?'

Elizabeth crossed and then recrossed her legs. 'I assume you already know the answer to that question, Inspector.'

'I do.'

'And you are asking me, just as you asked Maisie here, because you have become aware that I was not entirely truthful about my whereabouts.'

'Again, that is correct.' Danny referred to his tablet. 'Here it says that you told Constable Harker you arrived here at around six-thirty this evening, in time to listen to Christine's verdict on the ballad.'

Elizabeth nodded. 'I did say that.'

'But the CCTV coverage of the hotel car park shows that you arrived last night and didn't leave.'

Hari peered up from where she'd been staring at the table, and asked, 'You didn't leave after Frank introduced you to us last night?'

'No.' Elizabeth folded her hands together in her lap. 'I stayed.'

'Where?'

'With a friend.'

'I'm going to need more than that.' Danny poised his stylus over the tablet ready to add in the details Elizabeth was clearly reluctant to share.

'I was with Frank, and, before anyone jumps to conclusions, it's a twin room and I was working most of the night.'

'That's true,' Frank confirmed.

Hari didn't think he looked terribly pleased about having an attractive woman make it quite so clear that they'd had separate beds.

Danny levelled his eyes on Elizabeth. 'It would have been better if I'd been told the truth earlier.'

'Why?' Elizabeth stared straight at him, her face unflinching. 'I'd believed there'd been an accident. I wasn't aware a crime had been committed on the premises while I was here, and neither my private life nor my working life are any concern of yours, Inspector.'

'The hotel may not be thrilled to know they have not one, but two unregistered guests here, but I suppose they must be used to people sneaking in for liaisons.'

'They might be, but I was working.'

'So you said, Miss Jeffries.'

Frank sat forward. 'Elizabeth is one of the Midlands' leading experts on antique books and manuscripts.'

'Is she now? Not just an expert on old books – but manuscripts as well?' Danny refocused his gaze on

Elizabeth, who was currently giving Frank a glare that was pure ice. 'You didn't think that would also have been useful for us to know? The fact you're an expert in these matters as well might have helped us. You could have looked at the ballad.'

'I offered to view it last night.' Elizabeth wrinkled her nose as if she'd smelt something unpleasant. 'But was denied the chance.'

'We told you, Jez wanted to save them for today – but then, of course, things changed with poor Sharman and everything,' Christine protested. 'I couldn't have shown you the real thing by then. It was on its way to London. Plus, you hadn't said you were an expert.'

Elizabeth snorted by way of response.

Hari was trying to make sense of a nagging feeling that was making itself known at the back of her mind, when Penny spoke up. 'Sharman was an expert on old books, too. She sold quite a few antique volumes. Specialist stuff.'

'Really?' Hari asked. 'I thought she sold new and second-hand books?'

'They are second-hand – really second-hand.'

'You mean Sharman had access to books as old as, say, the sixteenth century?'

Clara nodded. 'She'd get really excited about some of the finds. Her father started her passion for old things, especially books. That's why the shop is called *Parchment and Paper*. Some of her books are collectors' items.'

'Are you telling me,' Danny took a visible deep breath, 'that Sharman was also an expert on ballads?'

'The selling of them, certainly,' Penny concurred. 'Not the manufacturing of them.'

Hari was about to open her mouth, but Lee got in first. 'I should say, Inspector, if we are telling you things we didn't think important but might be – especially now we know someone deliberately hurt our friend – that I've had a few virtual visits to Sharman, and I can confirm that Clara and Penny are correct. Her shop did have some very old volumes in it.'

'Including those written on parchment?'

'Occasionally, yes.' Lee paused before adding, 'I'm sure you're wondering, as I now am, if the parchment from this fake ballad might have come from there?'

'Could it?'

'It has to be possible.' Lee tried to picture the shop. 'She had some rare pieces for sale. But, if that's the case, and someone did buy one of her oldest works for the purpose of damaging it, she'd never have known that was their motive for the purchase. Sharman was passionate about Robin Hood and history. No way would she have compromised herself like that. Not knowingly.'

'Thank you, Mr Stoneman. I'm grateful for that information. Does Sharman have an assistant in the shop?'

'No, it was just her.' Penny sighed.

'Did she have her laptop here with her, one she used for business?'

'I think so, yes.' Penny looked at Clara, who nodded in agreement.

Danny turned to Dawson as he picked up his mobile phone. 'Did you find a laptop in her room?'

'We did. You want me to get onto the tech boys?'

'Please. I want to see her business records, everything that involves the sale of manuscripts or books dating from the sixteenth century made between this time last year and last month.'

'Sir.'

As Dawson went to leave the room to make the

call, Danny added, 'And when you've done that, Sergeant, place a call to the police in Oldham. I want someone to search the shop.'

Once Dawson had gone, the inspector sat down on his chair and asked the group, 'Apart from Mr Stoneman, has anyone else been to Sharman's shop? Penny, Clara?'

Penny shook her head. 'I've not been. I've seen some of the interior online, behind Sharman's head when we've had video calls, but I've never made it to Oldham.'

'Same here.' Clara cuddled her arms across her chest. 'We always meant to visit her up there, but it's so far away.'

'How about you, Miss Hann?'

'Never.' Scarlett shook her head. 'I knew Sharman by sight, obviously. I came to the Robin Hood Club last year for the first time and met her then. She's so distinctive, with her brightly-coloured hair. A loyal fan, of course, but beyond that, I didn't know her.'

'Where was the last club meeting?' Danny asked.

'Oxford,' Jez answered before Scarlett could. 'We had a country hotel on the outskirts of the city, towards Woodstock.'

'Sounds nice.' Danny took some notes as he asked, 'And that had a nut-free kitchen as well?'

'Yes, as I said, all the hotels I book do. It's such an awful allergy, with potentially disastrous results.'

'Clearly.' Maisie's entire body exuded boredom. 'I never knew her at all, Inspector. I can't see why you are so insistent that I remain. I've apologised for not attending the hall like a good little schoolgirl, but now I'd like to go.'

Slinging her handbag over her shoulder, Maisie Flowers stood up. 'I've work to do. Roger has got his place in *Anything Goes*, but, as I said, there are better roles in the musical and I'd like—'

'Sit down, Miss Flowers. Now, please.' Danny turned his back on the grumpy agent, instead placing his focus on Frank. 'Mr Lister, do you recall what Mr Barnes said earlier when he was talking about the ballad?'

Frank's eyes narrowed. 'Jez has said a lot about that blasted ballad. I thought you wanted to talk about Sharman and what happened to her?'

'If you don't mind, Mr Lister, I'll decide on the direction of the questioning.' Unfazed, Danny continued, 'During the panel earlier, Mr Barnes said he was going to speculate on what sort of impact the ballad, should it have been real, might have had on any future stories you and your fellow authors might decide to write.'

'So?'

'Mr Lister, the fact that you have, to all intents and purposes, already written a ballad about a carter has not passed me by. I've read your book about Robin Hood which includes a carter.'

Frank was on his feet in less than a second. 'How dare you accuse me of forging that document! I'd never—'

'Mr Lister, I did no such thing.'

Danny's sharp shout sent the older man thumping back onto his seat, his arms folded tightly around his chest. 'It damn well sounded like that's what you were implying.'

'If you would let me finish—'

'I don't see why I should! Why are you focusing your fire on me? What have I done? Why aren't you speaking to Harriet like this? It's bloody obvious she's behind this.'

'What?' Dot rounded on Frank. 'Hari would never—'

'Oh yeah? Really? You're so sure of that, are you?'

'One hundred and ten per cent.' Dot took hold of Hari's arm.

Thankful that she was sitting down, Hari felt her legs tremble as she listened to Frank. He was furious.

'I'd never do anything like that.' Hari felt her throat go dry as she addressed Danny. 'I'll admit I physically could do it. In fact, I've said as much before, but—'

'You have the skill to mix the inks,' Frank cut in.

'Well, yes, but—'

'You have the ability to write the story. You know where to find the types of books or manuscripts to steal the parchment from. Forget Sharman's shop, you'll know plenty of places to find such materials.'

'Yes, but why would I? And when the hell would I find the time?'

'You'd have found the time. What do you do all day but write a few words?'

Hari was so cross her words froze in her throat. 'I…'

'And you, as a known expert, would have been given access to any such aged documents by any number of people or associations desperate to get a *celebrity* writer's opinion. I bet you were banking on being the one to authenticate it! No need for expensive lab tests if the sainted Dr Danby has said it's real!'

Not caring for the scorn in his use of the word "celebrity," Hari felt sick as Frank switched his calculating expression back to face the policemen. 'I repeat, Inspector, why is Dr Danby not being made subject to the same questioning as everyone else?'

'I can assure you, Mr Lister—'

'Can you, Inspector Shaw?' Frank's face creased

into a self-righteous sneer. 'Or can you simply confirm that you've got a bit of a crush on the Robin Hood Club's current flavour of the month?'

'That's enough!' Jez rounded on his guest. 'That is an entirely unprofessional accusation, and I don't think Hari is worthy of it. Honestly, Frank, it's one thing for you to be envious of Hari's good fortune with the television deal, but to accuse her of faking a historical document... it's preposterous!'

Elizabeth looked up from where she'd been staring into her lap. A small smile played at her pink lips. 'No one seems to be denying that the inspector is sweet on the good doctor though, do they?'

Feeling her cheeks glowing as pink as Elizabeth's jacket, Hari said, 'Please. This is insane. I have been helping Inspector Shaw because he wanted to ask me about Sharman working with me.'

'Over a cosy dinner for two?' Roger's tone was positively sugar-coated.

Danny didn't even blink at the accusation, leaving Hari wondering if he'd already been wondering if someone had spotted them eating together in the pub.

'We were hungry, Mr Striver, and time is of the essence in such situations. I offered Dr Danby the chance to eat while we spoke. If I hadn't been able to eat then, I wouldn't have had a meal until very late, and believe me, I work much better — and faster — on a full stomach. Something that will benefit all of you.'

Frank shook his head. 'And I'm the one accused of being unprofessional!'

'Mr Lister, if, as is being implied, I had wanted to enjoy a private, cosy meal for two with Dr Danby, I would *not* have picked a Wetherspoons, nor would I have sat us at a table in full view of the world, including Mr Striver. And, I'd like to think I'd have come up with a conversation that was more interesting than – and no offence to you, Miss Henderson – the ingredients used by her friend, and the cookie flavours that Sharman had said she liked.'

'All that is as maybe.' Roger exchanged a meaningful look with Maisie. 'But that does not mean that the gorgeous Dr Danby, the creator of my most cruel of potters, did not forge the ballad. In fact, I can prove she did.'

'I beg your pardon?' Hari felt the heightened colour drain from her cheeks, stealing the rest of her body heat away with it. 'How can you prove something I did not do?'

Ignoring Hari, Roger asked, 'Have you read this supposed new ballad, Inspector?'

'I have not.'

'You will know it is called *Robin Hood and the Carter*.'

'Yes, and I know that it is similar to *Robin Hood and the Potter* at the beginning.'

'Correct.'

'You have already said that the ballad echoes many of the story traits found in Frank Lister's novels.'

Danny held a palm up to Frank to prevent the outburst of protest he could see about to explode from the author's lips as he asked, 'What are you getting at, Mr Striver?'

'The rivalry between Frank and Harriet is well known. Who else would be so calculating – and have the literary and historical skill base – to put such a story together? The very essence of which underscores Frank's story. Should it have been unquestionably accepted as genuine, Frank's books would surely have plunged back to popularity, but she is clever – very clever. Hari here knows that the ballad would be subject to tests, and so be seen as being a fake.'

'Then why on earth would she bother?' Penny frowned. 'Which Hari wouldn't, anyway.'

'Oh, she'd bother.' Roger grinned as he saw approval in Frank's eyes. 'Because the ballad was bound to be found to be a fake. And by making it chime so well with Frank's work, she could easily lay the blame on him.'

'That's insane.' Hari looked imploringly at Danny. 'Something like this would have taken months to set up. Longer, even. And I have no problem with Frank, apart from the fact that he has a problem with me.'

Roger casually flicked a hair from his forehead. 'You can't deny that if Frank's work was off the scene, then your sales would be even better.'

Hari couldn't believe what she was hearing. 'But Roger, Frank being arrested for forgery wouldn't magically stop his books being popular. Quite the reverse, I imagine. Folk would be fascinated and would want to read outlaw books written by a criminal! Plus, going to prison doesn't stop a person from writing. Remember Jeffrey Archer? He wrote a bestseller while he was doing time.'

Dot broke in. 'Actually, Frank being caught out for faking the ballad would help his career more than Hari's. Everything you're saying, Roger, makes it less – not more – likely that Hari is behind this.'

Trying to steady her rapid pulse, Hari was relieved when Danny suddenly changed the subject and addressed Maisie. 'Ms Flowers, you, like Miss Jeffries, have admitted your presence in the hotel without a reservation, but unlike Miss Jeffries, you claim you were not an overnight guest. Correct?'

'I thought we were in the midst of accusing Dr Danby, Inspector.'

'I'm aware of the accusation. I will return to it shortly. First, however, I wish to find out where you've spent the last two nights.'

'I've already told Sergeant Dawson that.' Maisie picked at her long, red nails. 'And I'm not claiming anything. I am stating it as fact.'

'And now I'm giving you the chance to rectify your statement in case we've misunderstood.'

'You have not misunderstood, Inspector. I was not here last night. I was in London sorting things out for Roger, as usual.' Maisie squared her shoulders as she placed her phone out on the table around which they were all now sat. 'I hope you won't mind me recording the rest of this conversation, Inspector. I have my client's interests to protect here. Your insinuations suggest my protection might well be required.'

'You are not Mr Striver's lawyer, Ms Flowers, nor has he been accused of anything.'

'Nonetheless, Inspector, I wish to have a record of this conversation.'

Hari, hoping Danny had just been humouring Maisie when he'd said he'd return to Roger's accusation, was surprised when he didn't deny her request.

'If it makes you feel better, you may record our conversation. You have not responded to Dr Danby's suggestion that the ballad's fabrication benefits Mr Lister.'

Maisie flexed her hands, her talon-like nails glistening in the subdued light of the otherwise abandoned bar. 'I agree that the only person who'd benefit from the ballad being so like Frank's work is Frank. But why would he? The only reason I can think of is to try and resecure a television show for his stories – but he is no fool. He knows that such an effort would be pointless. There'll be no TV series for him. Even if the ballad was real, there wouldn't be. Not for at least a decade, anyway.'

'Why not?' Scarlett broke her silence.

Maisie gave her a patronising smile. 'Because, Miss Hann, every generation has their Robin Hood. Or Mathilda, in this case. The ship has sailed. There's only room for one at a time. You only have to evaluate the bad timing of the Kevin Costner and Patrick Bergin films in the early 1990s to see that. The lesser – but bigger budget – movie won the day. Even now, only die-hard Robin Hood fans watch the Bergin film.'

'A sweeping generalisation, but I take the point,' Scarlett admitted.

Frank glowered at Danny. 'Maisie is right. I would not stoop so low to get my TV series. And, if you're thinking that you can use me as your scapegoat for this, you can't.' He spun around, jabbing a finger towards Hari as he snapped, 'I was set up by this woman. I'm sure of it, Inspector.'

'But then she ruined it.' Roger spun back to stare at Hari. 'Couldn't help yourself.'

'What?'

Roger's expression suddenly resembled that of a lion about to eat its prey. 'I said I had proof, Inspector, and I meant it.'

Hari shook her head fast as, for one horrible second, Danny and Dawson's mutually uncertain expressions fell on her. Dawson seemed ready to arrest her there and then, but worse still was the flash of doubt in Danny's eyes.

'Inspector, Sergeant,' Hari pleaded. 'If I was the sort of person who could desecrate old documents for my own gain, then I suppose I'd be able to fake a manuscript. But that does not mean I would. Not in a million years.'

Roger shook his head. 'You gave yourself away.'

Dot put her hand back on her friend's arm. 'What are you talking about?'

'There is a particular line in the ballad. Just one. It will be familiar to Harriet.'

'The line! That's it!' Hari's hand clapped to her mouth. 'I knew I'd read a little of the ballad before! I knew it, but I couldn't fathom where it came from.'

'Oh, come off it!' Frank shook his head. 'You can't pull that one now that you've been found out.'

'I'm not pulling anything. Truly! I've been racking my brains, trying to remember where I'd read the line before and—'

'Okay. Enough!' Danny slapped a palm against the table. 'First, what line are you all talking about? Dr Danby, can you explain, please?'

Not missing the use of her surname rather than her first name, Hari avoided looking at anyone but Danny. 'When I first saw the ballad in the archive with Neil — Professor Frampton—'

Sergeant Dawson interrupted as he referred to his notes. 'On Saturday around six in the afternoon?'

'Yes. We, Professor Frampton and I, met Christine there at six. We were shown the ballad almost straight away. We'd left by seven at the latest.'

'Thank you.' Dawson nodded. 'Do go on.'

'I read it a few times. Skimmed it for the most part the final time. But there was one line that kept coming back to me after we left, and it bugged me. I searched online for it, but I couldn't see it in any of the other original ballads. But now…'

Dot placed a hand on Hari's arm. 'You've remembered where you'd read it before?'

'Remembered!' Roger scoffed. 'Well done! That

was a heck of a performance. Bloody hell, woman, you should be on the stage. You could have played Mathilda yourself!'

Danny stood up. 'Mr Striver, will you please stop with digs and jibes and spit out what you are insinuating.'

'The line she recognised. The one *she* is pretending bugged her. It's hers! It's a direct quote from her very first book! It's from *Mathilda's Sherwood!*'

Chapter Twenty-eight

'I have never been so embarrassed in my life.' Hari ran her hands through her hair as she looked at Danny across the hotel manager's desk. 'You don't believe Roger, do you?'

'It doesn't matter what I believe. It's what we can prove.' Danny stirred a finger through a pot of paperclips that sat on the desk as he asked his sergeant, 'Dawson, could you get me a coffee, I'm gasping. Hari?'

'Oh, um. Please. Black. One sugar.'

'But, sir—'

'Don't worry. I won't start the interview until you're back.'

A flash of annoyance crossed the sergeant's face as he left the office that the hotel manager had offered to the police so they could interview people in private.

'Also, could you make sure the remaining members of the Robin Hood Club are confined to their rooms until we're ready to talk to them again. And take their mobiles. I don't really want them conferring for a while.'

As soon as Dawson had gone, Danny said, 'We don't have long on our own, so quickly, before it's on record; why didn't you tell me about the line in the ballad?'

Hari's shoulders sagged. She felt as if the stuffing had been knocked out of her.

This is what you get for admitting to yourself you find someone attractive. I should stick to fictional boyfriends. They can't hurt you!

Feeling the burn of his brown eyes on her, Hari asked, 'Do you believe I could have done this?'

'No, but I have to be able to prove you didn't now

that the allegation has been made.' His eyes looked sad as he repeated, 'The line, Hari?'

'It's like I said, I knew I'd read the line before, but couldn't think where. It's not even a significant line – which makes me wonder why the forger put it there.'

'What was the line?'

'It's in *Mathilda's Sherwood,* like Roger said. It's from the first altercation in the series, before Mathilda meets Will; between Mathilda and the felon, in this case—'

'The carter.' Danny nodded. 'I've read it at least eight times.'

'Oh. Really? I knew you liked them, but *eight* times... wow!' Not allowing the tiny shaft of hope she felt in her chest to blossom, she said, 'The line is, *"...the carter pushed her down, his ruddy face scowled in anger..."*'

'Frank's books feature a carter.'

'They do,' Hari agreed. 'But the line is mine.'

'And you truly felt no sense of recognition of it being yours when you read it?'

'Nope.' Hari shrugged. 'I've written five more novels since then, plus I've adapted that book, and two more, into scripts, something that – while using the same story – can take you a fair way from the original text on a dialogue level.'

'Same meaning, different words?'

'Exactly. But I can't see how I can prove I didn't do this.'

'Which is why my job is so difficult.'

'I'm sure.' Hari glanced towards the closed office door and sighed. 'I understand why you'd think I forged the ballad, but I didn't. I had no reason to, and I certainly didn't kill Sharman. In all honesty, I'd have thought that was the crime that needed your attention the most.'

'And you're right. You're also the person who convinced me that the two crimes were linked.'

Hari hoped Dawson would need to queue for their coffees, giving them a little longer alone. 'And now you think I've concocted some sort of elaborate double bluff. By making you think I'm after justice for Sharman rather being the person who caused her death?'

Danny groaned. 'Hari, I'm sorry. I have to—'

'I know. It's just...' Hari suddenly sat still. 'How did he know?'

'Pardon?'

'How did Roger know that line in the ballad came from my book?'

'He must have read it. Means he's a fan, too.' Danny paused. 'Hang on, was he in the episode of your show where that line featured?'

'No, the potter wasn't in that one. I don't recall the line being used in the TV series anyway. It would have been a scene that was shown – the words wouldn't have been spoken. I'd have to check the script to be sure, though.'

'Could I ask you to do that now, please? I assume it would be on your laptop.'

'It is. I'd have to fetch it from my room.'

'I'll get Dawson to collect it shortly.' Danny paused. 'If it was in the script too, then whoever used it to implicate you could have got it from either your show or your books.'

'The books, surely.' Hari closed her eyes and focused on breathing properly. 'But you're missing the point.'

'I am?'

'Only me, Neil, Christine and two other local

historians saw the ballad prior to it going to London. And, when Christine had the photos of the work here, Roger was not around. And Jez never had the chance to put them on display.'

'So, Roger couldn't have known about that line being in the ballad unless someone told him, or he saw it?'

'Or he wrote the ballad!' An ache formed in Hari's chest as she went on, 'No, Roger wouldn't have the knowledge, but he knows people that do. Danny, I have a horrible feeling I know what happened. Can we… would you mind if I asked you a few questions?'

'Questions I shouldn't really answer? Those sorts of questions?'

'They're the sort of questions I was referring to, yes. And then, when I've asked them, I think we need to check on a few things.'

'Now?'

'Now. Because if I'm right, then the person who is at the bottom of all of this will be gone by tomorrow!'

'Okay. But if I can't answer anything for legal reasons, then I won't.'

Hari felt a smile edging away some of her disquiet. 'Deal.'

The sound of the door opening brought Sergeant Dawson back into the room, three cups of coffee balanced on a tray in front of him.

'Thank you, Dawson.' Danny picked his cup up as the tray was placed on the desk. 'You have arrived just in time. I will fill you in on what I've learnt from Dr Danby, but first, she has some questions for us.'

'She is questioning us?' Dawson's disapproval was plain.

'I mean no disrespect, Sergeant, but I think I know what happened to Sharman and why.'

'How could you know, unless it was you who—?'

Not wanting to hear another accusation, Hari quickly said, 'Because, if I'm right, the crimes here have been constructed like a murder mystery story.'

Not letting Dawson voice his disapproval of the fact he'd been talking about the case to a potential suspect, Danny asked him, 'Has everyone been confined to their rooms?'

'Everyone except Miss Spencer, Ms Flowers, and Miss Jeffries. The hotel has put them in separate vacant rooms on the first floor. Numbers one, two and four.' Dawson sniffed. 'They weren't too gracious about it.'

'I'm sure.' Hari sipped at her coffee, recoiling a fraction as the liquid burnt the tip of her tongue.

'The mobiles are here.' Dawson held up a large, see-through bag.

'Excellent. Thank you, Sergeant.' Danny checked the time. 'It's getting late, and I for one would like to get this tied up today if we can. You had questions, Dr Danby?'

'I did. Can I ask you, Sergeant, in the hotel kitchen here, did you find any trace of nuts?'

'I can confirm that, according to the staff, no nuts have been used in dishes cooked here in the last two years,' Dawson said.

'Thank you.' Hari crossed that point off her mental check list and changed the subject. 'Is there CCTV in the hotel corridors?'

Danny rolled his eyes. 'There's supposed to be, but it hasn't worked for some time.'

'Would the guests have known that?'

'I can't see why they would.' Danny looked at Dawson, who shrugged. 'I suppose Jez Barnes may have been aware.'

'Umm…' Hari picked her cup back up and blew

across the surface of her coffee. 'Perhaps he did… and if he did and told someone…' Hari turned to Dawson. 'When you get your colleagues to examine Sharman's laptop, concentrate on a period of say, one to four weeks after Jez announced when and where this Robin Hood Club event would be held this year. See what was purchased from her shop in that period, and by whom.'

Dawson crossed his arms. 'You think our victim was involved in the ballad?'

'Too much of a coincidence for her not to be.' Draining her drink, Hari spoke fast, 'I did not fake the ballad, Sergeant, nor did I kill Sharman. But the culprit is in this hotel now.'

Dawson tutted. 'You think you're some sort of Miss Marple, do you? It does not work like that! Tell her, sir. You can't just change the rules so you can play at *Midsomer Murders*!'

Danny's eyebrows rose. 'My, you do watch a lot of cosy crime drama, Sergeant!'

A little embarrassed by the awkward atmosphere, Hari said, 'I suspect you will either find there will be no records of anything at all, or—'

'Nothing at all,' Danny suddenly saw what Hari was saying, 'nothing recorded, yet a book or manuscript will be missing, despite being in the stock record.'

'Yes!' Hari's confidence faltered. 'Or… maybe there'll be a book in the shop that is of the right age, recorded as intact, but is actually damaged stock because—'

'Its flyleaves are missing.' Danny sat up straighter. 'Dawson, can you call the police in Oldham back? Ask them to hunt for books of the right age that have been damaged. Tonight, if possible, but first thing tomorrow if their overtime budget won't stretch.'

'Right, sir.'

Danny leant across the desk 'You *are* sure about Sharman's involvement in this, Hari?'

'Let's just say, I think I'm on the right track.'

Pausing for a moment, Danny asked, 'What are you suggesting we do next? And please, bear in mind that Dawson is right, we do have to adhere to the law as we work.'

'Of course. But think about it. Everyone here likes stories. They either invent them, act them out, research them, share them, or make money out of other people writing them. All I'm suggesting is that we — you — treat this like a story.'

'A *Poirot* moment, you mean!' Dawson banged his cup into the saucer with a clatter. 'Come off it! I was joking about *Miss Marple*.'

'Maybe you were joking, but it's still an excellent idea, Sergeant.' Danny stood back up. 'These people respond to drama. Let's give them some.'

Chapter Twenty-nine

Hari flicked through her notebook as she waited for Danny. The answer to everything that had happened was burning at the back of her mind.

I have no proof... what if I'm wrong?

She desperately wanted to speak to Dot, but as Danny had left the office, he'd asked her not to contact anyone, and she'd reluctantly promised not to. Nonetheless, Hari was buzzing with nervous energy.

What am I doing? Dawson's right, I'm no Miss Marple. I'm meddling in a police investigation.

Pulling her ever-present pen from her pocket, Hari smoothed out a new page in her notebook.

Danny clearly trusts me to help.

She started to write down a list of names, leaving gaps between each one so she could make notes as she went.

If I'm really going to go all amateur detective on this, I need to address each person separately. Innocent until proven guilty.

'Frank, Roger, Elizabeth, Maisie, Scarlett, Lee, Christine, Penny, Clara...' Hari's pen hovered over the page before she reluctantly added, 'Jez, Neil, Dot.'

I'll approach this as I would a research project; double checking all my sources. Then, I need to get crime plot thinking, just as I would when I'm weaving a crime into one of Mathilda's books.

Closing her eyes, she pictured each person on her list one at a time. 'What do you each have to gain or lose from Sharman's death?'

Seconds later, she crossed Dot, Penny, and Clara off her list.

'Dot can only lose from this. Everything she has worked for could go if it came out that someone died via one of her cookies.' Hari opened her eyes again. 'Anyway, she'd never hurt a fly.'

She scribbled a second line through her best friend's name.

'Penny and Clara are so distraught it can't be them.' She paused. 'No, that's fluffy thinking – being distraught is not proof of innocence.' She focused on her notes. 'The fact that neither of them has anything to gain is more pertinent. Plus, they only see Sharman at the Robin Hood Club, and they have no links to the ballad world that I know of. Dot said Penny was an admin clerk and Clara a teaching assistant.'

Next, she ran her pen around the name Neil, circling it in black ink. 'No way could it be him. And the police haven't asked him to stay, so they can't think he's involved.' She hesitated. 'Okay, he could have done it, just as I could have. But what would he get out of it?' Hari kept up her solo commentary. 'A new ballad to study? He was coming to Buxton at the right time, so it was not surprising he was asked to see the ballad. I'd never have been invited if it wasn't for Neil…' A treacherous thought crossed the back of her mind. 'And because I saw it, it would be easier to think I was involved in the forgery… or would it? If I'd forged it, I'd want to keep my distance…'

Hari tapped her pen against her notebook. 'Neil was at the last Robin Hood Club meet, so he already knew Sharman. He knows all there is to know about ballads and can make up authentic inks. He's the one who taught me to do it!'

Hari felt sick.

What if it's him… and not…?

Forcing herself to move on, she underlined the name Christine. 'She has lots to gain in kudos, career wise. Although, in practical terms I'm not sure what that would lead to, beyond being shown to be a quick thinker when it came to acting after the discovery of the document.'

Wondering how Danny was getting on, Hari continued to talk aloud to herself. 'If Christine did set all this up, then why did Sharman have to die? They'd never met.'

She was about to put a cross through the archivist's name, when she remembered the issue of getting the ballad hidden in the archive's back room in the first place. 'Christine was away on holiday the week before the discovery. Anyone who gave her colleagues the slip and snuck into the workroom area could have planted it. But maybe Christine told that person where to put it?'

Feeling less sure of herself by the moment, Hari put a question mark next to Christine's name, and then – reluctantly – did the same by Neil's.

'Scarlett?' Hari shook her head and crossed the actress's name out. 'No. I'm still sure it isn't her. Too much to lose and nothing to gain. Mathilda is a stepping stone for her, this won't be her best role. I can't see why she'd do this, even if it has put the spotlight on the Robin Hood story for a while, and so our show by association.'

Turning the page of her notebook, Hari redrafted her list.

'That leaves Frank, Elizabeth, Roger, Maisie, Jez, and Lee, plus the logistics to consider... I need to recheck my timings and locational thinking.'

She quickly drew a plan of the hotel corridor that had contained Sharman's bedroom. *I wonder how close her room was to the stairs or fire exit?*

The sound of the office door opening announced Danny's return. He was talking before he reached his seat. 'You were right. There is a sixteenth century parchment pamphlet listed on Sharman's laptop as being in perfect condition, but that same item, according to the boys in Oldham, has its flyleaves missing, one from the front and the back two.'

'They've checked already?'

'Shop's not far from the station, believe it or not.'

'Handy.' Hari chewed on her bottom lip. 'So, Sharman either had no idea the pages had been ripped out, or she did know, but hadn't had the chance to update her records.'

'Or maybe, she was party to the flyleaves being removed, and had no intention of amending the record?'

'Also possible.' Hari considered her notes. 'I've been trying to work out where everyone was during the disco and why they'd want to forge a ballad.'

'It's looking like Sharman had to die because she knew where the parchment came from.' Danny sat next to Hari.

'But did she know from the start, or did she find out? She didn't see the ballad after it was discovered.'

Danny noticed the map on the open notebook. 'The fire escape is next to Sharman's room. The lift is at the other end of the corridor and is next to the official staircase.'

Hari nodded. 'And the fire escape, as I discovered when I ran away from Lee, is easily accessible to all, and can take anyone out to the hotel's garden.'

'You ran away from Lee?'

'Long story, and nothing to do with this.'

'Sure?'

'Positive.' Hari ran a finger over the list of names at the top of her page. 'Either way, it means that whoever swapped the cookies could have done so with little risk of being spotted. They'd just have to go through the fire door, and then quickly back out again.'

'You still think you know who did it and why?'

'Let's just say, my process of elimination so far is keeping me set on my idea, but I'd very much appreciate your input. I could be seconds from making a total fool of myself. Oh, and Professor Frampton should join us if he's still here.'

'You think your old tutor is involved?'

'I really hope not.'

'Dot, you don't have to be here,' Hari whispered in her friend's ear as, back in the hall, they stood together by the door.

'I know, but I need to find out who tried to ruin me.'

'I'm not sure that was the motive.' Hari put a hand on her friend's shoulder.

'Maybe not, but it could certainly have been a consequence. It might still be!'

Hari swallowed as Danny led the others into the hall, choosing where each person would sit, as if choreographing a play. 'I'm in over my head here, Dot. Danny could get into a lot of trouble for letting me help – and what if I'm wrong?'

'Then it'll be proved you're wrong. At least by sifting through all the evidence like this, you'll be helping Shaw and Dawson get on the right track.'

'That's a bit like implying I don't think they can do their jobs properly.'

'I'm sure they can. But you know this world, and they don't.' Dot squeezed her friend's hand encouragingly.

'I've been treating it like the plot to a book.'

'Sensible.' Dot mumbled under her breath, 'Then, after all this is over, you can make it into an actual story.'

Hari sighed. 'Maybe one day. When it isn't all so real.'

Frank was not best pleased at being sat, as per the detective's whim, three seats away from his nearest companion, Elizabeth. And he wasn't the only unhappy person in the hall.

'Inspector, why are we being herded back in here like children in detention?' Maisie slumped onto her allocated seat. 'I'm not part of the Robin Hood Club, so I'd like to go home, please.'

Elizabeth stood back up. 'I couldn't agree more. This is ridiculous.'

Danny raised his hands, as if in peace. 'No one here is being forced to stay. Yet.'

'Yet?' Roger crossed his arms over his chest. 'There's an edge of menace to your voice, Shaw.'

'Not menace, Mr Striver. Simply regret. Regret that, during what should have been a weekend of fun and friendship, a young woman was killed.'

Frank waved a hand towards Hari and Dot as they waited by the doorway. 'Why aren't they being sat down like we are, Inspector?'

'Because it can be proved they aren't involved.'

'Implying we could all be involved?' Christine looked offended as she regarded Hari from across the room.

'Only in that everyone here, in some way, has the ability needed to be involved in either the forgery of the ballad, or in the death of Sharman,' Danny explained. 'In some cases, both. Normally, I would not work like this, but this is an unusual situation, and as you all live in differing parts of the UK, and will be leaving soon, time is against us.'

'In other words, Inspector,' Jez played his hat brim through his fingers. 'You want to get justice for Sharman before the chance slips away, along with the culprit.'

'Precisely, Mr Barnes.' Danny gestured for Hari to join him on the stage, while Dawson took up a position by the double doors, a uniformed constable next to him.

'Now hang on,' Frank protested. 'What makes you so sure one of us is responsible? It could have been anyone from Sharman's life. I assume she had a life beyond the Robin Hood Club.'

'I will come to that, Mr Lister. I will also stress that I know full well that you can't all be guilty. I simply assumed you'd care about the outcome.'

Neil regarded the detective. 'Absolutely, Inspector. Thank you for inviting me back in to find out what's happening.'

Feeling guilty that she'd had to consider her friend as a suspect, Hari couldn't look at Neil as Danny gathered the meeting to order. 'Now then, let's recap the situation.'

'What the hell for?' Roger grumbled. 'I've got to leave! It's gone ten already, and Maisie's got me a meeting tomorrow morning in London with the director of the musical.'

'I'm very pleased for you. If you stop interrupting, we'll be done faster.' Danny, his voice calm, took out his tablet and tapped on the screen a few times. 'So, a ballad was discovered in the Buxton Archive a short time prior to the arrival of the Robin Hood Club's scheduled stay at the Harmen Hotel. A venue that is a short walk away from said archive.

'As coincidences go, it's a big one, but if you are going to find an undiscovered ballad, an archive is not so strange a place to do so. What *is* strange is the added coincidence of where, within the archive, that ballad was found.'

'In the pile of books waiting to be mended, Inspector Shaw?' Christine asked.

'Not so much that, but the particular book in which it was found. As Hari pointed out to me, it was discovered within the pages of a volume of *Knighton* – volume four, in fact.'

Neil raised a hand. 'The very volume that covers the period of history often associated with the ballads of Robin Hood.'

'Precisely, Professor Frampton,' said Danny. 'I gather that copy of *Knighton* was near the top of the pile when you found it, Miss Spencer, rather than in the haphazard mending heap you remember leaving behind before you had a holiday?'

'Yes, Inspector. I got back from a week away the day I found the manuscript.'

'And your fellow staff members did not attend to any book maintenance while you were away in—?'

'Cornwall.' Christine tutted. 'The chance would be a fine thing, Inspector. We're often short-staffed, and holiday cover is as rare as hen's teeth. No one had time to do anything beyond the daily running of the library and the archive. Anyway, no one else is qualified to mend spines apart from me.'

'Understood. So, you returned from holiday and, having a full complement of staff for once, you decided to grab the chance to catch up on some jobs in the workroom?'

'Yes. Thinking back, it was the fact the mending pile was tidy that attracted me to it. Normally it's something of a heap, each book taking its chance as to which would be mended first.'

'Do you know who tidied it up in your absence?'

'I do not. No member of staff recalls doing so, and as there is no security video in the workroom, then I am at a loss to explain it. At the time, I didn't think about it.'

'But someone must have been there to plant the ballad. And then left things tidy to draw you to said pile.'

'It's rather an odd thing to do, but yes, I suppose they must have, Inspector.'

'Which would involve smuggling it into the archive building, passing the staff and getting into the workroom, unseen.'

'That wouldn't be so difficult. You'd only have to wait until all the staff were busy elsewhere and slip into the back room. As I said, we have no security cameras on the premises.'

'It would have taken nerve, though.' Danny thanked Christine, and moved to where Neil was sat. 'Professor Frampton, you were with Hari when you studied the ballad.'

'I was. We were both invited to view the document.'

'Because you were coming to Buxton anyway?'

'No, Inspector. Christine did not know we were coming here. We were asked because we have a known academic track record in that area.'

'Another coincidence.' Danny frowned.

'They do happen, Inspector,' Elizabeth cut in. 'All you're doing now is making me think that the professor and Dr Danby were behind this. Together, probably.'

'I can see why you might think so. In fact, the circumstantial evidence against Hari really does stack up. Consequently, Sergeant Dawson and I interviewed Dr Danby again. A fact you are all aware of.'

'And yet you say she is in the clear, Inspector?' Jez

smiled at Hari and Dot. 'I'm very glad to hear it. You think Hari was set up?'

'I do, Mr Barnes. It is for that reason that I have taken the unusual move of taking advice from Hari. She is, as we have heard, knowledgeable about ballads. She and Miss Henderson, Dot, also worked with Sharman for a short while.'

'And this advice has led you to bringing us all here?' Jez's eyes widened as he looked again at his guest author.

'It has.' Danny beckoned to Hari. 'Perhaps you would join me?'

As Hari, her heart beating fast, joined Danny on the stage, Frank called out, 'Oh really, Shaw, this is too much. I grant you that the woman is good at her job, but a detective she is not.'

Chapter Thirty

Hari's throat went dry as she stared out at the scattering of people in the auditorium before her. There may only have been ten faces looking back at her, but she felt far more intimidated than she had when facing three hundred *Return to Sherwood* fans.

Perching on the edge of the stage, rather than sitting on one of the seats placed behind her, she glanced at Danny, who gave her a quick, encouraging dip of his head.

'Right, well… I'm no expert, of course, but—'

'Damn right, you're not.' Frank crossed his arms over his poorly-fitting shirt and leant back in his seat. 'This is a farce.'

'No, Mr Lister. This is one citizen helping the police in the course of their duties. All I am asking Hari to do is to run through the situation as she sees it. You have already done that yourself, making it clear that you see Hari as the culprit, have you not?'

'Yes, but—'

'Then I simply ask you to give your colleague here the same courtesy.' Danny nodded to Hari. 'Please, continue.'

'Okay…' Hari took a deep breath. 'To my mind, the ballad and Sharman's death must be linked. As Inspector Shaw said, there are simply too many coincidences for one not to be connected to the other.

'I've been considering the matter; two crimes under the umbrella of one aim. An aim that included laying the blame for all this at my door, with the added implication that my best friend, Dot, was involved, by the use of a cookie as the murder weapon.'

Sitting down next to Hari, Danny interjected, 'As you all know, Sharman was allergic to nuts. Fatally so.

She made no secret of it; therefore it was an obvious assumption that she would carry an EpiPen just in case she did encounter a nut.'

'But,' Penny wiped a tear from her cheek as she looked across at an equally distraught Clara, 'she'd left her pen in her bag in our room.'

'She had.' Danny gave Penny a sympathetic smile. 'When Sharman was found, her room was in disarray. At first we assumed her attacker had trashed her room, but I think it is a safe assumption that it was Sharman herself who made the mess while hunting for her pen.'

Feeling her confidence rise as she heard Danny echo her own thoughts, Hari added, 'Penny, Clara, and Sharman were old Robin Hood Club friends. They met at whichever location the event was held at each year and had three days of outlaw-related fun. Between times, they stayed in touch via video calls and messages. They've not met up in person between events.

'The evening of the disco, Sharman joined Penny and Clara in the twin room they'd booked. They were all trying on clothes ready for the dancing. It was supposed to be a night of fun. But, unbeknownst to Penny and Clara at the time, it had more meaning to Sharman.'

Clara gripped Penny's arm for support. 'We only found out she had a man here later.'

'A bloke? Sharman?' Frank was shocked.

Not wanting to reveal Lee's secret to those who didn't already know unless she had to, Hari made sure she avoided looking in the actor's direction. 'Sharman had been seeing someone from the Robin Hood Club. The relationship was in its tentative stages, and I have been led to believe that Sharman was unsure as to how serious the gentleman in question was about her. She didn't even confide in her friends, yet circumstances have meant that said man has since revealed himself to Penny and Clara.'

'Plus the discovery of Sharman's notebook—' Danny added.

'You found it!' Frank interrupted sharply.

'Yes, we found it, Mr Lister.' Danny went on, 'In her notebook, her positive feelings for the gentleman in question were clear. She was simply wary that he might not care for her as much as he claimed.'

Roger was incredulous. 'No accounting for taste.'

Dot scowled. 'That was a cruel comment.'

'It was.' Elizabeth glared at Roger. 'Inspector, surely her would-be beau ought to be here.'

Danny said nothing.

'Ah, I see. Interesting.' Elizabeth immediately regarded each of the men present, as if assessing their suitability for the role. 'He *is* here.'

Not giving anyone time to speculate aloud, Hari took her pad from her bag and gripped hold of it like a security blanket as she launched back into her enquiry. 'Penny, am I right in recalling that Sharman had told you and Clara she was tired during this dress-up session?'

'Yeah. She'd been working long hours lately to keep the shop going. What with that, having fun here, and helping you out on your stall, she was shattered.'

'That was why you weren't that surprised when she didn't show at the disco?'

'Yeah. We... we didn't know she had a man to turn up for at the time.' Clara gulped.

Inspector Shaw gave Clara a reassuring smile. 'You told Dawson that Sharman left you and went to her room at around seven o'clock?'

'Yes.'

'Time of death has yet to be confirmed, but our pathologist's initial thinking is that Sharman would have died fairly soon after that.'

Hari took back over. 'As Inspector Shaw said, when the police found Sharman, her room was in a mess – a mess made while she hunted for her EpiPen. But she was hunting in vain, as the pen was in a bag she'd accidentally left in Penny and Clara's room.'

'But,' Jez chipped in, 'the killer couldn't have known that.'

'They didn't, which is why I think,' Hari paused, 'and this is just a guess, you understand, that Sharman was not meant to die.'

Danny's eyebrows rose. 'Hari?'

'No one could have known she'd forget her bag, or that she only had one EpiPen with her.'

'You think the poisoner meant for Sharman to be ill, but not killed?'

'As I said, I'm not sure.'

'But?'

Hari's eyes flicked to Dot as she said, 'It'll sound silly, but if this was a story I was writing, then the cookie would have been meant to unnerve Sharman. She would have grabbed the EpiPen and been alright.'

'Having been left shaken and scared.' Lee spoke for the first time since they'd been corralled back into the hall. 'And probably quite sick.'

'Exactly.'

'But what on earth for?' Maisie's unimpressed expression remained firmly in place.

'Either because Sharman needed teaching a lesson; frightening, perhaps, or because the killer wanted to implicate Dot – blame her for the death, or allergy triggering – for some reason. Or, as we've said before, to point the finger at me, via Dot.'

Silence filled the hall. Hari could see everyone thinking, digesting what she was telling them.

When no one had spoken for a few seconds, Hari continued. 'Sharman's business was in difficulty. She loved her shop, *Parchment and Paper*. It had been her father's. She was also hoping to take up the chance she'd been given to do a part-time PhD on medieval literature. Money, however, or lack thereof, was very much an obstacle.'

Jez laid his hat in his lap as he chipped in, 'She'd recently got some money to help her. At least, she told me she had.'

'And she had.' Again, Hari took care not to look at Lee. 'A friend had given her the money to do her PhD.'

'She'd wanted to do that ever since I met her.' Jez gave a rueful smile. 'Sharman was a very clever lass.'

'She was. And that was the problem.' Hari surveyed the faces before her with more certainty. The more she spoke, the faster all the pieces fell into place in her mind. 'Sharman did not give the impression that she was as capable as she was.'

Danny said, 'You said you don't think murder was the intention.'

Hari took a sip of water from a glass on the table behind her. 'I think that Sharman suspected that the parchment used for the ballad came from her shop – although why I'm not sure.'

Danny added, 'We won't know for certain until the book the flyleaves were ripped from are analysed, along with the ballad. Our people in Oldham are arranging delivery of the book to London as we speak.'

'You have the source of the parchment?' Frank asked, his expression suddenly unreadable.

'Yes, sir. We do.' Dawson took a step nearer to the stage.

Hari held up her notebook. 'Sharman had a notebook not unlike mine. Whereas I jot down ideas that would make good stories, Sharman recorded ideas that might spark her future research, books she might hunt down to sell in her shop and, more recently, her suspicions and her musings as to her potential boyfriend. Sadly, the full extent of her suspicions were never written down, but she knew all was not well. Her last note said, *"All is not right at RHC"*.'

Jez drew a sharp breath through his teeth. 'You think she knew who was behind the ballad forgery?'

'She had a felon in mind, yes.'

'Who?' Frank had lost his hostile front.

'You, Frank.'

'I beg your pardon!'

'I suggest you listen, rather than bluster, Mr Lister.' Danny held up a hand. 'Go on, please, Hari.'

Hari spoke quickly. 'Sharman was at a weekend with friends, with the chance to spend time with the man who'd recently told her he loved her, but instead she spent her time sitting at my book stall. Why?'

'Because she wanted to watch Frank,' Dot volunteered. 'His stall was opposite ours. He could see everything we did.'

Hari nodded. 'And Sharman, while she sat there, could see everything Frank did.'

'Why the hell would she want to do that?' Frank was looking worried. 'I haven't done anything.'

'Sharman believed you had, though,' Danny added. 'Although I think we can assume you weren't her only suspect, or she'd have set up permanent camp at Hari's stall, rather than only helped out now and then.'

Hari felt her pulse beat faster as she said, 'You can swap things around, of course. If Frank could be watched from my trade stand, then he could watch me and Dot from his.'

'Why would I want to do that?' Frank rubbed a hand over his face. 'Your success is hard to take at the best of times. Why would I want to study it?'

'*You* wouldn't. But you might know someone who does.'

'What?'

Hari turned to face the seats before her. She was rather alarmed to find she was enjoying herself. 'Let's think creatively. Except for Penny and Clara, we are all connected with the creative arts in some way. If this was a book or drama plot, then the first thing the writer of said plot would be figuring out would be the motive for the crime they were going to commit to paper. In this case the motive can be said to be money.'

'Money?' Christine appeared surprised. 'If that was the case, why not simply sell the fake to a private buyer? It wouldn't have been so easily detected as a fake – especially if someone unreputable could have been hired to claim it was real.'

'A question I've asked myself,' Hari stated. 'But the financial gain planned here would have come from the consequence of the ballad's existence, not of the sale of the ballad. Also, whoever forged it would surely have been paid by the person who asked them to do it – assuming they are not one and the same.'

Danny jumped up and indicated his sergeant. 'Dawson has secured permission to see the bank accounts of everyone in this room first thing tomorrow morning. If any one of you has recently been in receipt of a large injection of cash, we will soon know about it. So, any volunteers?'

Chapter Thirty-one

Every eye was focused on Danny, but no one obligingly admitted to a financial windfall after doing a spot of forgery.

'Let's think logically.' Hari broke the silence. 'We all need money, but some of us here need it more urgently than others. Jez, you told me that the Robin Hood Club is expensive to run, and you make no money from it, is that correct?'

'What? Nothing at all?' Maisie swung round, regarding Jez as if he was mad.

'Love, not money. That's what this is about.'

'But you could make a fortune from this!'

'I could, Maisie, but then none of the real fans could afford to come.' Jez shrugged. 'I didn't forge the ballad for money, though, nor did I kill one of the RHC's most loyal supporters.'

Danny pressed the screen of his tablet and scrolled through the page before him. 'Jez, you say you last saw Sharman while she was at Hari and Dot's stand on Saturday afternoon. And during the seven until eight period in which we believe she died on Saturday night, you were in the bar and disco area setting up for the evening ahead?'

'That is correct.' Jez sighed. 'As I said to Sergeant Dawson, others can vouch for me. The bar staff, DJ, and so on.'

'And they have done.' Shaw nodded. 'Yet, that does not mean you didn't help whoever did this.'

'I suppose not.' Jez banged his hat back on top of his head. 'But I didn't. I was thinking this would have to be the last Robin Hood Club. Now I can't see any way it can go on.'

'Oh no!' Penny and Clara exclaimed together.

'People are already talking about a memorial event in honour of Sharman.'

'So I've heard, but I'm sorry. The cost of this is crippling, as is the workload. My bank manager will no longer be appeased. A sad end to something that has, until this weekend, only brought joy.'

'I'm so sorry, Jez, why didn't you say?' Frank's forehead creased with what appeared, at least, to be genuine concern.

'Would you have believed me if I'd told you this didn't make a profit?'

'Well, ummm… no. You're always so generous and I know you pay the stars well and on time. You make it look so easy.'

'Thanks, Frank. That's always been the plan. But that's not important. I didn't hurt Sharman, and I am not involved in the ballad. I'd have loved it to be real.'

'As would we all, Jez.' Hari turned to her fellow author. 'Frank, I'm sure you in particular would have liked *Robin Hood and the Carter* to be the real deal, for reasons already stated.'

'I would.' Frank sounded wary. 'But if you're about to say I'm behind it again—'

'I was merely going to say that, as the ballad supports your stories, it would have given you a boost in sales, and perhaps it could have led to your opinion being sought on the ballad. You're very knowledgeable about these matters. We have seen for ourselves how galling you find it to be overlooked every time an expert on medieval literature is sought.'

'Sometimes it is. Such situations as the finding of a new ballad aren't common though, are they.'

'True enough.' A fresh notion arrived in Hari's head, and she found herself saying, 'I do wonder, though, how would you have felt if Sharman had got her PhD. Yet another person, younger than you, would be better qualified in the subject.'

'Better qualified doesn't mean they know as much as I do!'

'Exactly. It must be endlessly frustrating.'

'Oh, nice try!' Frank clapped his hands. 'Not frustrating enough to kill over it. Not by a long stretch.'

Dipping her head in acknowledgement of Frank's protest, Hari switched her focus. 'Miss Jeffries — Elizabeth — as we know, you are a specialist in rare books and manuscripts.'

'I am, but before you read anything into that, Little Miss Poirot, I can assure you that is just a coincidence.'

'Another one?' Hari turned to Danny. 'Aren't they just stacking up, Inspector.'

'Don't be sarcastic.' Elizabeth pulled her latest pink jacket closer around her shoulders. 'I know Frank because of his interest in old books.'

Danny moved towards Frank. 'You did not tell us you had such an interest, Mr Lister.'

'Because it's bloody obvious! I'm an historian, albeit one without letters after my name. I've got an interest in anything old!'

'Fair enough.' Danny shifted his gaze to Elizabeth. 'But you, Miss Jeffries, could, should a request from a client be made, get your hands on the parchment necessary to make the ballad?'

'I suppose I could, but I didn't.' Elizabeth frowned, making wrinkles destroy the illusion of youth across her foundation-covered forehead. 'Didn't you just say that the parchment came from Sharman's shop?'

'I said we suspect it might have done and enquiries are in progress. Sharman thought it might have, though, and that's what matters here.' Hari nervously licked her lips before speaking to Frank again. 'You made a phone call yesterday. During that call, to someone you referred to as darling, you said "I need it to be seen to be real." What needs to be seen to be real, Frank?'

Frank gawped like a stunned fish.

When he didn't answer, Hari went on, 'I assume you were talking to Elizabeth. I've heard you chat with a good many people over the weekend, but she is the only one you've referred to as darling.'

Confirming Hari's suspicions, Elizabeth's response was only just short of venomous. 'And what gave you the right to eavesdrop on our private conversation?'

'I didn't.' Hari moved on quickly before Dot came under suspicion in the spirit of guilt by association. 'Please tell us, what needs to be seen to be real?'

'That's none of your business.'

'The obvious conclusion is that you were referring to the ballad.' Danny got up and paced towards Frank.

'The obvious is wrong.'

'Then tell us the un-obvious.'

'That was a personal conversation, Inspector,' Elizabeth snapped. 'You've no right to insist.'

Hari broke in, 'After the police had finished questioning me, and while I was waiting for you all to gather in here, I did some checking. I studied a plan of the hotel, making a note of where all the rooms are and how many beds are in each one.'

'Fascinating.'

'It was fascinating, Miss Jeffries, because it got me thinking. I dismissed the idea at first, but the more I considered it, the more sense it made.' Hari paused before asking, 'We know you were in the hotel longer than you originally said, but can you tell us why you pretended not to have been here overnight?'

Elizabeth pulled at her jacket as she muttered, 'Why do you think? I didn't want people to know I'd spent the night with Frank!'

As Frank's complexion went from a ruddy red to a pale puce, Hari shook her head. 'But you didn't spend the night with Frank, did you?'

'I did. I told you that there is an extra bed in the room and—'

'No. That isn't what you told us. You said it was a twin room. But it isn't. It's a double room.'

Elizabeth's eyes widened and her mouth dropped open as if to speak, but Hari had already swung around to face Frank.

'Normally I'd say who you had in your room last night was none of our business, Frank, but I suggest you share that information, because this is very much *not* a normal circumstance.'

'It isn't, but it has nothing to do with—'

Danny interrupted. 'Mr Lister, please, answer Hari's question.'

With a deliberate precision of movement, Frank got up and moved to sit next to Maisie.

A communal raising of eyebrows later, Jez said, 'That's why you always come whenever Roger does one of my events! It's not because Roger hangs off your every word, it's because you're seeing his agent, and she sticks to her charge like glue! And there I was thinking you were simply a loyal Robin Hood Club member.'

'I am!' Frank placed a hand on Maisie's thigh. 'And Roger does not hang off my every word!'

Danny raised a hand. 'That's neither here nor there. Nor is the question of why your relationship is hidden – although that is a little odd. What *does* matter is where everyone has been during the weekend, and three of you have lied to me about it. Ms Flowers, when did you really arrive at the hotel to stay with Frank?'

'On Saturday.' Maisie tapped her red fingernails on the arm of her chair. 'Just before lunch.'

'And how did you enter the hotel?'

'Fire exit in the garden.'

Hari felt another piece of the puzzle slip into place. 'A route that would have taken you up some back stairs and into a corridor with no cameras.'

'I didn't know about the lack of cameras.'

'So why sneak in?'

Maisie's eyes narrowed. 'To grab some time to myself before Roger saw me and started demanding things.'

Roger flinched as if he'd been struck. 'You were avoiding me?'

'Yes! You're bloody hard work.' Maisie blew out a sharp breath between her ruby lips. 'I wanted to get some work done – on your behalf – without you interfering!'

'And to see Frank in private?' Hari asked gently.

'Not until later. He was at work too, remember.'

'He was.' Hari turned to Elizabeth. 'So, if it wasn't the ballad that needed to be seen to be real, it must have been your fake relationship with Frank. One that you weren't happy with, but could see the sense of going along with.'

'I told you—'

'It's personal. Yes. But as we have established, it is Maisie who's with Frank. You knew of their relationship.'

Elizabeth said nothing.

'You knew, but it served all three of you to let everyone assume Frank was with you. Odd, as you've also made it publicly obvious he isn't to your taste. So, why would you indulge in the charade when you so clearly don't like him very much?'

Elizabeth pursed her lips but remained quiet.

Hari flicked her gaze from the book seller to Roger. 'What time did you arrive at the hotel?'

'You already know. You saw me when I arrived in Reception.'

'I did. But before your appearance in the reception, I saw you in the pub garden. I wasn't sure it was you at first – thought I was seeing things, but you were there, weren't you?'

Roger sighed. 'Yes, I was there.'

'And the audition for *Anything Goes*? Was that real, or just an invented alibi?'

The actor's cheeks flushed. 'It was real! *And* I got the part.'

'But the audition wasn't when you claimed it was.'

'No,' Roger conceded. 'It was the day before. I caught the early morning train from London to Birmingham and then got an Uber from the station to here. Damn pricey it was too.'

Not commenting on how Roger chose to spend his money, Hari said, 'So you arrived at the Harmen Hotel around midday, presumably to meet someone secretly before you were officially here.'

'Yes.'

'Who?'

'Do I have to—?'

'You do have to tell us, yes.' Danny was already moving towards Roger.

'Actually, Inspector,' Hari chipped in, 'I think I can guess. While we are all busy being persuaded — not entirely successfully — that Miss Jeffries and Mr Lister are together, *Roger* is the gentleman who's actually with Miss Jeffries.'

Roger said nothing as he got up and sat next to Elizabeth.

Danny frowned. 'Two questions, Mr Striver: Why lie about the audition timing, and why keep your liaison secret?'

'Because nothing I have is private, Inspector. I just wanted to have a relationship that no one knew about, because then it might not go wrong.'

The detective's eyes narrowed. 'If the gossip columns are to be believed, you're known to have had a string of disastrous relationships.'

'Yes. And I wanted this one to be different. To last.' He offered his hand to Elizabeth, who took it willingly. 'I also wanted to spare her the celebrity magazines and social media jibes about our age gap. It's only fifteen years, but you know how cruel people can be.'

Elizabeth gave Roger such a gentle look that Hari was taken by surprise. She'd only seen Elizabeth in ice maiden mode before.

'And the massaging of audition timings?' Danny prompted.

'Simply so we could have some time together in secret. Nothing more than that.'

'That's two couples here, pretending they aren't couples. Interesting.' Hari turned to Frank. 'Can I ask you, why – seeing as Elizabeth isn't exactly subtle about not finding you attractive – you agreed to be seen to be trying to court her?'

Frank was silent for a second, before focussing on Roger. 'I promised him I'd act as if I was interested in Elizabeth so no one would guess they were together. As Roger said, there isn't much privacy in his world.'

'And why would you do that for him?' Danny asked.

'Roger has always been very supportive of my work. Talks it up a lot, even though he never did get to be my Robin Hood. I owed him.'

'Or Maisie thought you owed him and persuaded you to go along with the charade.' Changing tack before Frank could respond, Hari turned to Jez. 'Can I ask, did you know that the CCTV cameras in the hotel's corridors aren't working?'

'I did. The manager told me when I arrived on Friday.'

'And where were you when the manager told you?'

Jez closed his eyes as he tried to remember. 'In the foyer, I think. Yes, he was talking to me while one of the porters helped me put up the display banners.'

'And were any of the people here around when you were told that?'

Opening his eyes again, a troubled Jez peered around him. 'Not that I noticed.'

'Thank you.' Hari felt the questions building in her mind as she switched her attention back to Roger. 'When you mentioned the fact that the inspector and I dined together in the pub yesterday evening, it was assumed you saw us yourself, but you didn't, did you? It was someone else who saw us, and they told you.'

'Well, umm...'

Danny's eyes narrowed. 'Who saw us, Mr Striver?'

Roger shrugged. 'I can't see it matters, but if you must know, it was Maisie who saw you and told me.'

'I did,' the agent confirmed. 'I'd nipped out for a bottle of gin. The prices here are criminal.'

'Just gin?'

'Frank already had tonic,' Maisie barked. 'And if you are going to give me a lecture about cheating the hotel out of bar sales, then save it.'

'The idea never crossed my mind.' Hari glanced at Danny. 'When the rooms were searched, did you find gin and tonic in Frank's room?'

'A couple of empty bottles were located, I believe. Sergeant?'
'Yes, sir. In the bin along with other bits and bobs.'
'Including cookie box packaging, by any chance?'

Chapter Thirty-two

Frank sat up straight. 'I imagine everyone here has a Cookie Creations box in their wastebin. I've been working opposite the stall. Dot has sold as many cookie boxes as Harriet has sold books. More, maybe.'

Danny turned to Dot. 'You've sold a lot of biscuits?'

'Everything I brought with me and more that I ordered in.'

'Only from *Pearce Bakes*?'

'Yes, Inspector.'

'And you purchased some cookies from Miss Henderson, did you, Mr Lister?'

'Me? No.' He grunted as he patted his stomach. 'Supposed to be watching the weight.'

'How about you, Miss Jeffries?'

'No. I wasn't at the RHC event, remember?'

'Indeed.' Danny swung round. 'How about you, Ms Flowers? Did you buy any?'

'No.'

'But did someone give you some cookies?' asked Hari.

'Yes.' Maisie stared straight at her.

'What flavour were they?'

'Some sort of chocolate.'

Hari turned to Dot. 'How many flavours do you have containing chocolate?'

'Fifteen and counting.'

'Who gave you the cookies, Ms Flowers?' Danny asked as every eye focused on Maisie. The atmosphere in the room felt thick with static.

'I did.' Roger raised a hand. 'Maisie has a sweet tooth, and well, I owed her for getting me the audition for *Anything Goes*. They were a thank you.'

Maisie grunted. 'Weeks of negotiating, reassuring the producer and director you wouldn't cock it up, and you buy me cookies!'

'Really good cookies!' Roger coloured. 'Everyone here loves them. It was just a token gesture. I hoped you'd like them.'

Danny moved from where he'd been stood and sat back next to Hari. 'And did you like them, Ms Flowers?'

'Yes.'

'You ate them all?'

'What if I did?'

'I am not judging you for that, Ms Flowers. Miss Henderson's cookies are delicious.'

'Then why ask the question, Inspector?' Frank's expression suggested that his brain was tackling a maths problem he didn't believe the answer to.

'Because I think that's when the idea came to Ms Flowers.'

'What idea?'

Danny ignored the question. 'You like cookies, don't you, Ms Flowers? Cookies in general, I mean.'

'That hardly makes me unique.'

'True. While Sergeant Dawson was searching everyone's room for Sharman's notebook, I asked him to take particular note of everyone's wastebins.'

'How fascinating.' Maisie's tone became caustic.

'Can you tell me where you disposed of the packaging from the cookies you consumed in Mr Lister's room?'

'I can't bloody remember. In the bin, presumably.'

'Really, Inspector!' Frank was incredulous. 'Where else would she put the rubbish?'

'An excellent question. You are correct, though; it was in the bin.'

'*Quelle surprise!*'

Dawson fixed his eyes on Frank. 'The point is, *sir*, that there was a wrapper from another brand of cookies in the bin, too.'

'So what? We've just established that Maisie likes cookies.'

As Frank stared at the detectives, then at Maisie, and then back again, Hari said, 'Ms Flowers, if I were to ask Dot to go to the supermarket near the pub, where you purchased your gin, would I be right in thinking she'd also be able to buy cookies there? The shop's own brand chunky cookies, maybe? A range which bears a striking resemblance to Dot's biscuits in style and consistency and, as it happens, only came into being after the countrywide success of Cookie Creations.'

Maisie scowled, but said nothing, as Hari went on.

'And if she went, would Dot find that one of the flavours available would be chocolate and nuts? Some sort of ground nuts, to be precise?'

Shaw signalled to the constable on the door, who immediately left the hall, Hari presumed, to hot foot it to the supermarket next to the Wetherspoons.

Frank's jaw dropped as he blustered, 'I don't like what you are implying, Dr Danby! We've already established that Maisie likes biscuits. Who doesn't? What if she did buy more from the supermarket?'

'I was merely wondering which flavour your partner would favour, Frank.'

'You were not!' Frank's cheeks flushed in anger. 'You're saying that…' He gulped suddenly as he saw the solemn expressions on both Hari and Inspector Shaw's faces. 'You can't be saying that she…'

As what was being suggested sank in to everyone present, Roger became as alarmed as Frank. 'Maisie?'

With every set of eyes in the hall on her, Maisie, her face taut, her lips pursed, swivelled her position so she could focus her over-kohled eyes on Roger. When she spoke, her words were little more than a hiss. 'You had so much potential, and you blew it – not just once, but again and again with your showing off and your massive ego! Frank and I worked our butts off; networked like you would not believe, to make sure you were the only one in the running to be his Robin Hood, and it was working – it was actually going to happen for you – for us! Then *she* came along,' Maisie swung round, jabbing a sharp nail in Hari's direction, 'with her oh-so-PC version of the legend, and wham – you don't even need a Robin Hood for a Robin Hood story anymore!'

Hari's lips opened and closed mutely in the face of the small woman's ire.

'Is that why you did all this?' Danny waved an arm at Dawson, who stepped closer to Maisie. 'So much effort, just to frame Hari because her books took away your meal ticket's chance of worldwide success.'

'Roger's career should have been immense – skyrocketing towards the stars, but it's over before it has begun.'

Finding her voice, Hari spoke softly. 'And you thought – despite your claims to the contrary earlier – that if I was accused of this crime, then my work might be rubbished, and my TV show cancelled. If that happened, Frank's series might have been made instead, and Roger might have become Robin Hood, after all.' Hari took a ragged breath as she ploughed on. 'This was all to make sure you had one last shot at making your client a household name.'

Danny gave Hari the tiniest dip of his head as he picked up the line of questioning. 'Ms Flowers —

Maisie — would you like to comment on Dr Danby's suggestion as to your motive?'

'It's not worthy of comment.'

Roger scowled at Hari. 'Especially as it suggests that my best acting years are behind me. I'm still in my twenties!'

'Late twenties.'

Suddenly something that had been bothering Hari slotted into place. 'Maisie showed you the ballad, didn't she, Roger?'

'No. No, I swear, she didn't.'

Hari's confidence faltered. 'But you have seen it – you must have, or you wouldn't know about the line in it that belonged to my book.'

'Frank told me about that,' Roger blurted out.

'And how did you see it, Frank?'

The other author sighed as he confessed, 'The photos. The ones Miss Spencer took for Jez.'

Hari was confused. 'I didn't think you'd seen those.'

'I did.'

Christine tentatively raised a hand. 'I showed them to Mr Lister. Sorry, Inspector, I should have said, but what with the young woman's death, I'd honestly forgotten about it.'

'Not to worry. So, when did you show Mr Lister the ballad photos?'

'On the way out of the hotel on Sunday night. He stopped me and asked,' she stammered, 'he was rather insistent on taking a look.'

'I ought to have been consulted from the start,' Frank cut in grumpily. 'As Dr Danby rightly assumed, it can get frustrating having my opinion ignored just because I don't have a host of degrees.'

Hari quietly asked, 'And you noticed the line from

my work?'

'Yeah.' Frank lowered his eyes.

The detective was doubtful. 'Three pages of old script and you spotted the only line from Hari's book, just like that?'

'Yeah.' Frank's eyes flickered to Maisie and back again. 'I've read the books – a few times.'

'You've read *my* books?' Hari was amazed.

'They're good.'

'Oh.' Floored by the revelation, Hari spluttered, 'But you... you accused me of stealing your ideas. If you'd read my books, then you'd know I didn't. I'd never steal anything.'

'I know. I'm sorry.' Frank shut his eyes for a split second, as if gathering himself. 'I was so close to having it all and then you came along and that was it. The dream was gone.'

Jez cleared his throat. 'Is that why there hasn't been a new book, Frank?'

'Yeah. At first it was just a case of getting the script for the television show written – the non-television show, as it turned out. Then, suddenly, with Hari's books flying off the shelves, there seemed no point anymore. I tried to write, but nothing happened.'

Not sure what to say, Hari felt floored by Frank's admission and pricked by guilt at stunting his creativity.

Seeing that Hari needed a moment to rally her thoughts, Danny took back the questioning. 'And you told Roger about the line in Hari's book, Frank?'

'Yes, Inspector. We were... we were having a grumble about her success, and I mentioned it.' Frank looked up at Roger. 'Although you did alright out of Hari, so you were okay, really. It was frustrating, though, after all the work Maisie put in. As she said, we put the right word in the director's ear, the producer, the casting director and so on.'

It was me. Hari felt the last few pieces of the puzzle slot into place. *It was me Maisie was talking about when she said, "You did alright out of her."*

The tension in the hall was electric as Hari took a deep breath and asked Jez, 'When did you decide that it would be my work that was featured at this year's event?'

'In Oxford, on the last day of the last event.'

'But you didn't ask me until only a few weeks ago. All the banners and everything showing scenes from *Return to Sherwood* would have taken time to put together.'

Jez coloured slightly. 'It was always going to be about the show, but, ummm… well, I wasn't sure the budget would run to paying you to come as well as Lee, Scarlett and Roger. I'm sorry, Hari.'

'Not at all. The fans are far more likely to come to see the stars than the writer. But you did invite me.'

'I always wanted to. Then when…' Jez's voice faded away as an unpleasant realisation came to him.

'When what, Mr Barnes?' Danny prompted.

'When Maisie said not to worry about paying for Roger to come, I had money to invite Hari and reinvite Professor Frampton — Neil. Actually, now I think about it, it was Maisie that suggested I invite you both – although I was planning to already, if the budget allowed.'

Roger's head snapped up. 'But I *was* paid!'

'You paid Roger's fee, didn't you?' Hari twisted around to face Maisie. 'You needed me to be here.' Not sure how she kept her voice level, she went on, 'And what a stroke of luck for you that Dot came with me.

'You saw the box of cookies left outside Sharman's door on the way to see Frank. You then took the cookies from the box and replaced them with the ones you had brought yourself from the supermarket, before placing them outside Sharman's bedroom door. How thrilled you must have been to see the thank you note from Dot that neatly proved the cookies were not from you.'

Before Maisie could react, Lee leapt to his feet. 'You killed her! You killed my Sharman!'

Frank's jaw dropped open. He blurted out, 'You? You and Sharman. *Seriously?* But you're a star and she was—'

Lee thrust a hand forward, his finger jabbing the air. 'Don't you dare judge Sharman, Frank Lister. Don't you *dare*.'

'I'm sorry for your loss, Mr Stoneman.' Danny spun around on the soles of his shoes to face Maisie. 'Do you have anything to say?'

'I brought those biscuits to eat myself; and eat them I did.'

'I am sure eating them was your original intention – but then you saw how you could use them. Use them to make Sharman stop and think before going to talk to the police.'

'Come off it, Harriet! This is getting ridiculous. Why would I want to stop her doing that?'

The tension in the room heightened further as Danny asked, 'Ms Flowers, how much did you pay for the ballad to be made?'

'I didn't!'

'And yet you made sure that Sharman was given cookies that could poison her system.'

'How?' Maisie's voice was little more than a squeal now. 'Even if I did swap the cookies – and I'm not saying I did – I couldn't force her to eat them, could I?'

Hari exhaled as she said, 'Sharman was looking

forward to them. They were a treat from Dot. A thank you – in her favourite flavour. She had no reason to think she couldn't eat them – had planned to enjoy them while she got ready for the disco. All you needed for her to do was take one bite from one cookie. And she did.'

'But—'

Danny shook his head. 'Let's leave the rest of this for an official conversation at the station, shall we?' He stepped forward. 'Maisie Flowers, I'm arresting you for the murder of Sharman Peterson and the forgery of a ballad. You do not have to say anything, but it may harm your defence if you do not mention, when questioned, something which you later rely on in court. Anything you do say may be given in evidence.'

Roger jumped to his feet. 'Don't be such a fool, Shaw! Maisie would never… and forgery, as well as murder? You never said that – it was all about Sharman, and now you're saying—'

Danny broke through the actor's shocked tirade before it fully broke. 'If you'd excuse us, Mr Striver. I have work to do and you, I'm sorry to say, need to find yourself a new agent.'

Chapter Thirty-three

Hari felt exhausted.

After the police had escorted Maisie away, a hush of disbelief had coated the hall. All she wanted to do was go back to her room to think. She was sure Danny had been right to arrest Maisie. *So why do I feel that we are missing something?*

Now, sitting in the bar, Dot at her side and a large whisky in front of her, Hari found herself the centre of attention once again.

A pale-faced Lee sat next to Scarlett. Her hand held his tightly as Penny, Clara, Jez, Christine, and Neil joined them. A moment later, an oddly quiet Frank, a brandy in his hand, sat with them. Then Roger, with Elizabeth at his side, approached the table.

'May we join you? I would understand if you'd rather we didn't.'

'Please.' Dot patted the vacant seat next to her.

'How could Maisie have done this?' Roger sat down with a thump. 'And how can I have not known about it? Not realised?'

Frank sniffed as he looked across the table at Hari. 'Tell me about it!'

Dot sipped from a large glass of pinot. 'I can't believe Maisie replaced my cookies with the ones from the supermarket. Worse, with ones that particular supermarket chain only sells now because they are trying to make their biscuits as good as mine – they basically ripped me off!'

Roger ran a hand through his hair. '*I* can't believe she put them in the box of cookies that *I* gave her.'

'I don't think she did,' Hari mused. 'She ate the ones from you, Roger. I think you giving her the cookies simply gave her the idea of how to put some pressure on Sharman. She used the box left outside Sharman's door. She wanted to give her a fright.'

'But not kill her?' Lee asked.

'I can't be sure, but I don't think so. Sharman was getting too close to the truth concerning the ballad. Maisie wanted her to have something else to think about other than the fact the parchment for the ballad came from her shop.'

'Being seriously ill would certainly do that!' Penny was close to tears again.

'She wouldn't have been more than temporarily ill if she'd had her pen.' Dot sighed. 'But how did Sharman know the parchment was from her shop?'

'I suspect she guessed and confronted Maisie. Even if Maisie denied it, the seed of suspicion will have been sown.'

'Makes sense – but why watch Frank?'

'All I can think is that it was because Roger is always hovering around Frank, and Roger is a direct line to Maisie. But, in truth, I doubt we'll ever know what Sharman's thinking was.'

'Such bad luck. If she'd never left her bag in her friends' room…'

'Exactly.' Hari sent a sympathetic look in Penny and Clara's direction. 'Maisie came and went via the fire exit. She knew about the lack of CCTV from you, didn't she, Frank?'

'I'm afraid so.' Frank sighed. 'Sorry, Jez, I heard you and the hotel manager chatting. I was already in situ and, well, I was feeling rather self-pitying, so I eavesdropped...'

'And you told Maisie about the security issue.'

'Just in conversation. She didn't directly ask me about it.'

'I doubt she had any intention of hurting Sharman

at that point.' Hari sipped her drink. 'Inspector Shaw told me that Sergeant Dawson spoke to the hotel receptionist who delivered the biscuits to Sharman. He was in a hurry, so simply left them on the floor outside her bedroom door.'

'And then Maisie saw them – and also saw an opportunity and took them to her room?' Lee asked.

'Maybe, or maybe she made the swap in the corridor. Either way, she swapped the contents with the cookies she had bought. Perhaps she was already planning to give nut-filled biscuits to Sharman – but now she had a box that had a personalised message from Dot on it. My best friend – giving her a way to imply that I was responsible.'

Dot found herself trembling. 'You really think all this was to frame you?'

'To frame me, or to cause me maximum embarrassment. Or both.'

Frank scrubbed both of his palms over his face. 'This is all my fault!'

'You?' Lee gripped his glass so tightly that Hari feared it might shatter.

'If I hadn't told Maisie that Sharman was allergic to nuts…' Frank's voice trailed off as he took solace in his drink.

Hari nodded. 'I had wondered if she'd found out about the allergy from you.'

'Again, it just came up in conversation – something about how awful the food was in this hotel and how glad I was I hadn't got my choice of meal limited further by being veggie or…'

'Or had allergies?' Hari suggested as Frank's round face creased into even more carelines.

'Yes.'

Scarlett put a comforting arm around Lee's

shoulder as Christine asked, 'Am I understanding you right, Hari? Are you saying that Maisie forged the ballad *and* killed Sharman?'

Hari put her hand on her notebook as it lay before her on the table. 'I'm saying I think so, but I'm not a detective. And…'

'And what?' Lee took a hefty sip from his whisky.

'I'm not sure, it's just…'

'Hari?' Dot laid a hand on her friend's arm. 'What is it?'

Hari sucked in her bottom lip as she wondered how to explain her sense that there was something missing.

'Frank, you know when you write a book, and you get to the end of a first draft. It's okay, but it isn't good yet – it's not quite done. There's always a vital bit of the plot that needs to be adjusted or added to or rewritten completely?'

'Yes. But what's that—?'

'I have a feeling that that's what we have here. Inspector Shaw has the murderer in his hands, but that's not the whole story.'

Frank's eyebrows rose. 'You are saying there's a chapter missing?'

'The closing chapter. The one where everything falls into place. The real link between the ballad and the death.'

Roger frowned. 'And do you know what happens in this closing chapter?'

'I wish I did.' Hari got to her feet. 'If you'll all excuse me, I really need some sleep.'

The aroma of fried breakfast sent Hari's stomach churning as she entered the dining room in a desperate hunt for decent coffee. She wasn't surprised to find that Lee was already there.

Her leading man was staring into the middle distance. She could only imagine what stolen future he was saying goodbye to.

Despite the gurgle of her empty stomach, Hari skipped the food counter and went straight to the coffee machine.

Unsure whether she should join Lee or not, Hari had the decision taken away from her by the arrival of Scarlett, who immediately sat next to Lee and waved her over.

'Hari. You okay? Have you slept?'

'Morning, Scarlett.' Hari pulled out a chair and sat down, but kept her coffee cup in her hands, needing its comforting presence as much as the contents. 'I can't have got more than an hour. You?'

'Bit more than that, but not loads.' Scarlett looked at Lee in concern. 'How are you doing?'

Picking up his espresso, Lee downed the contents of his cup as if he was downing a shot of tequila. 'How the hell do you think I'm doing?'

'Sorry. I—'

Immediately contrite, Lee placed a palm over Scarlett's hand. 'No, I'm sorry. I just can't believe she's gone, that's all.'

'It's okay.' Scarlett freed her hand and stood up. 'I'm going to get some tea and toast.'

As Scarlett moved away, Hari said, 'At least you two are getting on better now.'

'Yeah. She's alright when she's being a real person and not acting.'

Not sure what to make of Lee's statement, Hari was glad to see Dot come into the restaurant. Jez wasn't far behind her. By the time sleepy "good mornings" had been swapped, Neil had also arrived, followed by Frank.

There was no doubt that Frank looked awful. His eyes were blotchy and his skin pallid. However bad her night had been, Hari saw it had been nothing compared to Frank's, as he got to grips with the fact that his lover was a killer.

Sitting next to Hari, Dot whispered, 'Are you alright?'

'Ish. You?'

'Same. I just said goodbye to Penny and Clara. They said to say goodbye. They couldn't face seeing anyone.' Dot broke a piece of toast in half, letting the crumbs spray across the plate.

'Understandable.' Hari gave a sad smile. 'I'm sorry I didn't have the chance to say goodbye, though.'

Dot gestured to Hari's cup. 'Aren't you eating?'

'I couldn't. Not yet. Not until…' Hari stopped talking, dropped her eyes to her phone and typed, showing the message to Dot.

Can't say here. Been up most of night mulling it over. I think Danny and I made a mistake.

Dot's eyes widened as Hari typed another line.

Can you come through to the trading room? I need to talk to you.

A tiny dip of Dot's head saw Hari downing her coffee. 'If you'll all excuse us, Dot and I need to sort our boxes for packing in the car.'

As the two friends walked from the restaurant, they passed Roger and Elizabeth sitting in the bar, eating on their own, away from the others.

By the time they'd reached the trading room, Hari had connected a call to Inspector Danny Shaw.

With the knowledge that Danny would be with her as soon as he could practically get away, Hari ran through her ideas with Dot.

As she spoke, Hari half hoped that her friend would break in and tell her she was being silly. But she didn't.

'We have to go back to the others.' Dot gave up on her intention to actually take the boxes of stock back to the car. 'They're bound to head home after breakfast, and we need to keep them here!'

'Of course! Come on.' Hari dashed towards the door. 'How are we going to make them stay?'

'I've no idea.' Dot followed on Hari's heels. 'A goodbye coffee in the bar?'

'Why would they want one? If I was them, I'd want to get out of here at speed.'

'Me too.' Dot stifled a yawn. 'I'm desperate to get home to my own bed, and I've not been in the eye of the storm.'

'You almost were. Maisie made damn sure you could be implicated if she needed you to be.'

'And you.'

'Ummm…' Hari sucked in her bottom lip, 'and Frank.'

'Frank?'

Hari paused as her hand gripped the handle of the door that divided the trading room from the bar and Reception. 'Maisie didn't strike me as someone who doesn't think things through – she's an agent. Agents have an angle on every angle.'

'So?'

'If you were planning on poisoning someone with an allergic reaction, would you leave the wrapper of the cookies you intended to use in your own hotel bin?'

'No.' Dot's eyes widened as she realised what Hari was saying. 'She left it in Frank's bin because no one knew she was here!'

'Exactly. The police were supposed to think it was Frank's wrapper.'

'But, even if they hadn't already found out, surely Frank would've told the police that Maisie had been there the moment he was accused?'

'I'm sure he would, but is that enough to stop a cloud of suspicion landing on him? As it is, he's going to be tainted by this if it ever gets out that he's had a relationship with a killer.'

'Will it get out?'

'Bound to when the case comes to court.'

Dot nodded as she took a step nearer to the door. 'Are you ready?'

'Nope.' Hari pushed the door open. 'But let's go anyway.'

'This is kind of you, Hari, and I appreciate you wanting to buy us a cuppa before we go our separate ways, but I'd sooner go home.' Scarlett pulled out a chair at the same table they'd sat at the night before.

'Me too.' Roger, oddly unkempt, played a finger through the crumbs left on a plate before him, the only evidence that a Danish pastry had been consumed. 'I need to start the hunt for a new agent.'

Elizabeth gave him a sympathetic smile. 'What will you say though, darling? You can't tell people you're replacing Maisie because she's a killer. And you don't want people to think she's dropped you.'

While Roger let this horrifying idea sink in, Frank ran the back of a hand over his eyes. 'I think I'm going to need at least three more coffees before I'm remotely safe to drive.'

Hari gently ventured, 'I'm sure the police will want to talk to you again, Frank.'

'I haven't done anything!'

Neil spoke up first. 'Hari wasn't saying you had. She's right, though. You're Maisie's partner; they're going to want to know about her – confirm her movements this weekend and so on.'

Frank puffed out a ragged breath. 'Okay. Yes, I see that. Is that why you offered to buy us all a coffee, Hari? To keep us here until the police arrive?'

Everyone exchanged anxious glances as Hari blushed. 'I wanted to say goodbye to everyone properly, but now you come to mention it, perhaps it isn't a bad idea that we're all here like this.'

A brief quiet hung over them for a while, before Jez said, 'Well, despite the circumstances, I'm glad you're all here. I can thank you properly for coming this weekend – for giving your time to the RHC. Especially you, Frank. You've been a loyal member of the team for so long, and now it's over. There'll be no more Robin Hood Club meets.'

'I'm so sorry it ended like this.' Hari felt for their host. His bounce was all gone, and his expression was devoid of its habitual beam.

'Thank you, Hari.' Jez shook his head. 'I'm glad you could come. And I'm grateful to you, Scarlett, Roger, Lee, Neil, and Elizabeth, for making it last year as well as this year. Fans like new faces, but they like familiar ones, too.'

A cold trickle ran down Hari's spine as any lingering doubts about her theory disappeared.

'What is it, Hari?' Lee's eyes narrowed.

'Nothing. Really.'

'Nothing?' Frank looked doubtful. 'Are you sure? Or have you just worked out the last chapter?'

'Last chapter?' Scarlett asked.

'Remember what Hari said last night?' Lee turned to his co-star. 'That it was as if the last chapter of the story – of this situation – was missing.'

Jez leant forward. 'Do you know, Hari? Have you

worked out what was bugging you?'

Wishing that Danny would appear through the hotel door, Hari shifted awkwardly in her seat. 'It's not my place to—'

Lee put down his cup with a bang. 'Please, Hari. Tell us what you think happened.'

Hari felt helpless in the face of her leading man's broken-hearted expression. 'Okay, but promise you'll remember this is *just* my opinion. An amateur theory.'

'Promise.'

'Okay.' Hari cradled her own cup, letting its remaining warmth lend her strength. However, as she opened her mouth to speak, Scarlett cut in.

'Hang on. Should we do this? I mean, if Hari has discovered something that the police need to know, shouldn't we wait for them?'

'Well said.' Roger nodded.

'I'm happy to wait.' Hari felt a hit of relief. A relief that was promptly stolen as Lee got to his feet.

'No! I need to know now. I'm not waiting. They could be hours – even if they knew to come. We're only assuming they are coming back this morning.'

Wishing Danny would hurry up, Hari picked up her mobile. 'I'll message Inspector Shaw and ask if he intends to return.'

Lee slumped. 'I don't want to wait. Please, Hari. I'm going out of my mind here. I need to know – was Sharman… was she involved in the ballad forgery? I keep wondering if she knew about the flyleaves from her shop. I'm convinced she'd have hated the idea, but she needed money and—'

The sound of two sets of feet walking swiftly towards them cut Lee's request off midstream.

Hari was as relieved as she was nervous as they saw Danny and Sergeant Dawson stride into the room.

'Thank you for your message, Hari.' Danny took a seat from a nearby table and placed it opposite Hari, as Dawson strode behind him. 'As you can see, your assumption that I'd like to talk to everyone again this morning was correct.'

'Why didn't you tell us that last night, then?' Frank asked.

'Because, last night, I hadn't spoken to Ms Flowers properly.'

'And?' Frank paused, before asking, 'Has she confessed?'

'To the manslaughter of Sharman, yes.'

'Manslaughter?' Lee was horrified. 'It was murder! How can you—?'

Danny raised his hand. 'Be assured, Mr Stoneman, I will be charging her with murder, it will be up to the Criminal Prosecution Service. They'll say which crime I can charge her with.'

Lee said no more as the inspector approached Hari. 'You wanted to talk to us?'

'I had an idea, but I don't know if it's helpful or not.'

'In a nutshell, then?' Danny held up his arm, indicating his wristwatch. 'I'm on the clock. I need to charge Ms Flowers formally soon.'

'Understood.' Hari took a deep breath and blurted out, 'In short, I think you should charge Maisie with Sharman's death, but not the forgery of the ballad – not completely, anyway.'

Chapter Thirty-four

'What?' Frank and Lee shouted their disbelief at the same time.

'Gentlemen, please,' Dawson snapped before turning to Hari, who was glowing with embarrassment. 'Can you explain yourself?'

'I think so.' Hari gulped. 'First, I need to ask some questions of everyone here. Is that alright?'

'Please do.' Danny gestured to Dawson. 'Make notes of this conversation, please, Sergeant.'

Scarlett's usually clear voice wobbled. 'Does that make it official? If notes are taken?'

'Is that a problem, Miss Hann?'

'Of course not, Inspector. I was just asking.'

'Fair enough.' Danny looked across the round table at Hari. 'Then if you'd be so kind, Hari, please explain why you don't think I should charge my prime suspect with forgery.'

Not sure whether he was as open to hear what she was going to say as he had been before, Hari crossed her fingers in her lap as she faced Lee.

'Again, I'm very sorry for your loss.' Her eyeline swapped to Scarlett. 'It's good to see you supporting your co-star. I always got the impression you two didn't get on.'

Lee shrugged. 'We didn't not get on; we just didn't gel as friends. Scarlett's been lovely over the past few hours, though.'

Scarlett gave him a supportive smile. 'It's never a good idea to appear as if you are close to your co-star. Social media just has too much fun with speculation. It can make your life a misery. Best to be distant.'

'I understand that.' Hari focused on the hand that was laid on Lee's arm. 'You'd like it to be more, though, wouldn't you, Scarlett?'

'It would be lovely to be proper friends with Lee, but as I said—'

'Social media hassle.' Hari watched as Lee withdrew his arm from Scarlett's touch. 'Funny how many celebrity couples manage to cope with that, though, isn't it?'

'Well, I didn't want to.'

Lee frowned. 'Why would it be so bad to be seen as my friend?'

Hari answered before Scarlett could. 'Because someone might have seen the truth. You see, Lee, Scarlett is in love with you.'

'Scarlett?' Lee's eyebrows shot up his forehead. 'But you wouldn't even do an interview with me until this weekend!'

Scarlett coloured as Hari asked her leading lady, 'When did you guess about Sharman and Lee?'

'Last year... at least, I wondered.'

'And you were jealous.' Hari spoke faster as she sensed the unasked questions on her companions' lips racing to be spoken. 'Why would he choose her and not you?'

Lee pushed his chair back, putting a metre of distance between himself and Scarlett. 'You... you didn't help Maisie... please say you didn't—'

'No! Of course not.' Scarlett swung round. 'This is rubbish, Inspector! You can't let this woman accuse me of murder.'

'She did no such thing, Miss Hann.' Danny looked at Hari. 'You are going somewhere with this?'

'I am.' Hari took a deep breath. 'Someone in here helped Maisie do what she did. While Scarlett had a motive to get rid of Sharman – because she wanted Lee for herself – I'm sure she'd never stoop to murder.'

'Thank you!' Scarlett shuffled uncomfortably. 'If Sharman was still alive, I'd have left them alone. You can't force someone to love you.'

'True.' Hari swallowed a twinge of guilt as she turned to Neil. 'You, like me, could have forged the ballad.'

'Indeed I could, Harriet, but I did not.'

'A new ballad would have enhanced your career.'

'It would.' Neil tilted his head to one side. 'Yet, equally, being party to a forgery would destroy it.'

'And that's why, although you could easily have done the work, I don't think you were Maisie's accomplice.'

Neil leant forward. 'And did the fact we've been friends for years count for something too?'

'It did.'

'But if you believed me to be guilty, you'd have said so?'

'Sorry, Neil, yes, I would have.'

Pride crossed the professor's face. 'Good for you, Harriet. I'd have been disappointed in you otherwise.'

Hari switched her gaze to the convention's organiser. 'Jez, I don't doubt your affection for the legend, but at first I wondered if the timing had somehow gone wrong for those involved in the forgery. That the ballad was meant to be found while we were all here, not before we arrived. The media coverage would have been more focused on this event then – being so close to the place where it was found. Think how much good the publicity could have done the Robin Hood Club; forgery or not.'

Jez tugged at his hat. 'The publicity could have been good, but only if it was accepted as real.'

'Exactly. But the tests wouldn't have been done until *after* the weekend was over, so the whole time the

RHC was together would have been full of hopeful press speculation, something that could have done you good.'

Jez met Hari's eyes. 'I didn't do this.'

'I know you didn't.'

Frank's eyes narrowed. 'You accept Jez's word, just like that?'

'You would need a certain amount of money to set up a scam like this, and Jez is broke.'

'I am. Stoney.'

'I'm sorry I had to share that with everyone.'

'It's okay, Hari.' Jez placed his fedora on his head. 'I know why you had to.'

Roger placed both his palms flat on the table. 'You intend to assume we are all guilty until you've convinced yourself otherwise, Hari?'

'More to check I have my facts right, Roger.' Hari tried to ignore the fast beat of her pulse as she asked, 'Can I ask how long you've been seeing Elizabeth?'

'A year.'

'Frank introduced us,' Elizabeth confirmed. 'At the last RHC event.'

Jez rolled his eyes. 'You didn't pay for a ticket then, either, did you?'

'I'm sorry, Jez. We assumed you were raking it in.'

'Well, Roger, now you know better.'

Hari hurried past the awkward moment by turning to her fellow author. 'Frank, you and Maisie have been together for how long?'

'A fraction under a year...' Frank closed his eyes. 'I know she can be a bit abrasive, but she was kind to me. We had fun, we really did, and she was so interested in everything I did, and...' His voice trailed away as an unpleasant thought hit him. 'Oh God. I've been played, haven't I?'

'Maybe. I'm sorry.'

'Played?' Incomprehension was replaced by disbelief on Roger's face. 'You mean Maisie only dated Frank because of what he knew?'

'Because of whom he knew.'

'Sharman?'

'Yes.' Hari cupped her hands around her coffee and turned to Lee. 'Sharman was already having money troubles at the shop when you saw her at the convention in Oxford, wasn't she?'

'Yes.' Lee nodded.

'And that was just after it was announced that your Robin Hood series wouldn't be made, Frank.'

The author nodded. 'That happened two weeks before the convention in Oxford. Your show was doing so well that spending money on another one would be a waste of time.'

'I'm sorry.'

Frank grunted. 'It put a whole different feel on the RHC meet for me.'

'And for Maisie and Roger, I'm sure.' Hari exhaled slowly before going on. 'As we've learnt, Maisie had worked hard on making sure Roger was seen as the only actor suitable for the role of your Robin, in consultation with you, as the writer.'

'Yes,' Frank agreed. 'That's how we first met. She gave up her other clients, convinced that all her time would be needed by Roger. That he was going to be huge.'

'And I would have been!'

Hari ignored the actor's protest. 'Either way, Maisie and you were disappointed.'

'Wouldn't you have been?' Frank sighed.

'You became close to Maisie during that time.'

'Yes.' Frank shot a look at Hari. 'But you're now

telling me that it was a manufactured closeness on her part, aren't you?'

'I'm sorry, Frank.' Hari felt awkward. She wanted to say it might not always have been a relationship of convenience for Maisie, but the words stuck in her throat. Instead, she asked, 'And you introduced her to your friend Elizabeth while you were in Oxford?'

'Yes. That's where Elizabeth lives. Her office is there, too.' Frank sucked on his bottom lip. 'She and Maisie got on from the off.'

Hari turned to the woman next to Roger. 'And while you were in Oxford with Frank and Maisie, you asked to meet Roger?'

'Yes, I did.' Elizabeth placed a delicate hand on Roger's thigh. 'I'd seen him on television, and I'd liked what I'd seen. He'd had small roles in *Casualty, Midsomer Murders,* and so on.'

'Not that small,' Roger mumbled into his drink, showing Hari that he was still his old self, shock, or no shock.

Frank gave the actor a stolid stare. 'Elizabeth and Roger hit it off straight away, didn't you?'

'We did.' Elizabeth pulled her pink jacket across her chest.

Hari asked, 'Would you agree with that, Roger?'

'Absolutely. I couldn't believe my luck. Elizabeth is so clever and fun and beautiful. A bit older than me, I grant you, but—'

'Not that much older, darling!' Elizabeth gave him a warm smile.

Chuckling, Roger took his partner's hand. 'You got on with Sharman too, didn't you? So did Maisie.' He turned to Danny, oblivious of the dark shadow that suddenly crossed his lover's face. 'I can't remember how the girls discovered Sharman had a bookshop,

Inspector, but once they did, that was all they seemed to talk about.'

'That's not surprising.' Elizabeth's smile widened. 'I'm a book dealer and Maisie was always interested in people.'

'And Maisie visited the shop in Oldham,' Danny stated.

'Ah, she *did* go there then?' Hari lifted up the note to that effect she'd made in her book.

'She did,' Danny confirmed.

'Did she? I didn't know that.' Roger looked at Frank, who shrugged.

'Oldham police checked the CCTV records from Sharman's shop. You see, unlike here, she *did* have security.' The inspector watched Frank as he spoke. 'Maisie visited the shop only three weeks after the Oxford convention.'

'But why?' Frank appeared more confused by the moment. 'Maisie doesn't know the first thing about old books.'

'You do though, don't you, Elizabeth?' Hari shot a quick glance at Danny, who acknowledged the sense of the question with a dip of his head.

'I know a great deal about old books, but I've never been anywhere near Oldham!'

'You didn't need to go, Elizabeth. You'd already told Maisie what to find and how to detach the flyleaves. All of Sharman's manuscripts and books are listed online. It wouldn't have been difficult to direct Maisie to the correct document.'

'I did no such thing!' Elizabeth glared at Hari.

'I wonder why Maisie didn't just buy the book rather than rip out the flyleaves?' Jez asked. 'It can't have been easy to distract Sharman, so she didn't notice.'

Lee's voice seemed to come from far away as he fixed his eyes on Elizabeth. 'I can see how it would have been possible. It's a real nook and cranny-type shop. You'd only need to ask Sharman to go and find something for you, and she'd miss whatever you were doing.'

'If Maisie did that, it was nothing to do with me!' Elizabeth rounded on Danny. 'Plus, if she had, wouldn't her damaging the books be on CCTV?'

'Having watched the recording, we can see there was a moment when, carrying said volume, Maisie disappeared from view, just for a minute or two.' Danny kept his eyes on Elizabeth. 'As Mr Stoneman says, the shop is all corners and bends. Not every inch is covered by a camera. Maisie was in the shop just shy of an hour — long enough to suss out where to stand to do what needed doing.'

Roger was aghast as he swung around to Elizabeth. 'Please tell me you didn't help her do this.'

'Of course I didn't! Why would I?'

'To be the one to verify a rare manuscript, of course,' Hari said. 'It wasn't just Maisie that was playing Frank. You also used him, Elizabeth. Who better than Frank, who'd be at the RHC near to the archive where you planned to plant the fake ballad, to be the one invited to see it? But disaster – others were invited to verify it – not Frank.'

Danny asked, 'Are you saying Frank was involved, too?'

'No.' Hari gave the author a sympathetic look. 'But I imagine he would have been encouraged to verify it by both Elizabeth and Maisie to help his own career.'

Jez grimaced. 'But that still brings us back to the issue of the parchment and inks being the subject of tests.'

'It would,' Hari agreed. 'And then, when the parchment was found to be a fake, Frank's humiliation would have been complete. He'd be known as someone who misdated a forgery. His reputation ruined.'

Elizabeth had had enough. 'How dare you imply that—'

Danny stood up. 'Hari may not be officially able to imply anything, but I am. Elizabeth Jeffries, do you deny assisting Maisie Flowers in the forgery of a Robin Hood ballad?'

'I do! Why would I want to harm Frank? What's he ever done to me? If I forged something I'd sell it straight on!'

'And I'm sure you would have next time, but Sharman had become suspicious.'

Dot whispered, 'And that's why Maisie wanted to frighten her? To advise Sharman *not* to tell the police about her visit to the shop in Oldham?'

'Exactly.' Hari quickly added, 'Maisie got the flyleaves, brought them back to Oxford, and — I imagine — left them with Elizabeth, who wrote the ballad over the next few months.'

'Making it appear as if you wrote it, Hari, by adding in the line from your book.' Dot scowled.

'Yes. But you hedged your bets, didn't you, Elizabeth? You also put the spotlight on Frank – his books feature a carter, not mine.'

Frank grumbled. 'I bet that was Maisie's idea. Punishing me for not making her rich.'

Elizabeth said nothing as Dawson silently moved to stand behind her.

'It wasn't down to you to make her rich, Frank,' Hari said. 'But yes, if your TV show had come off, then Roger would have been a star, and so you'd have made Maisie wealthy by default. As I said earlier, this is all about money.'

'But why was Elizabeth involved?' Dot asked. 'I mean, why didn't Maisie ask Frank to forge the document? Frank is more in the know than Elizabeth when it comes to Robin.'

'I suspect Maisie offered to pay Elizabeth for helping her frame me – or Frank. In her vindictiveness, either of us would do. Face it, we could both have pulled this off. The only problem is, we love Robin Hood. Neither Frank nor I would ever have done this.'

'But Elizabeth doesn't need money.' Roger gazed at his partner; she was staring into space, her chin tilted up, her shoulders back. His tone betrayed his growing unease. 'She's always splashing out, buying the latest designer clothes, taking me to the best hotels. Everything she wants, she has.'

'I'd rather you all stopped talking about me as if I wasn't here!' Elizabeth suddenly broke her silence, her face almost the same colour as her jacket.

'Indeed you are here, but Roger's right, isn't he?' Danny moved to Dawson's side. 'You have a very lavish lifestyle, Miss Jeffries. A different designer pink jacket for every occasion, for a start! And your lifestyle caught up with you. We have received everyone's bank statements, just as we said we would. And you have a spending habit, Miss Jeffries, and not much income. It wasn't just Sharman's shop that was suffering from the recession.'

'I would never—'

'Miss Jeffries, in five minutes' time I am going to ask Sergeant Dawson to place a call to our colleagues in Oxford. They are going to visit your shop. Are you telling me that, during that forensic search of the premises, they will find nothing that will compromise your position?'

Elizabeth clamped her lips together. She said nothing.

'I see. So, perhaps it might be in your interests to start telling the truth — unless you want to be charged alongside your accomplice for the murder of Sharman Peterson.'

Chapter Thirty-five

Hari could see a small group of journalists outside the main doors. Each time a guest came in and out through the glass entranceway, Constable Matthews had to step forward and prevent at least one optimistic newshound from crossing the threshold. She wasn't sure who was the most frustrated — the constable, the journalists, or the hotel's manager, who must be rueing the day the Robin Hood Club ever booked to stay.

Before Danny had left with Dawson and a rather less than serene Elizabeth, he'd instructed the few remaining guests from the RHC to stay put until he returned, just in case he had further questions. This request had been greeted with a mixture of responses, the most unifying being that everyone was shattered after a broken night, and, having checked out of their rooms, had nowhere to rest in private, the Green Room having already gone back into general hotel use. The upshot had been a request from Danny to the hotel manager for the loan of eight bedrooms for them to wait in. A frantic search through the bookings had revealed only four free rooms, and it was in those that they all waited.

Hari counted her lucky stars that she was able to share one with Dot. She dreaded to think how Frank and Roger were getting on in theirs, while Jez and Neil shared one with Lee, and Scarlett had the final room to herself.

'How long do you think we'll have to wait here?' Dot laid back against her single bed and stared at the ceiling.

'No idea.' Hari leafed through her notebook. It was almost full.

***

Three hours later, Inspector Shaw and Sergeant Dawson stood to one side of the table as the few remaining members of the Robin Hood Club retook their seats in the bar.

'Please, Inspector, can you put us out of our misery?' Roger looked at Frank. Both men had the air of being haunted. 'Did they really do this? Sharman and the ballad?'

'I'm afraid they did. At least Maisie did. Elizabeth is technically an accessory to the death as she knew who was responsible as soon as it happened, but said nothing to the authorities.'

'Then Hari was right.' Frank gazed across the table. 'And on top of all that, they played Roger and me.'

'I'd have loved to be wrong about that.' Hari wasn't sure what else to say.

'*How* did they do it, though?' Scarlett glanced furtively at Lee, her expression making it obvious she had no idea where she stood when it came to her co-star. 'It must have taken a hell of a lot of planning.'

'It would have. And a long time to physically make the ballad. Not only did it need constructing on a stanza-by-stanza basis, but the parchment would've also needed preparing, the inks to be made, the quills fashioned correctly, and then it would need to be layered up. It wouldn't have been enough to just write on the parchment, it would need to be done carefully, making sure the work was perfect – but not too perfect.'

'So much effort, just to frame you, Hari.' Danny shook his head.

'I doubt it was just for that.' Hari shrugged. 'If this had worked, can you imagine how much they could have made from forging other documents?'

Neil agreed. 'They'd have made a fortune with such things overseas.'

'I wondered from the beginning why the ballad was hidden in this way, why it wasn't just sold privately.' Hari tapped her pen against the table. 'Without too much expert scrutiny, it could have made them a lot of money – not a fortune, not without having a provenance, but a fair bit of cash, certainly.'

'You still think they intended me to be the expert who said it was the real deal, Harriet?' Frank crossed his arms over his chest, hugging himself.

'I think they'd have tried to persuade you, yes. I'm not saying you'd have agreed to do it. In fact, I don't think you would have.'

'I wonder why they did things this way round?' Dot cradled a cup of tea she didn't want. 'If it had been me, I'd have gone for the private sale option from the off. Safer and more likely to yield an income.'

Danny pulled his coffee cup closer. 'The impression I get from the women is that Maisie saw a chance to humiliate the person who'd stopped her becoming a rich woman and Elizabeth saw a chance to dig herself out of the massive debt she'd spent herself into.'

'Maxed out every credit card she had?' Hari asked.

'I couldn't possibly say.' Danny nodded as he spoke.

Roger licked his dry lips before asking, 'Elizabeth *invented* the ballad? She has admitted it?'

Danny picked up his drink. 'She did. Once the team in Oxford had been to her office, she had no choice but to admit it. They found all the materials required to fake the ballad inks.'

Frank huffed. 'Finding that isn't proof, Inspector. I have such inks, and I bet Hari does.'

'I agree, Mr Lister, but they also found the missing corner from the ballad. If you recall, one of the parchment pieces had a corner ripped off.'

Neil inclined his head. 'A rip that was new, whereas the ballad appeared old.'

'Precisely, Professor Frampton,' Danny said. 'Apparently the parchment got caught in a drawer when Elizabeth hid the papers prior to treating it to get rid of any practice pieces. The lab will be testing it for fingerprints today. I'd be surprised if they didn't find Maisie and Elizabeth's on the ballad.'

Frank sank back against his chair, his last vestige of hope that his friend hadn't betrayed him, along with his lover evaporating. 'And I suppose they will test the ballad for DNA evidence now.'

'They will, sir, yes.'

A silence coated the room for a moment before Roger thrust his hands through his hair, raking it backwards. 'I still say Elizabeth would never have hurt Sharman! She liked her. Respected her work.'

'I think you're right, Mr Striver.' Danny looked at Hari as he spoke. 'Both women worked together on the ballad. Elizabeth used the original *Robin Hood and the Potter* as a template, changing the locations, seasons and so on as she wrote. Then Maisie gave her the line from your work, Hari – to add in to the tale. It was Elizabeth who told me that their plan – as Hari guessed – was to pull off a similar scam, once every couple of years, to top up their bank accounts.'

Jez pulled a face. 'Call me a cynic, but I bet they were only thinking of every year or so because it takes that long to get things right and too many fakes would be suspicious.'

'There may well be truth in that, Mr Barnes.'

'Was it Maisie who planted it in the archive?' Hari opened her notebook on the table in front of her, her finger tracing down the notes she'd been working on all day while trying to make sense of the order of events.

'According to Elizabeth it was.'

Neil crossed his long legs under the table. 'How did she get it into the archive workroom, Inspector?'

'Walked in when no one was about, saw the pile of mending, and slid the ballad inside the biggest book there.'

'Just like that?' Dot's eyebrows rose.

'Yup.' Danny added, 'It was pure fluke it was the volume of *Knighton* that mentions Robin Hood.'

Dot tutted. 'I'd never have the nerve!'

Roger grunted. 'Maisie has a lot of nerve. How do you think she got the director of *Anything Goes* to bump me up from being a minor character to the star?'

'She really did that, then?' Hari was surprised.

'She did.' Roger sighed. 'Killer or not, she was a bloody good agent. I've no idea what I'll do without her.'

Lee's eyes narrowed. Hari could see the effort it was taking him not to comment on his fellow actor's sudden lack of representation as he muttered, 'So, Elizabeth made the ballad from the parchment Maisie had stolen from Sharman's shop. How did Sharman find out? I know it wasn't unusual for her to have books on her shelves for years at a time, untouched and unsold.'

'I've been thinking about that, too,' Hari said. 'Even though it was damaged, Sharman's stock records detail the volume in question as complete and undamaged. I can only conclude that, while she was here, Sharman overheard Elizabeth and Maisie having a private conversation. We know she was already suspicious of Frank – but then she guessed what had happened and, I presume, asked Maisie if she had stolen the parchment from her.'

Danny nodded. 'Maisie's confirmed that is what happened. After we told her we'd found the ripped off corner. She knows we'll find her prints on it. She had no choice but to admit her part in the forgery, although she's still saying nothing about the death apart from that it was an accident.'

'Sharman had become suspicious that Maisie had used papers from her shop and challenged her.' Hari referred to her notebook. 'I wondered if she offered Sharman money to keep quiet, on the understanding she'd provide more parchment for Elizabeth to fake other documents on.'

'I don't think that's an unreasonable assumption.'

'Maisie isn't stupid, though,' Hari said. 'There are only so many old documents which could be "found" in Sharman or Elizabeth's shops. I wondered if they'd never meant the ballad to be taken as an *original* original, but as a fake all along – but an old fake. One made maybe two, three hundred years ago. That would make it valuable in its own right, but would need less work to make the fake one hundred per cent perfect.'

'I couldn't say.' Danny looked impressed by Hari's idea. 'Maybe they'd considered that option, or maybe they were too greedy to go for anything that would bring them less income. You could be giving them too much benefit of the doubt, Hari. Either way, Sharman wasn't having any of it.'

Dot grimaced. 'And so Maisie decided to punish her.'

'Yes,' Danny confirmed. 'At least we can prove it was just your box that was used. It was never your product that caused harm.'

'Thank goodness.' Dot shuddered.

Hari mused, 'It explains the timing of things, too. I wondered if there was a significance to Sharman not being around when the ballad photos were to show.'

'Maisie wanted to make sure she'd be too i... to see them?' Danny mused. 'And that she'd heed the warning and keep her mouth shut.'

'Poor Sharman.' Dot sighed.

'It all fits. Maisie is claiming manslaughter and Elizabeth's maintaining she had no idea about the cookie incident. She just knew that Maisie was going to, and I quote, "Have a word with Sharman."' Danny rose to his feet. 'I must go. As you'll appreciate, I have a lot to do. I wanted to let you all know what the situation was, and to tell you that we'll be in touch with you should we need you as witnesses when the cases come to trial. In the meantime, you are free to head to your respective homes.'

Frank and Roger were on their feet, ready to leave, before the inspector had finished speaking.

'You could have sent Dawson here to tell us all that, Inspector Shaw.'

'I could, Mr Lister, but—'

'But you wanted to see Dr Danby before she went home.' Frank gave Hari a knowing look. 'You get the TV show, you can still write, and, just as I lose my partner – a woman who I've now learnt lied her way into my life – you find a man. Dr Danby, you really do have the luck of the devil.'

Dot closed the boot of the car with a solid thump. 'That's it. Time to go home.'

Leaning against the side of the car, Hari stared up at the side of the Harmen Hotel. 'Not quite the weekend I'd imagined.'

'No.' Dot opened the car door. 'Poor Sharman.'

'Poor Lee. She would have been the perfect partner

for him. Would have kept his feet on the ground as he became more and more famous.' Hari felt her phone vibrate in her pocket. 'Oh.'

'What is it? We don't have to stay longer after all, do we?'

'Um, no.' Hari felt a pink blush light up her cheeks. 'It's Danny. He's asked if he can come to Salisbury next weekend to take me out to dinner.'

'Fabulous.'

'Is it?' Hari bit her bottom lip. 'After all that's happened, not to mention that I've been perfectly happy on my own for years and—'

'Stop it!' Dot tutted. 'Get in the car. It's time I got you home so you can report in to all your Robin Hood posters.'

Hari laughed. 'It's the longest I've gone without talking to them in months.'

'There you are, then. If I can't talk some sense into you, then I bet they can.'

'Maybe…'

Dot rolled her eyes. 'Send Danny a reply saying yes, and then get in the car. I'm not driving us anywhere until you've done that.'

'But what if it all goes wrong?'

'But what if it doesn't?'

'Always the optimist.' Hari smiled at her friend. 'Despite everything, I'm glad we came. Mind you, now I've done my bit, even if it did run again, I'd be in no hurry to come back to the Robin Hood Club. I'm sad for Jez, though; that it's to be the last one, I mean. Penny and Clara were right, it would have been lovely to hold an event in memory of Sharman.'

Dot inserted the key and ignited the engine. 'Actually, I've got something to tell you about that.'

'Really?'

'When you nipped to the loo before leaving, I had a chat with Jez.'

Hari bit her lip. 'Was he alright? He appeared so drawn earlier.'

'Well, he's smiling again now.' Dot winked as she steered the car away from the hotel.

Hari swivelled around to face her friend. 'What have you done, Dorothy-Ann Henderson?'

'I've offered to sponsor the next convention.'

'You haven't!' Hari's face broke into a huge smile.

'Yep! The Robin Hood Club will continue; now coming to you via Cookie Creations!'

'Oh my God! That's amazing.'

'I felt I owed it to Sharman.' Dot nodded. 'And in a way, it was her idea.'

'How do you mean?'

'When I was at the banquet with her, Penny, and Clara, we were chatting, and Sharman mentioned how well my biscuits and your books go together.'

'She was right.'

'I'm glad you think it's a good idea, because there's a catch.'

Hari chuckled. 'Isn't there always?'

'You'll have to come with me.'

'But *Return to Sherwood* has had its featured convention. It'll be someone else's go to be the lead draw. And besides, everyone's heard everything I've got to say.'

'Frank comes every time.'

'I'm not Frank!'

'Thank goodness.' Dot eased the car onto the main road towards the motorway. 'It won't be in Buxton next time. I thought Salisbury.'

'There's no Robin Hood link to Salisbury!'

'True, but it's where we live. I thought you'd like

to show a certain Inspector Shaw around the area. Although, that was before I knew he was already inviting himself over.'

'Dot! The chances of him holding interest in me for a whole year are zero!'

'Rubbish.' Dot glanced sideways at her friend. 'He said he wanted to come to a Robin Hood Club event as a regular fan, rather than accidentally attending as a policeman.'

'Well, yes, but—'

'But nothing!' Dot eased up to fifth gear. 'Put this weekend next year in your diary. The Robin Hood Club is coming home!'

Coming soon…

May Day Murder at The Robin Hood Club

About Jennifer Ash

With a background in history and archaeology, Jennifer Ash ought to be making good use of her PhD. She should be sat in a dusty university library translating Medieval Latin criminal records, while writing research documents that hardly anyone would want to read. Instead, tucked away in the Southwest of England, Jennifer writes stories of medieval crime, steeped in mystery, along with modern cosy crime, while taking the occasional side order of romance.

Influenced by a lifelong love of Robin Hood and medieval ballad literature, Jennifer wrote *Manuscript Mysteries at The Robin Hood Club*, (KDP, 2024), as well as *The Outlaw's Ransom (*Book One in *The Folville Chronicles)* – a short novel, which first saw the light of day within the novel *Romancing Robin Hood* (written under the name Jenny Kane; Pub. Littwitz Press, 2018).

Such was the success of this medieval murder mystery, Jennifer continued *The Folville Chronicles* with three further, full length novels, *The Winter Outlaw, Edward's Outlaw* and *Outlaw Justice.*

Jennifer has also penned a selection of audio stories and novels for the popular 1980's television show, *Robin of Sherwood,* including, *The Waterford Boy, Mathilda's Legacy, The Baron's Daughter*, *The Meeting Place, The Power of Three, The Servant* and many more (Spiteful Puppet, Chinbeard Books and AUK Ltd, 2017- 2024).

Between her Robin Hood inspired moments, Jennifer finds time to be bestselling romance and romcoms novelist, Jenny Kane.

@JenAshHistory
@JennyKaneAuthor

Jennifer Ash
https://www.facebook.com/jenniferashhistorical/
Jenny Kane
https://www.facebook.com/profile.php?id=100011235488766

Information about all of Jennifer/Jenny's work can be found at www.jennykane.co.uk

Printed in Great Britain
by Amazon